MEGA-DOGS OF NEW KANSAS

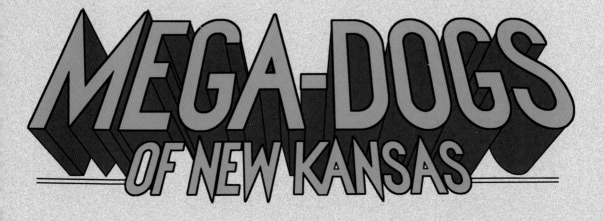

For Tracy, always —D.J.

To my folks, for letting me draw at the dinner table —J.K.

Graphic Universe™
An imprint of Lerner Publishing Group, Inc.
241 First Avenue North
Minneapolis, MN 55401 USA

For reading levels and more information, look up this title at www.lernerbooks.com.

Designed by Lindsey Owens.
Main body text is set in CCDaveGibbonsLower. Typeface provided by Comicraft.

Library of Congress Cataloging-in-Publication Data

Names: Jolley, Dan, writer. | Khouri, Jacques, illustrator.
Title: Mega-dogs of New Kansas / written by Dan Jolley ; illustrated by Jacques Khouri.
Description: Minneapolis : Graphic Universe, [2020] | Audience: Ages 7–11 | Audience: Grades 4–6 | Summary: "When an official threatens the mega-dog program, Sienna Barlow sneaks away with her dog, Gus, and begins an adventure across New Kansas." —Provided by publisher.
Identifiers: LCCN 2019039452 (print) | LCCN 2019039453 (ebook) | ISBN 9781541517332 (library binding) | ISBN 9781541599475 (ebook)
Subjects: LCSH: Graphic novels. | CYAC: Graphic novels. | Science fiction. | Adventure and adventurers—Fiction.
Classification: LCC PZ7.7.J65 Me 2020 (print) | LCC PZ7.7.J65 (ebook) | DDC 741.5/973—dc23

LC record available at https://lccn.loc.gov/2019039452
LC ebook record available at https://lccn.loc.gov/2019039453

Manufactured in the United States of America
1-44296-34557-3/5/2020

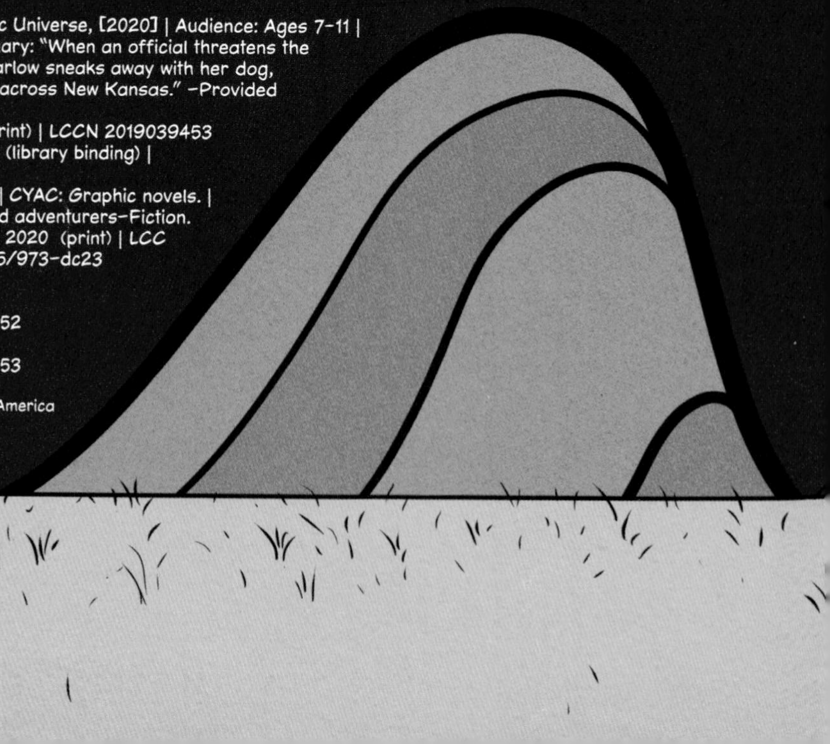

MEGA-DOGS
OF NEW KANSAS

DAN JOLLEY
JACQUES KHOURI

Graphic Universe™ • Minneapolis

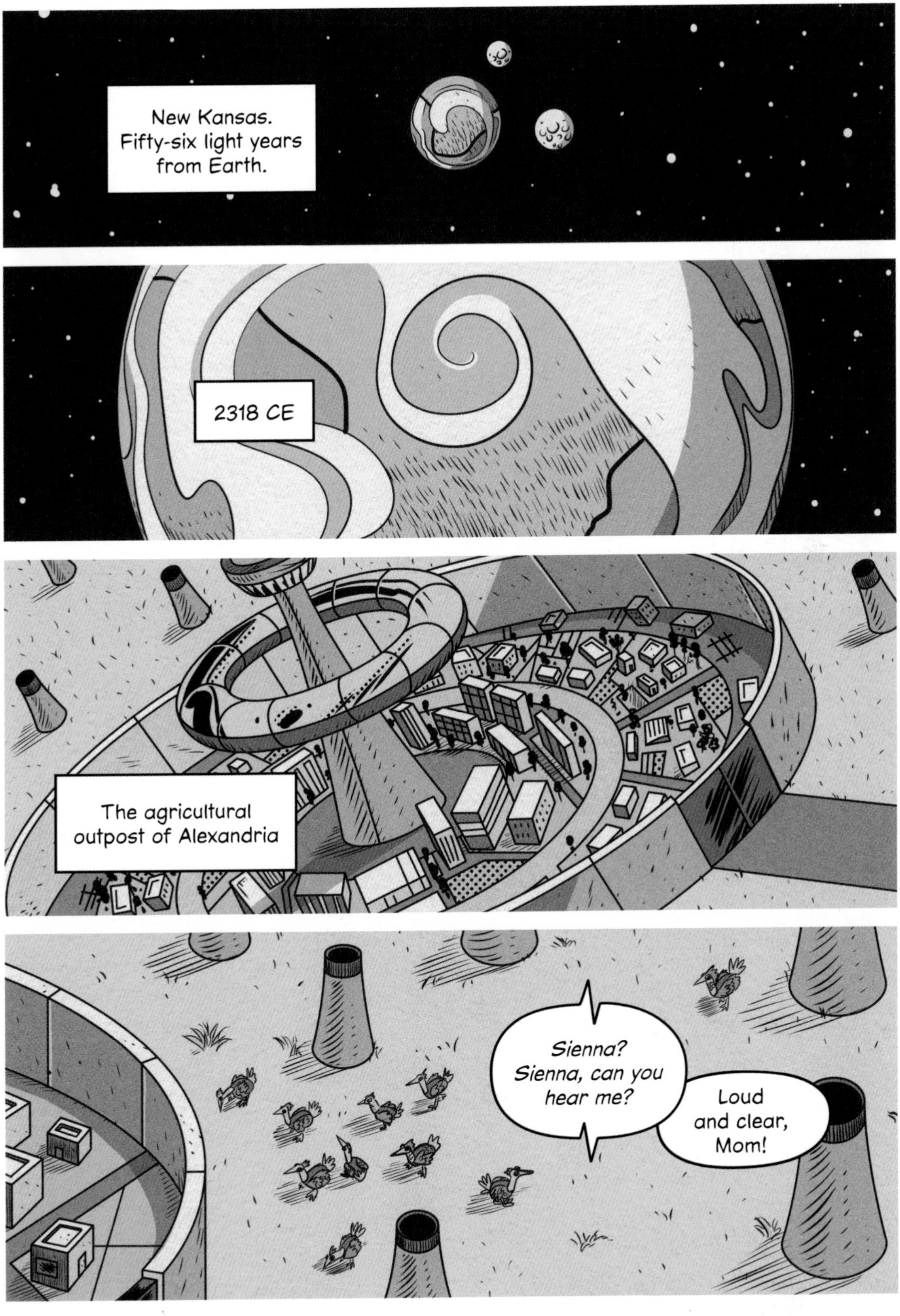
New Kansas.
Fifty-six light years
from Earth.
2318 CE
The agricultural
outpost of Alexandria
Sienna?
Sienna, can you
hear me?
Loud
and clear,
Mom!

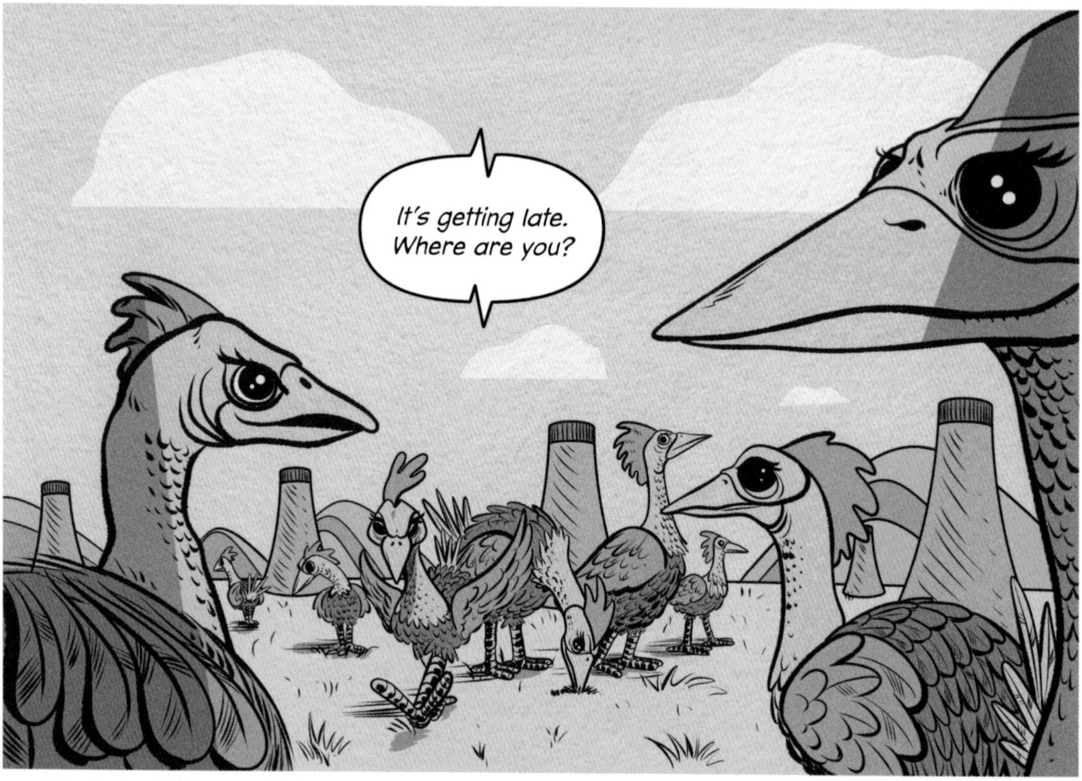
It's getting late. Where are you?

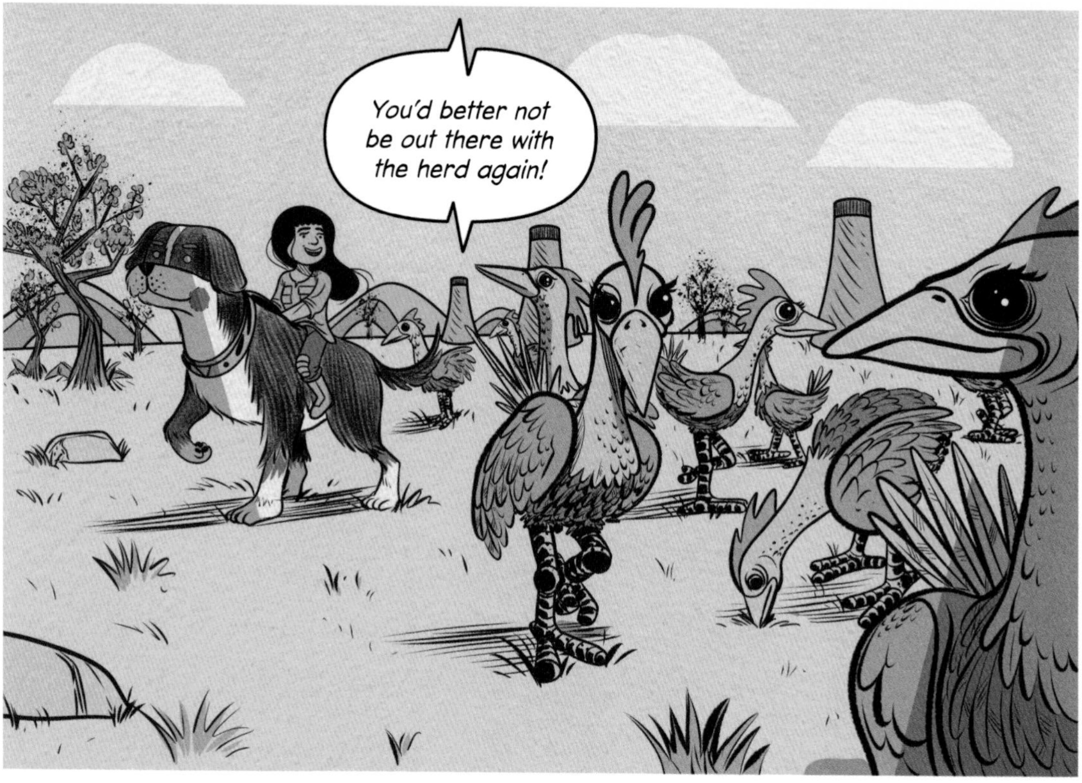
You'd better not be out there with the herd again!

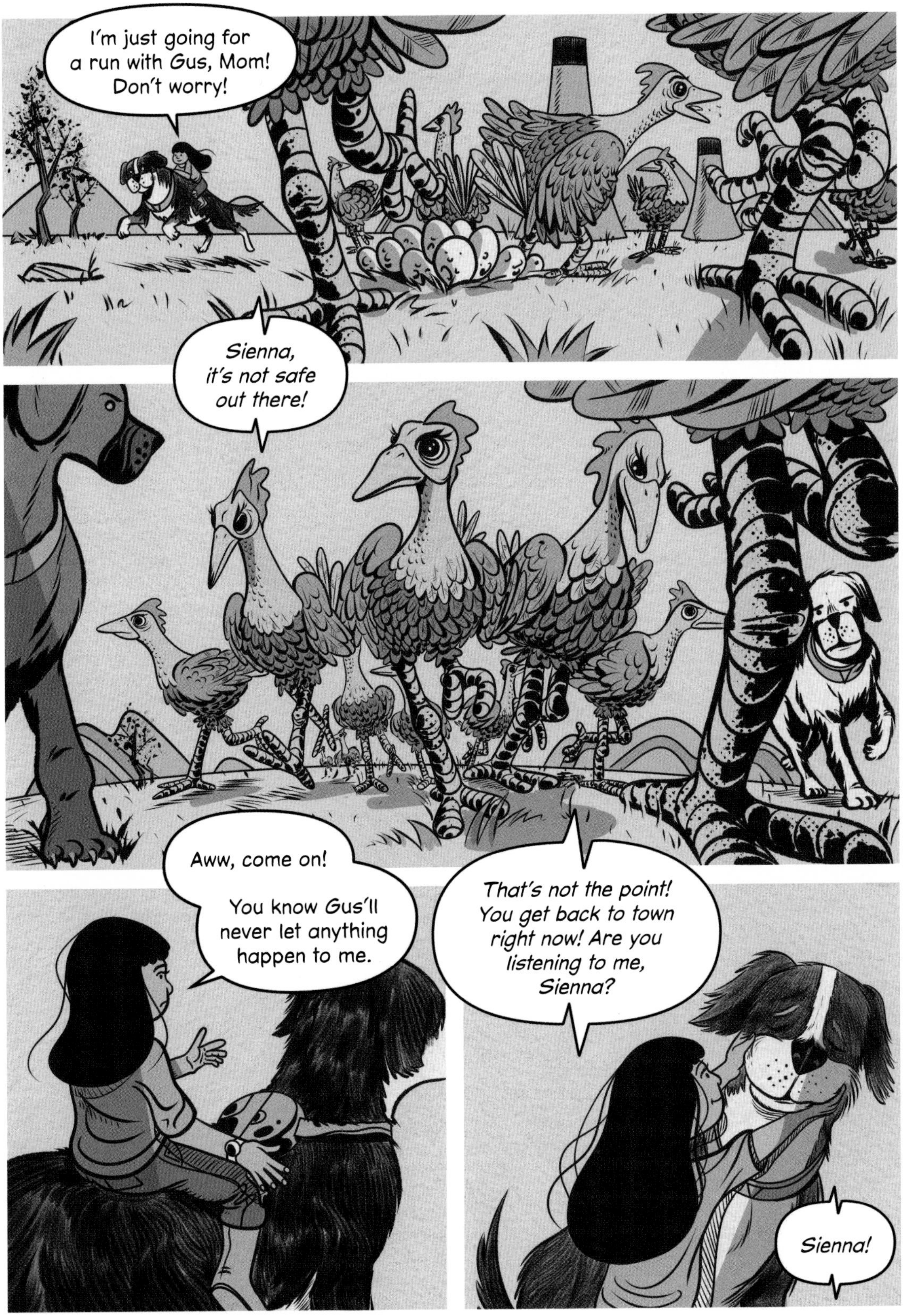
I'm just going for a run with Gus, Mom! Don't worry!
Sienna, it's not safe out there!
Aww, come on!
You know Gus'll never let anything happen to me.
That's not the point! You get back to town right now! Are you listening to me, Sienna?
Sienna!

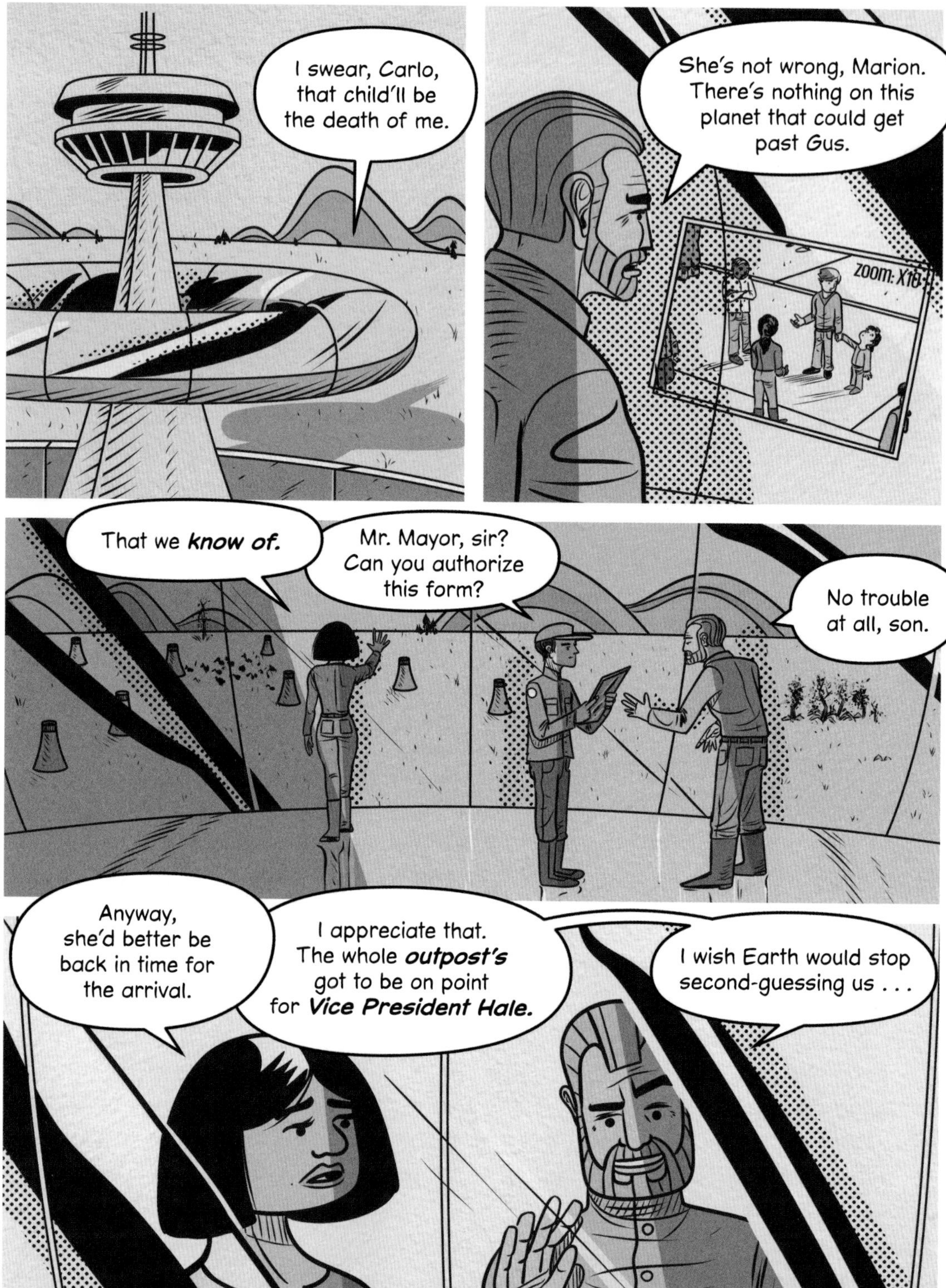
I swear, Carlo, that child'll be the death of me.
She's not wrong, Marion. There's nothing on this planet that could get past Gus.
zoom: X10
That we **know of.**
Mr. Mayor, sir? Can you authorize this form?
No trouble at all, son.
Anyway, she'd better be back in time for the arrival.
I appreciate that. The whole **outpost's** got to be on point for **Vice President Hale.**
I wish Earth would stop second-guessing us . . .

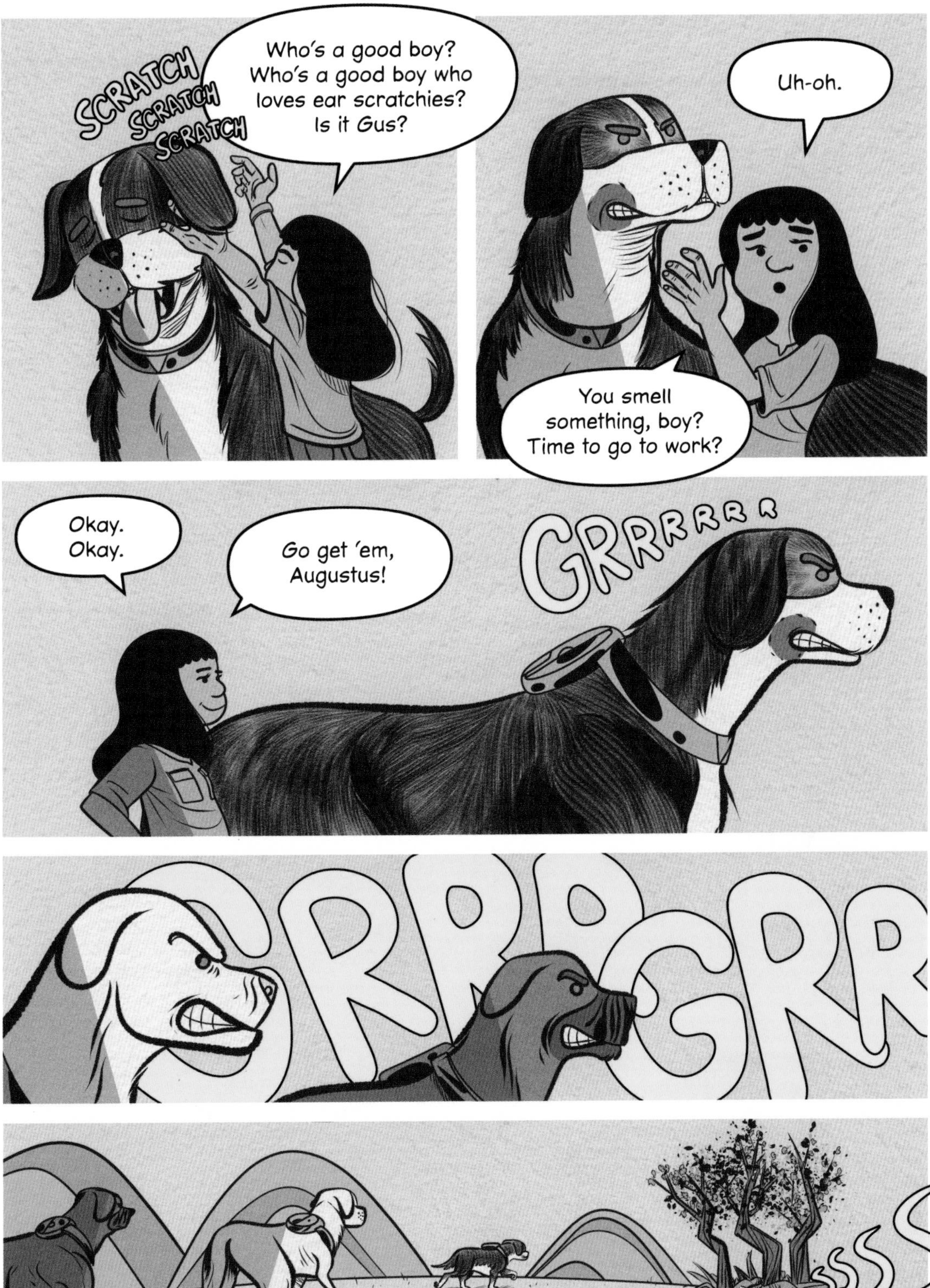
SCRATCH SCRATCH SCRATCH
Who's a good boy? Who's a good boy who loves ear scratchies? Is it Gus?
Uh-oh.
You smell something, boy? Time to go to work?
Okay. Okay.
Go get 'em, Augustus!
GRRRRRR
GRRGRR
SSSS

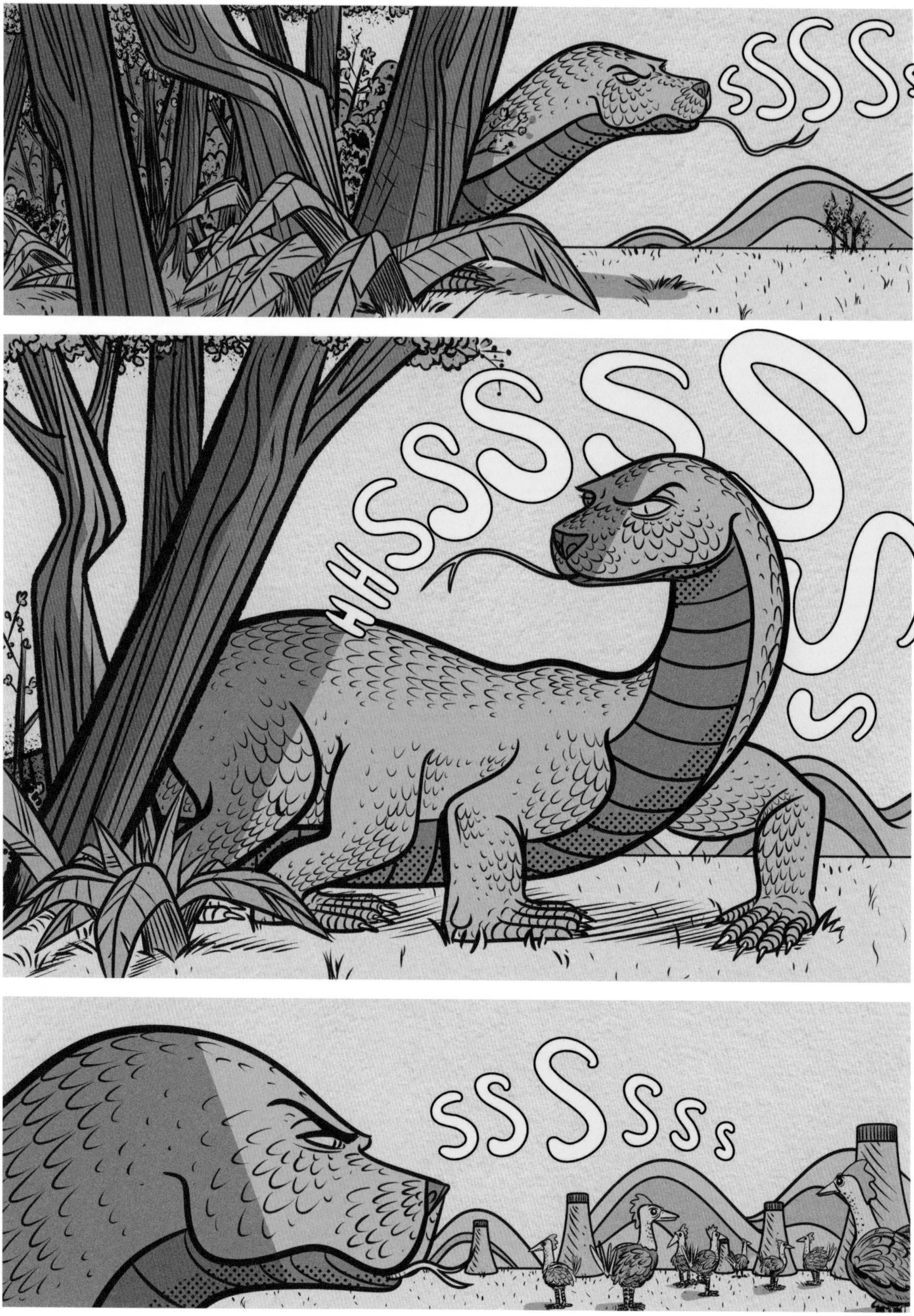
sSSSs
HSSSSSs
sSSSs

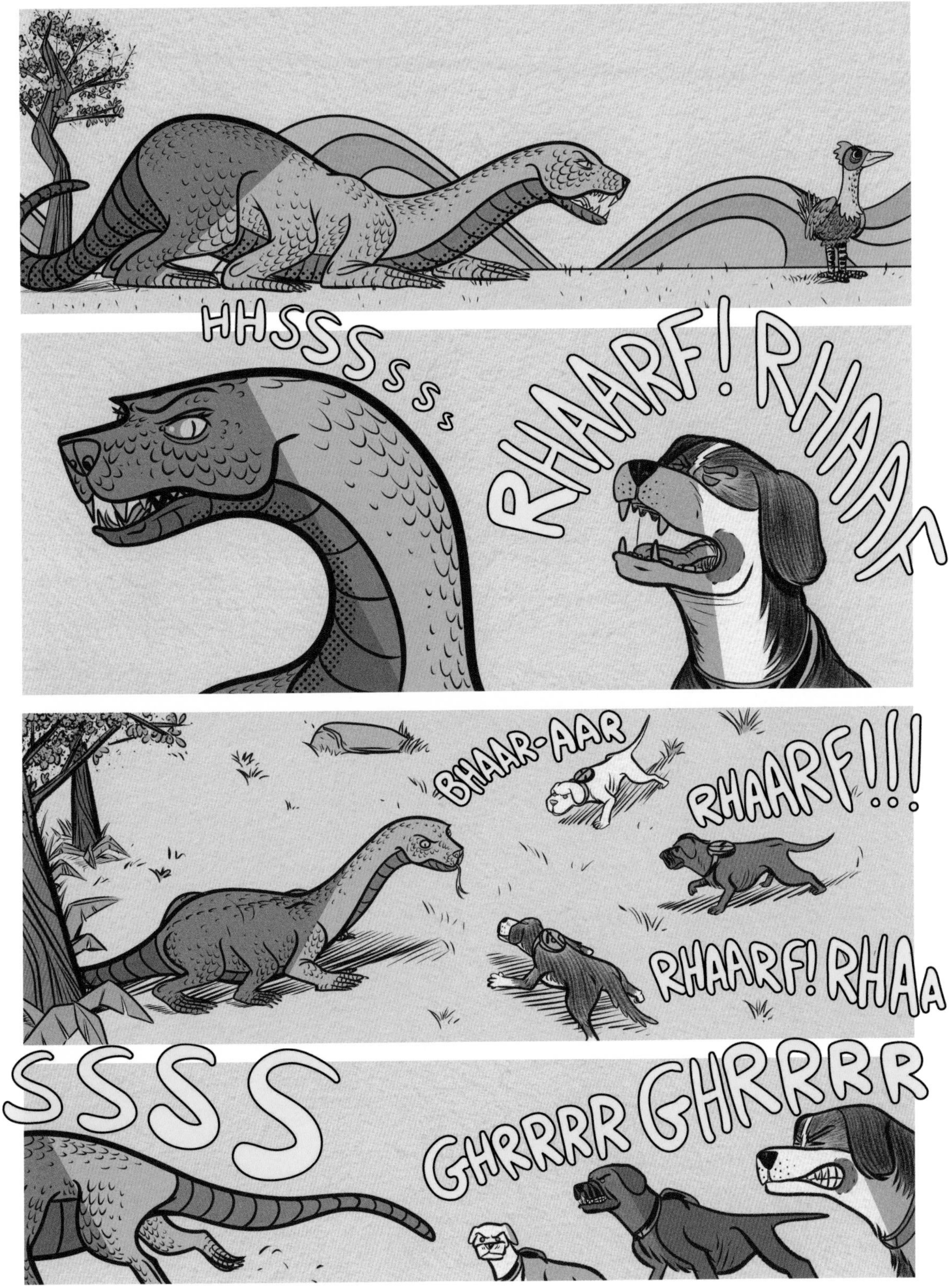
HHSSSSss
RHAARF! RHAAAF
BHAAR-AAR
RHAARF!!!
RHAARF! RHAA
SSSS
GHRRRR GHRRRR

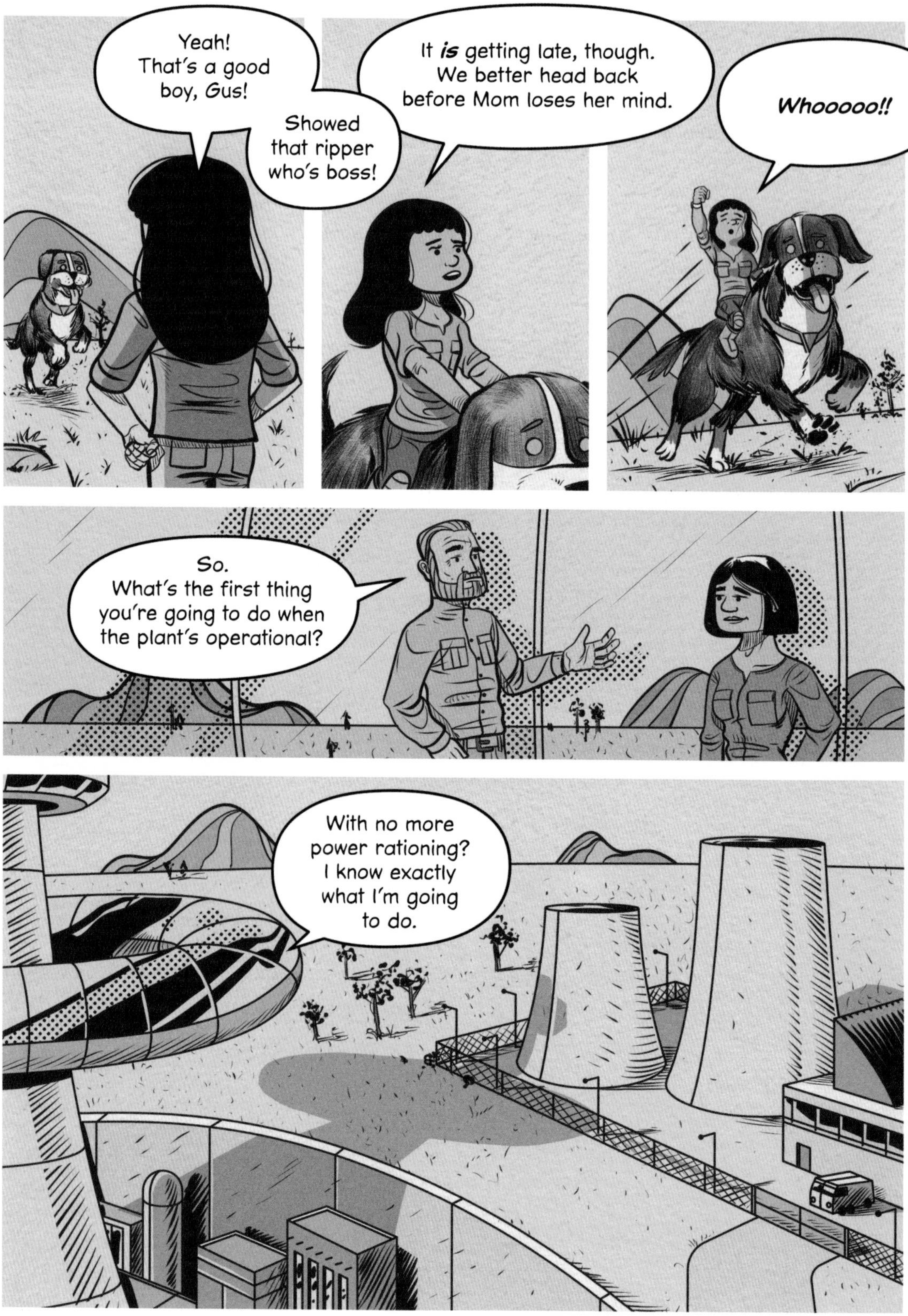
Yeah! That's a good boy, Gus!
Showed that ripper who's boss!
It *is* getting late, though. We better head back before Mom loses her mind.
Whoooooo!!
So. What's the first thing you're going to do when the plant's operational?
With no more power rationing? I know exactly what I'm going to do.

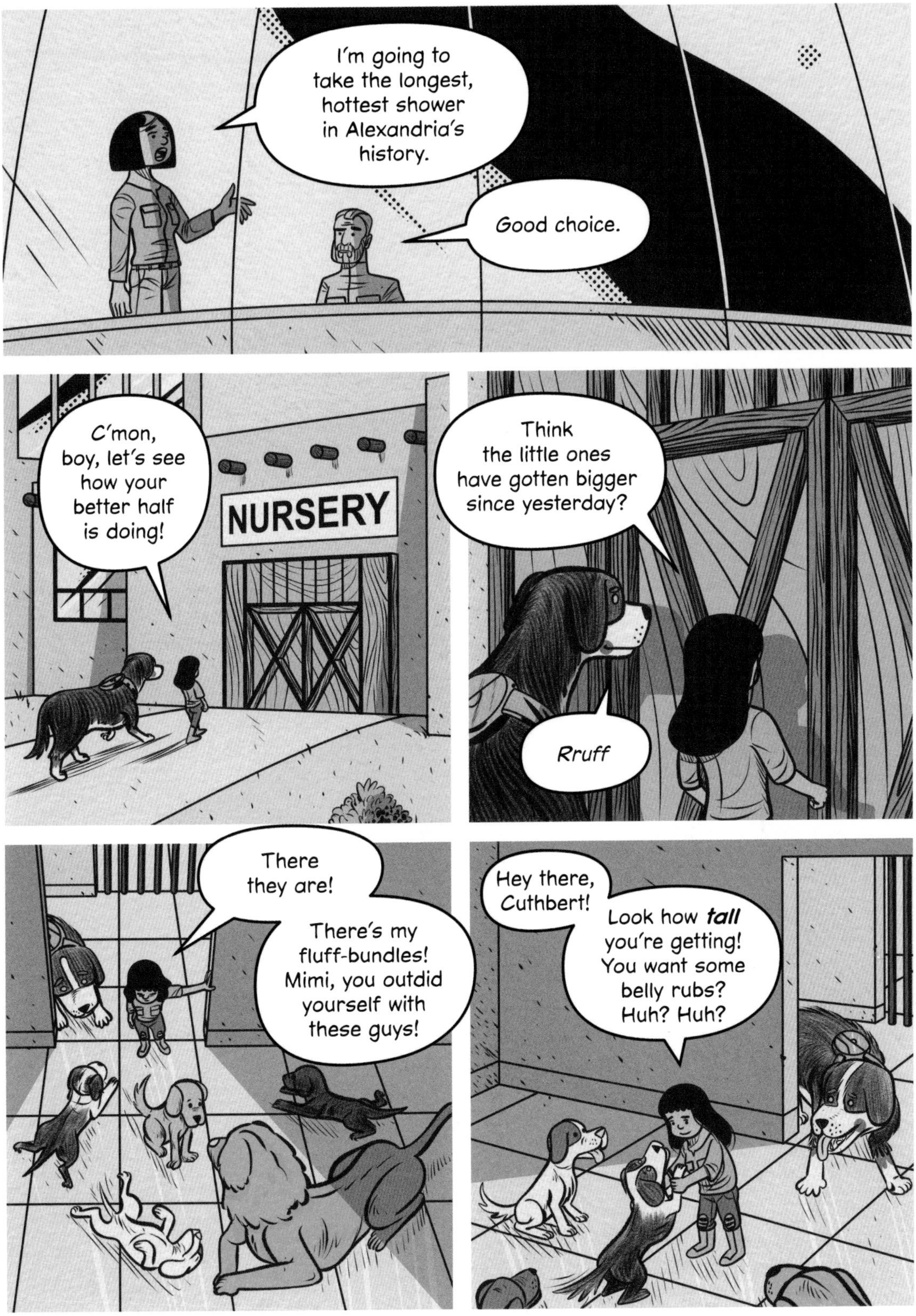
I'm going to take the longest, hottest shower in Alexandria's history.
Good choice.
C'mon, boy, let's see how your better half is doing!
NURSERY
Think the little ones have gotten bigger since yesterday?
Rruff
There they are!
There's my fluff-bundles! Mimi, you outdid yourself with these guys!
Hey there, Cuthbert!
Look how ***tall*** you're getting! You want some belly rubs? Huh? Huh?

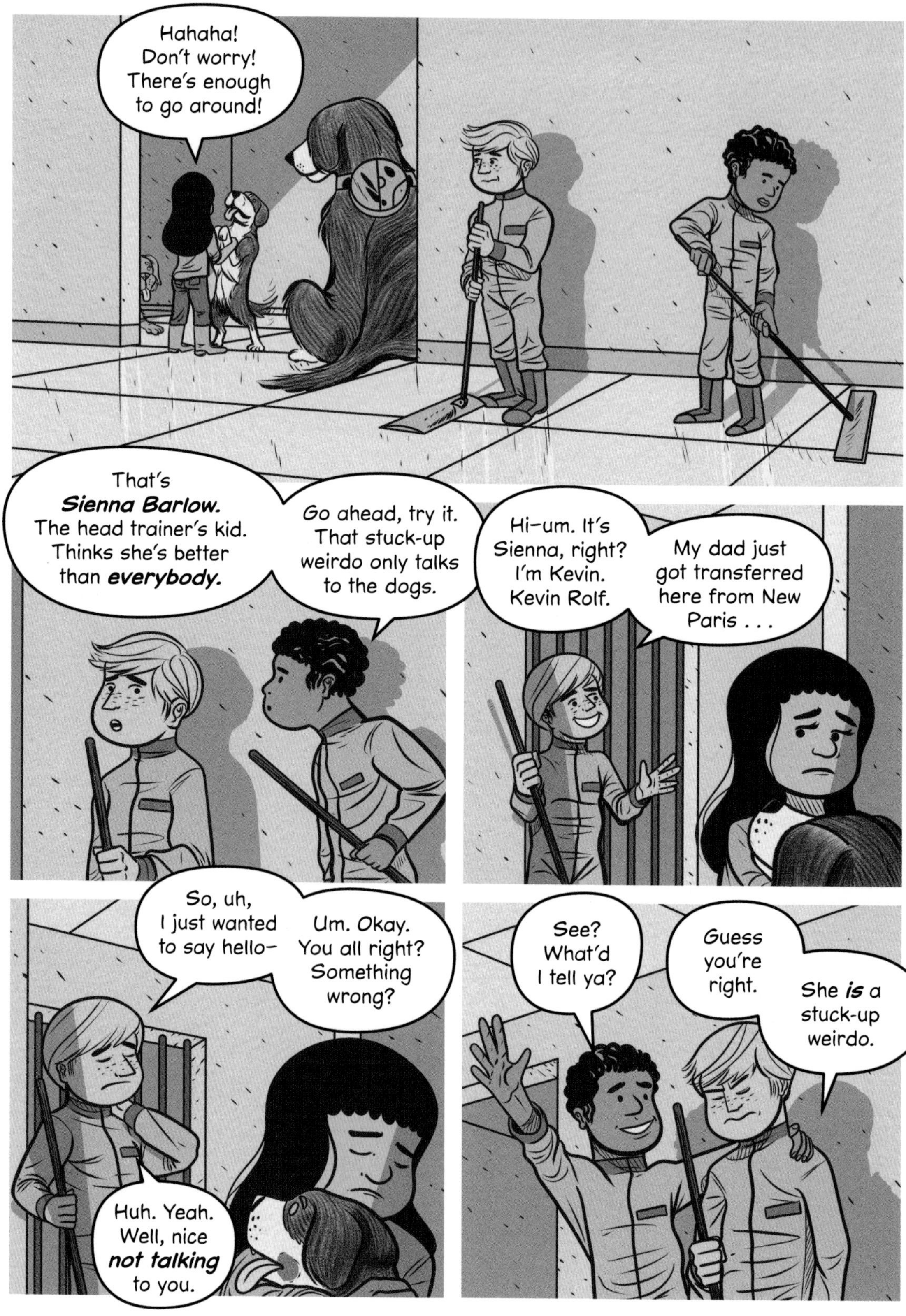
Hahaha! Don't worry! There's enough to go around!
That's **Sienna Barlow.** The head trainer's kid. Thinks she's better than **everybody.**
Go ahead, try it. That stuck-up weirdo only talks to the dogs.
Hi—um. It's Sienna, right? I'm Kevin. Kevin Rolf.
My dad just got transferred here from New Paris . . .
So, uh, I just wanted to say hello–
Um. Okay. You all right? Something wrong?
Huh. Yeah. Well, nice **not talking** to you.
See? What'd I tell ya?
Guess you're right.
She ***is*** a stuck-up weirdo.

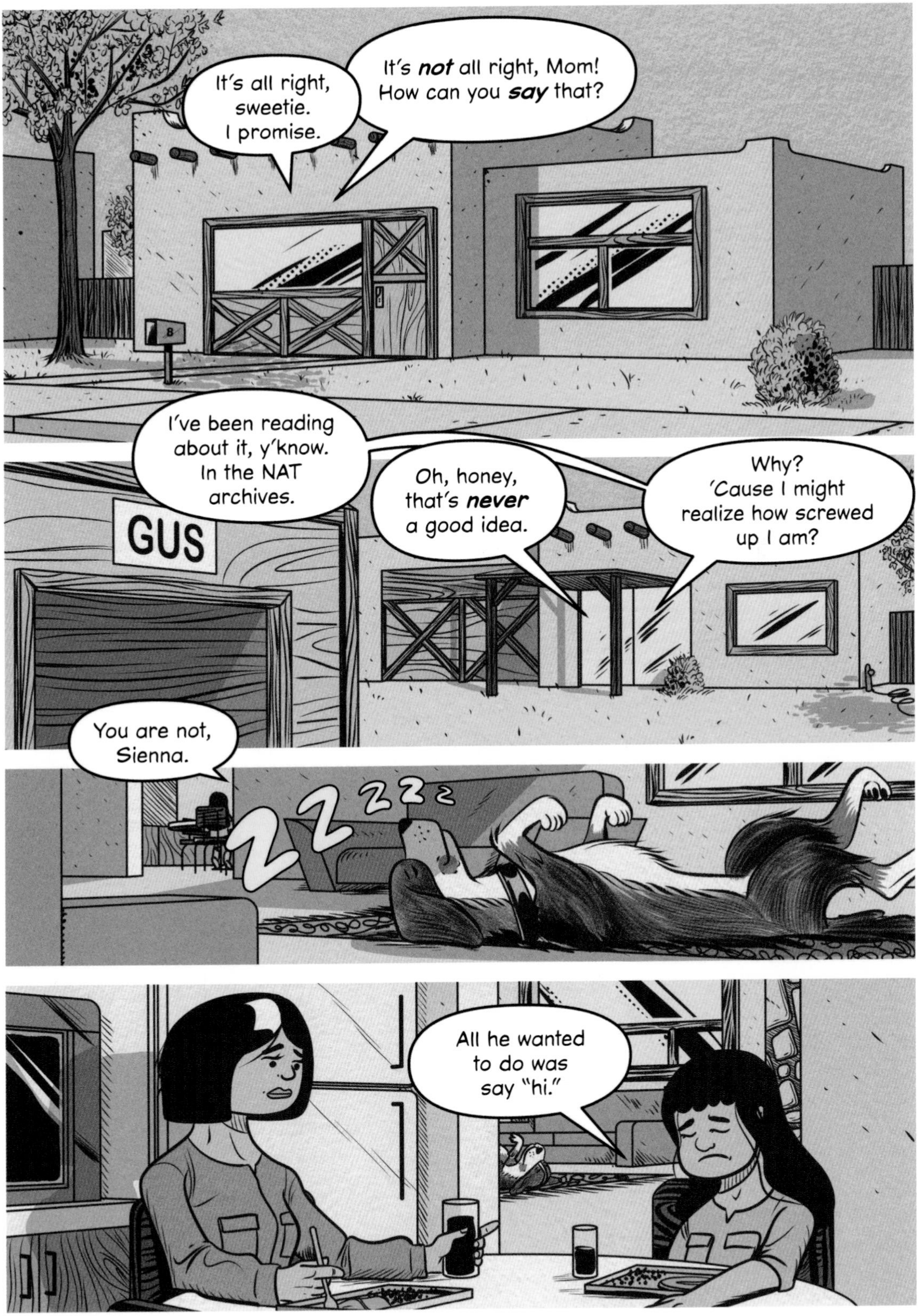
It's all right, sweetie. I promise.
It's **not** all right, Mom! How can you **say** that?
I've been reading about it, y'know. In the NAT archives.
GUS
Oh, honey, that's **never** a good idea.
Why? 'Cause I might realize how screwed up I am?
You are not, Sienna.
ZZZZZZ
All he wanted to do was say "hi."

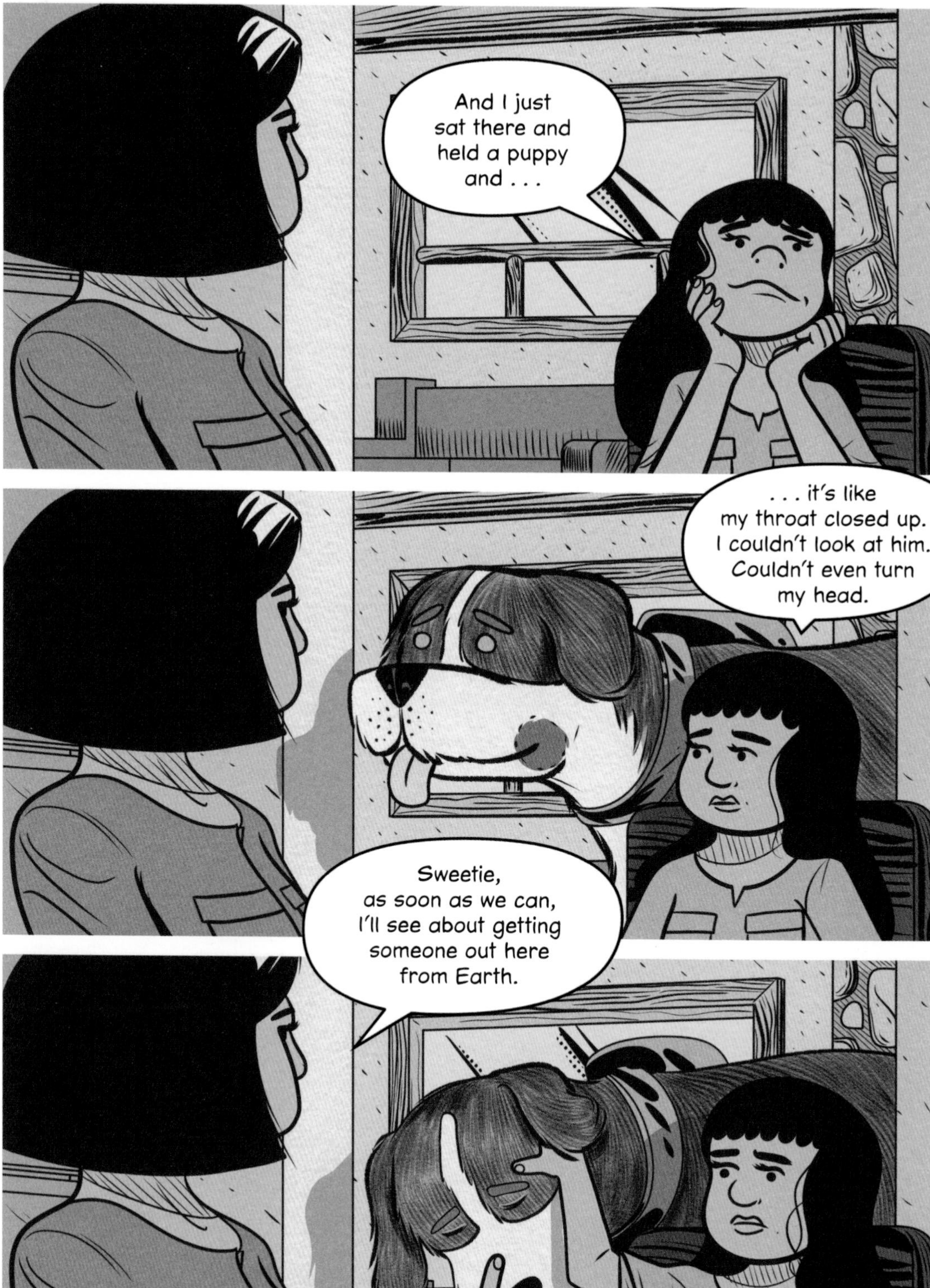
And I just sat there and held a puppy and . . .
. . . it's like my throat closed up. I couldn't look at him. Couldn't even turn my head.
Sweetie, as soon as we can, I'll see about getting someone out here from Earth.

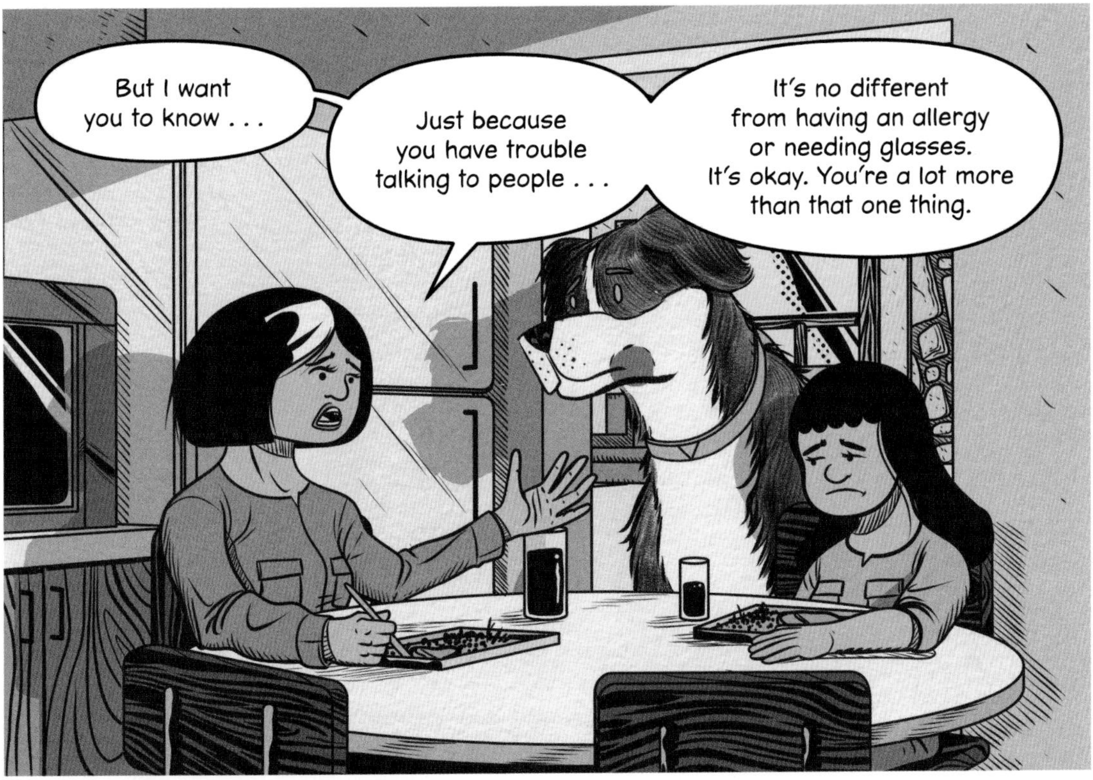
But I want you to know . . .
Just because you have trouble talking to people . . .
It's no different from having an allergy or needing glasses. It's okay. You're a lot more than that one thing.

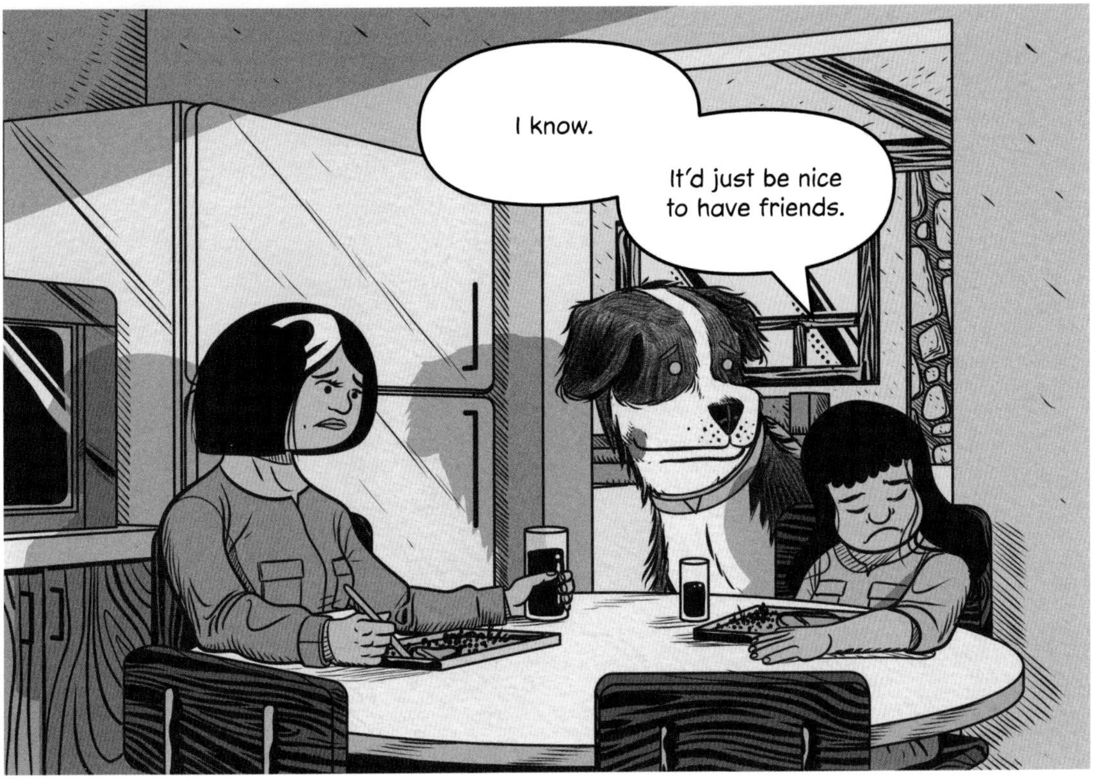
I know.
It'd just be nice to have friends.

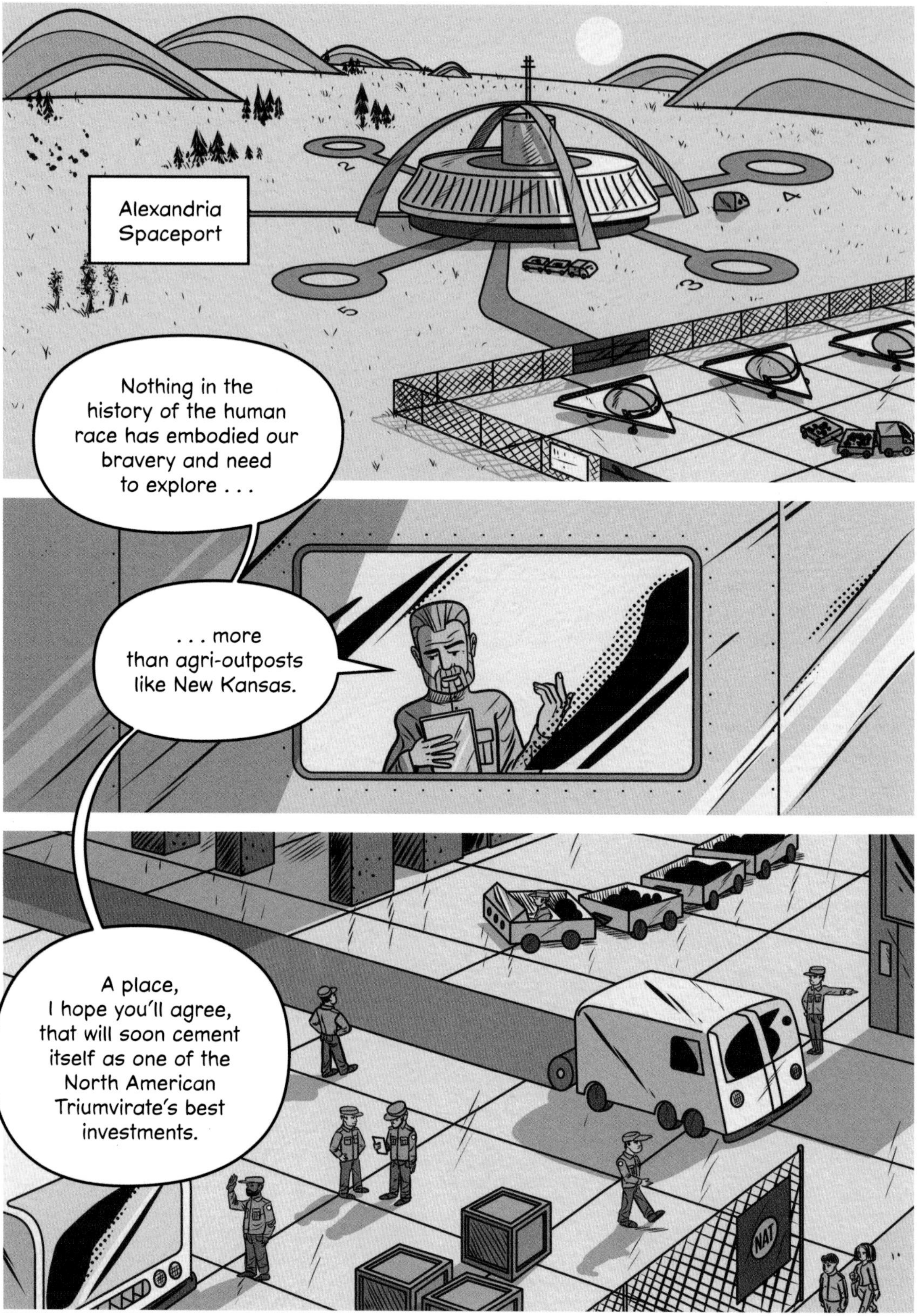

Alexandria Spaceport
Nothing in the history of the human race has embodied our bravery and need to explore . . .
. . . more than agri-outposts like New Kansas.
A place, I hope you'll agree, that will soon cement itself as one of the North American Triumvirate's best investments.
NAT

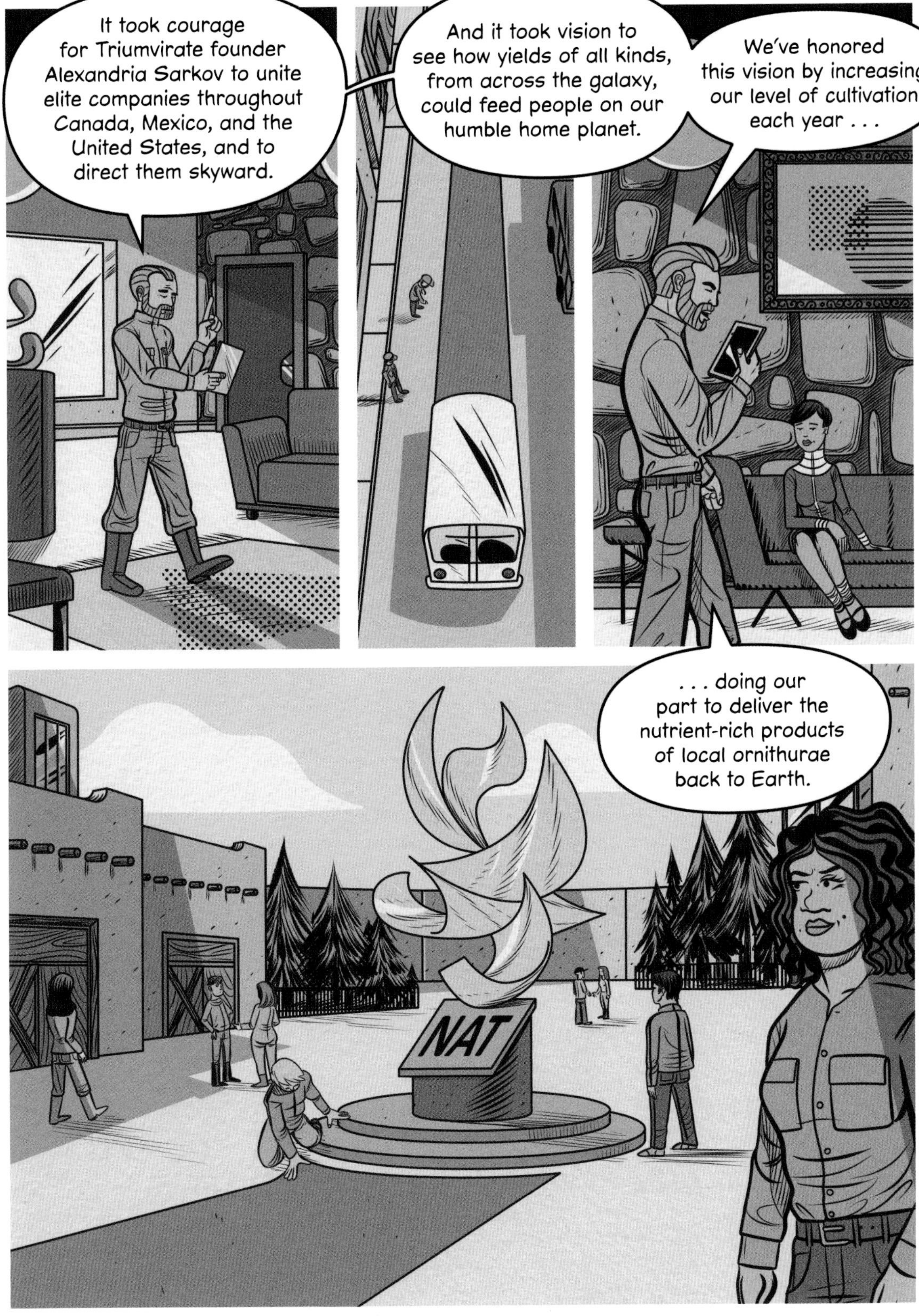
It took courage for Triumvirate founder Alexandria Sarkov to unite elite companies throughout Canada, Mexico, and the United States, and to direct them skyward.
And it took vision to see how yields of all kinds, from across the galaxy, could feed people on our humble home planet.
We've honored this vision by increasing our level of cultivation each year . . .
. . . doing our part to deliver the nutrient-rich products of local ornithurae back to Earth.
NAT

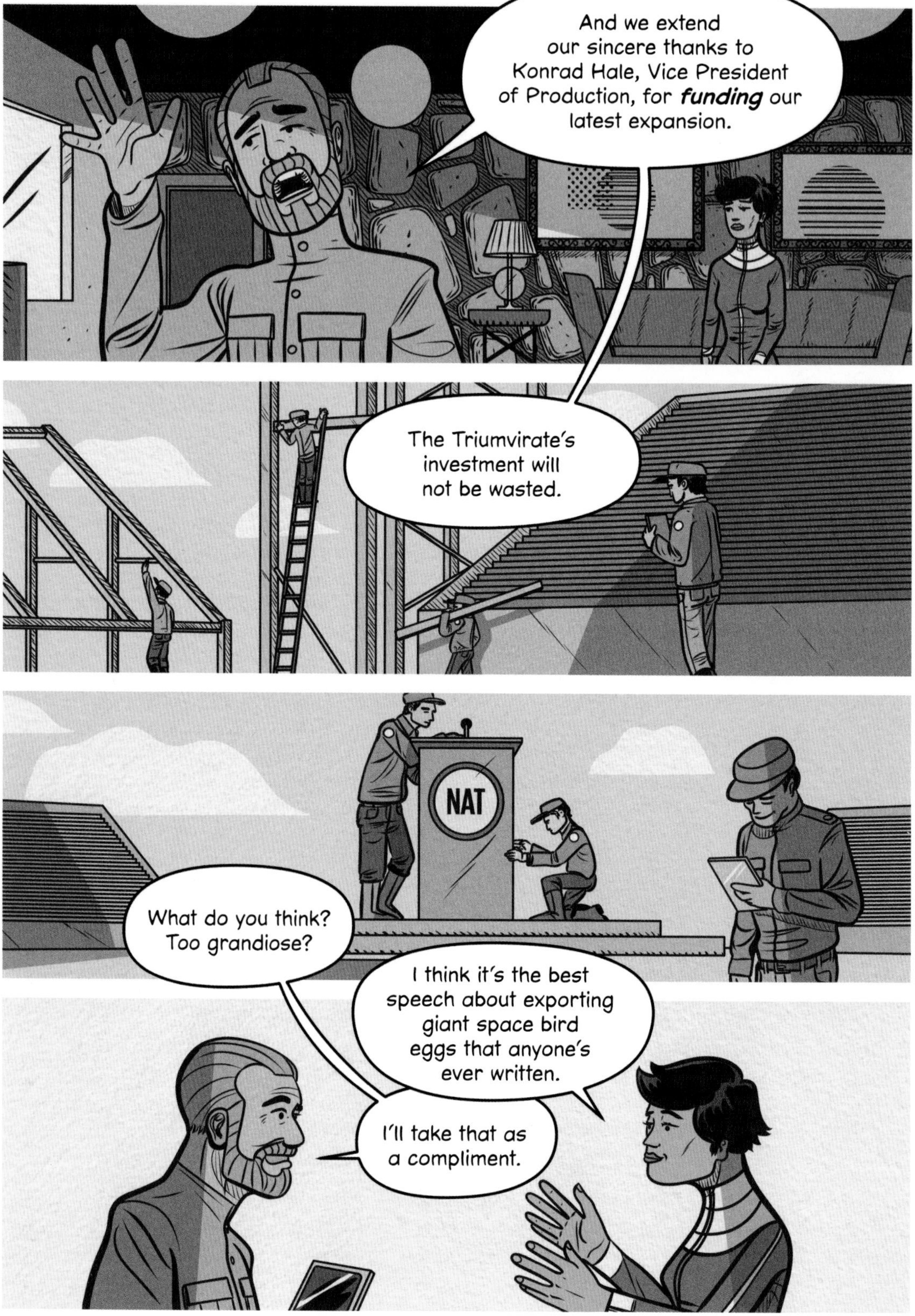
And we extend our sincere thanks to Konrad Hale, Vice President of Production, for ***funding*** our latest expansion.
The Triumvirate's investment will not be wasted.
NAT
What do you think? Too grandiose?
I think it's the best speech about exporting giant space bird eggs that anyone's ever written.
I'll take that as a compliment.

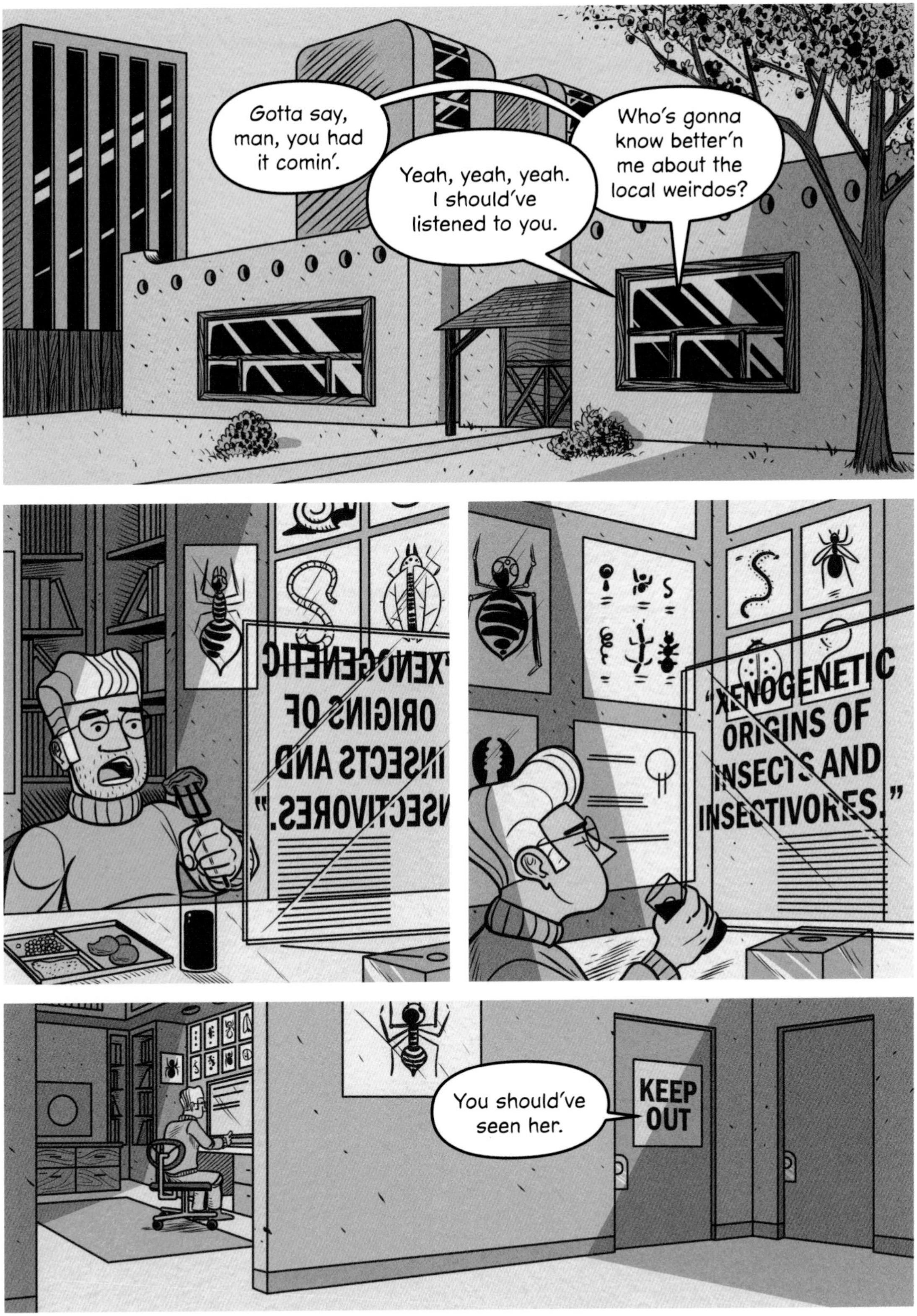
Gotta say, man, you had it comin'.
Yeah, yeah, yeah. I should've listened to you.
Who's gonna know better'n me about the local weirdos?
"XENOGENETIC ORIGINS OF INSECTS AND INSECTIVORES."
"XENOGENETIC ORIGINS OF INSECTS AND INSECTIVORES."
You should've seen her.
KEEP OUT

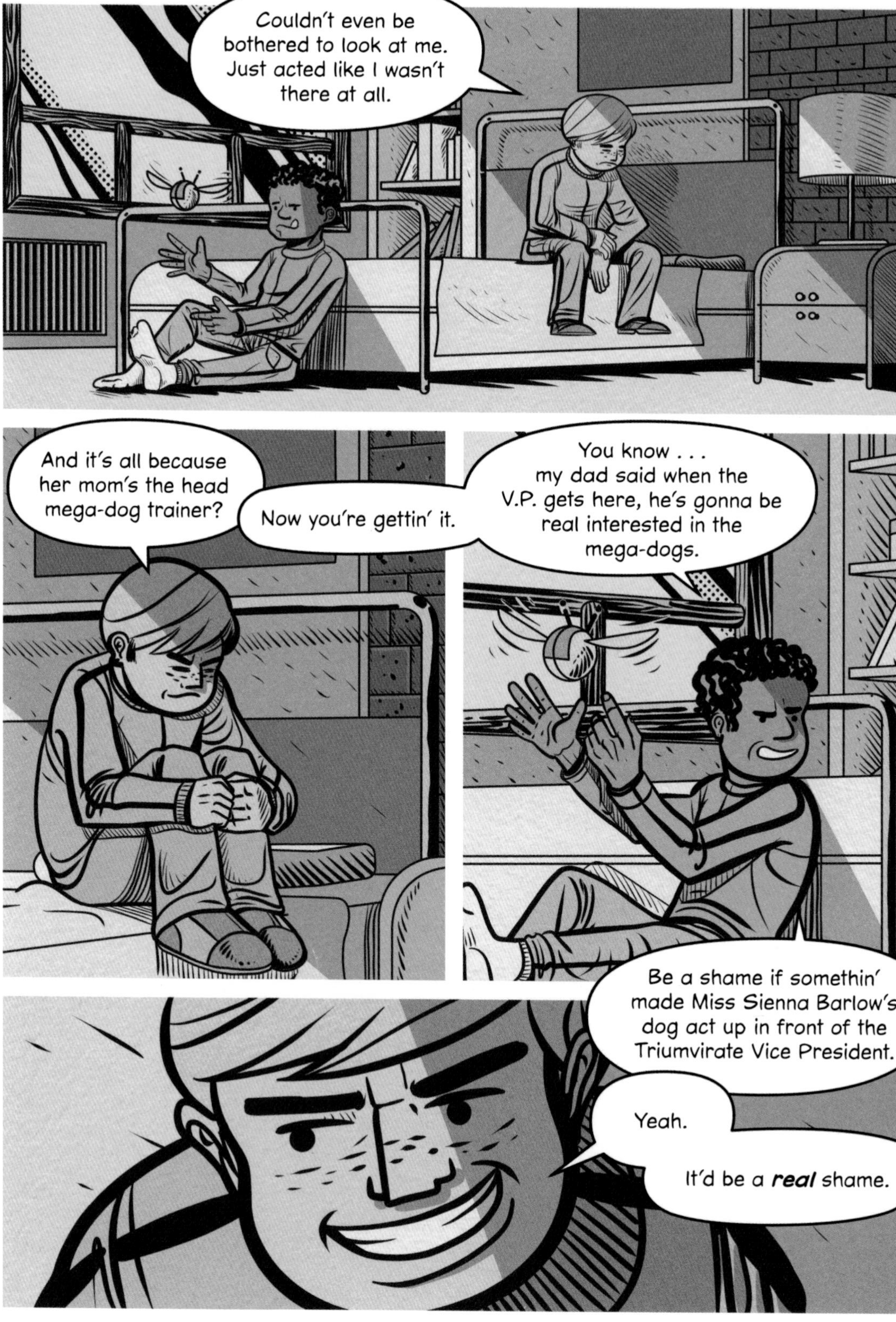
Couldn't even be bothered to look at me. Just acted like I wasn't there at all.
And it's all because her mom's the head mega-dog trainer?
Now you're gettin' it.
You know . . . my dad said when the V.P. gets here, he's gonna be real interested in the mega-dogs.
Be a shame if somethin' made Miss Sienna Barlow's dog act up in front of the Triumvirate Vice President.
Yeah.
It'd be a ***real*** shame.

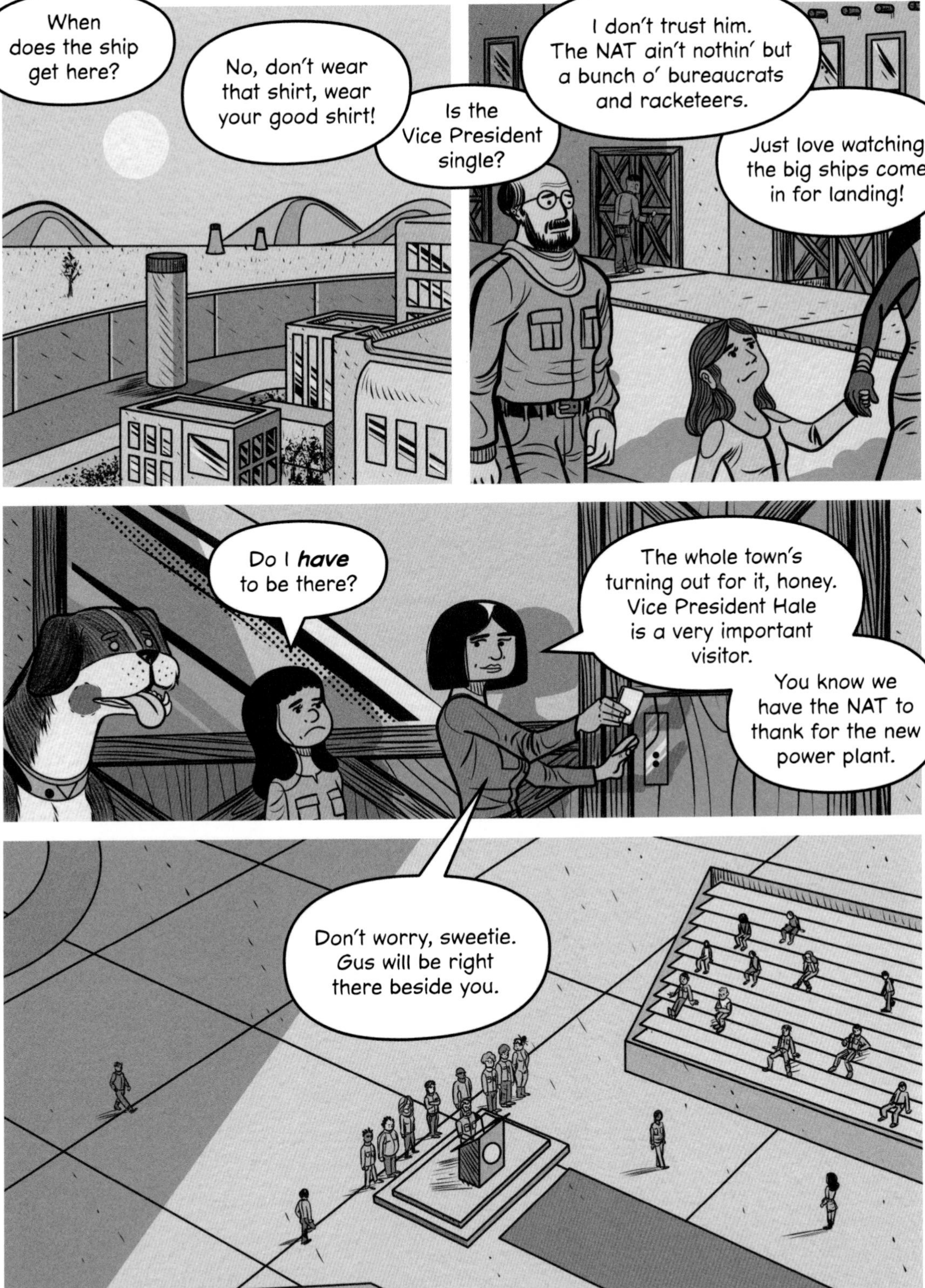
When does the ship get here?
No, don't wear that shirt, wear your good shirt!
Is the Vice President single?
I don't trust him. The NAT ain't nothin' but a bunch o' bureaucrats and racketeers.
Just love watching the big ships come in for landing!
Do I **have** to be there?
The whole town's turning out for it, honey. Vice President Hale is a very important visitor.
You know we have the NAT to thank for the new power plant.
Don't worry, sweetie. Gus will be right there beside you.

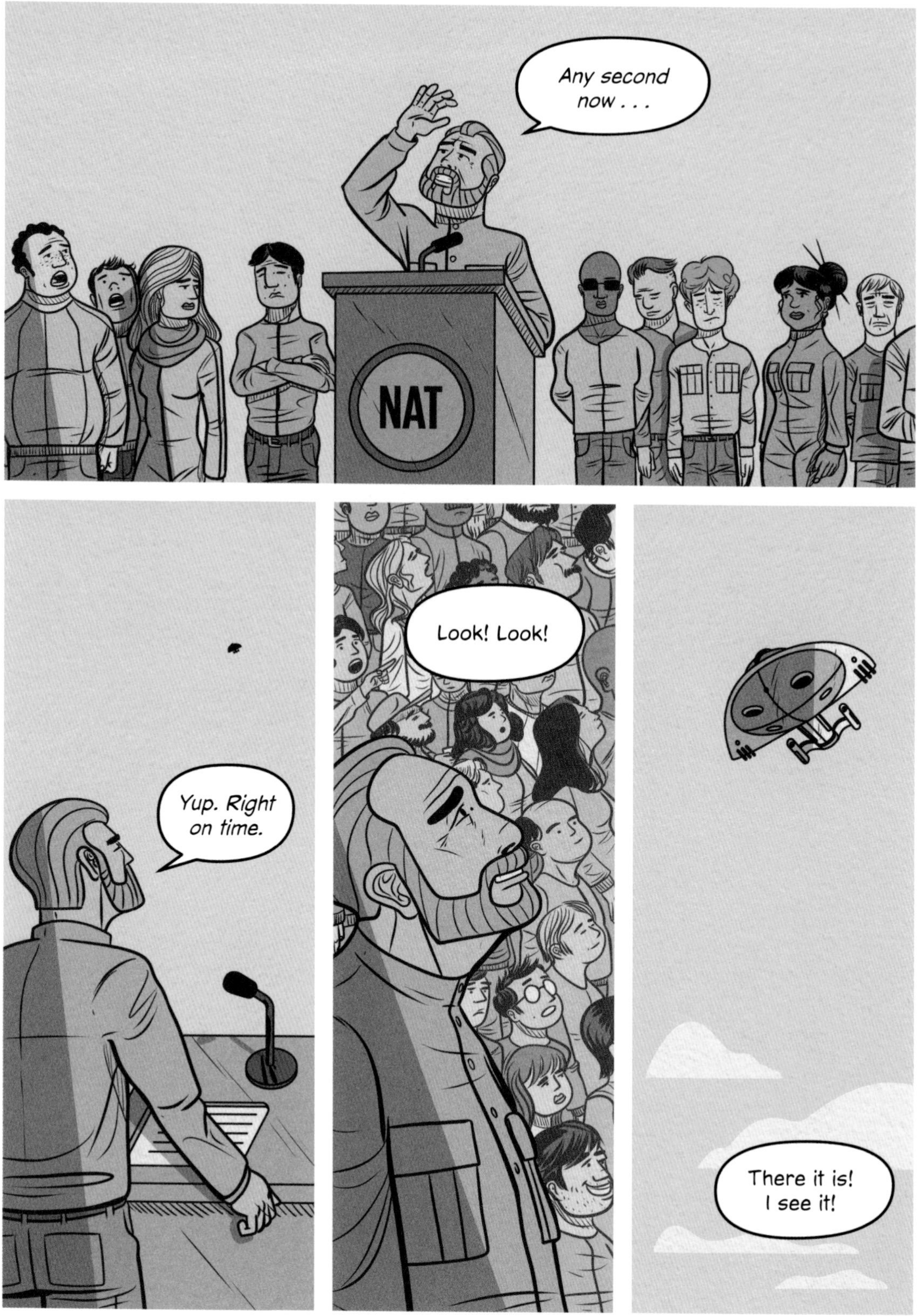
Any second now . . .
NAT
Yup. Right on time.
Look! Look!
There it is! I see it!

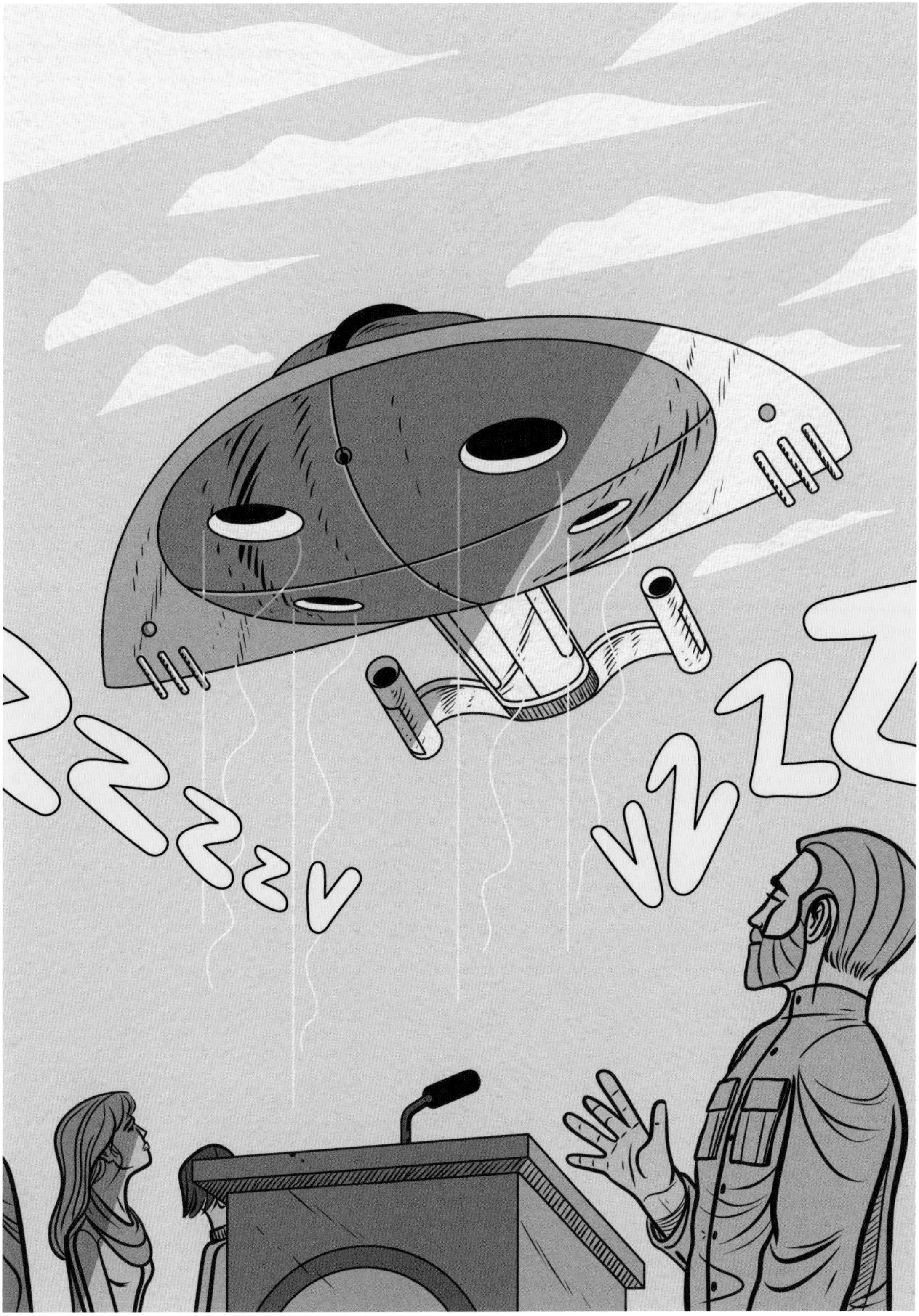
ZZZzv
vZZZ

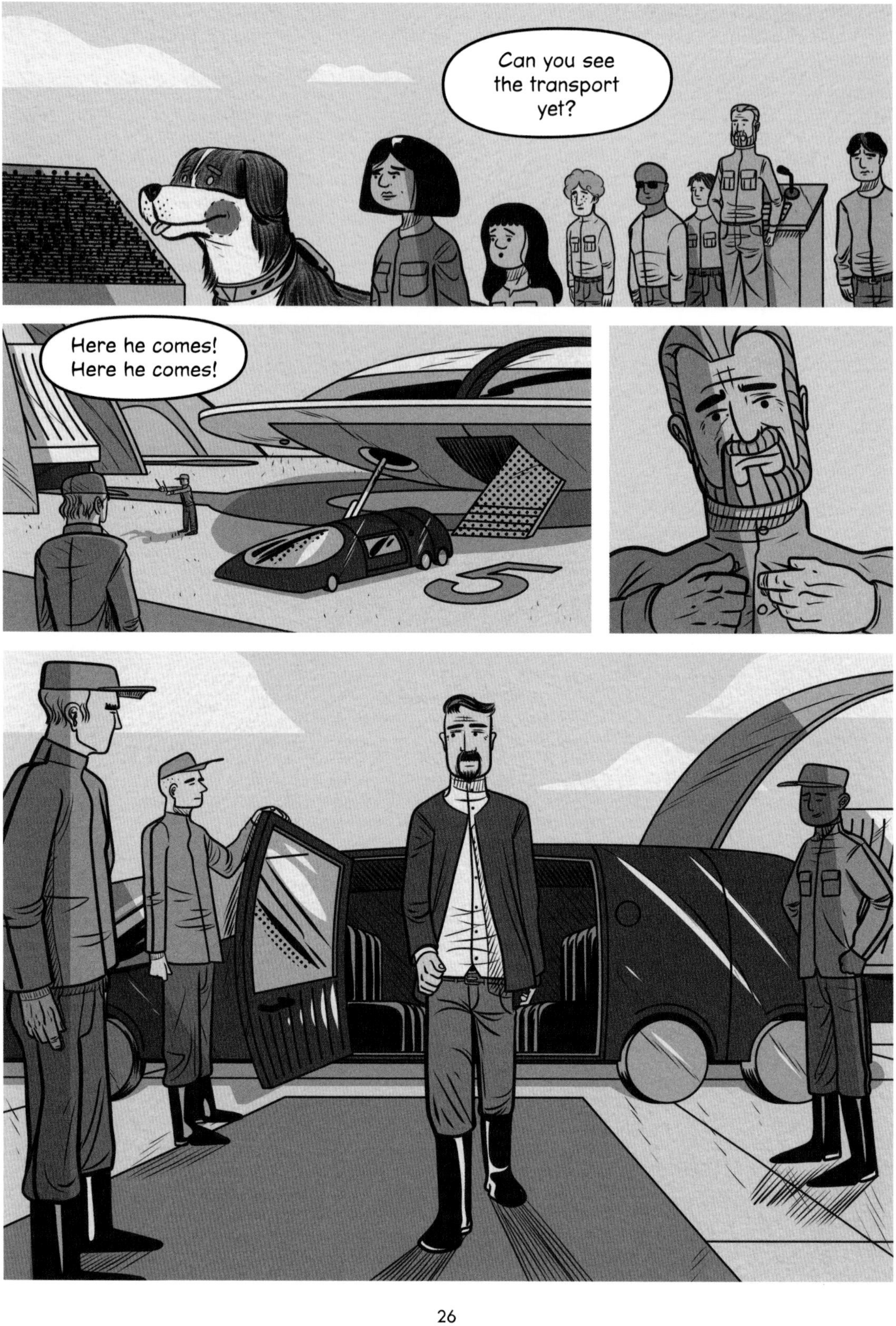
Can you see the transport yet?
Here he comes! Here he comes!

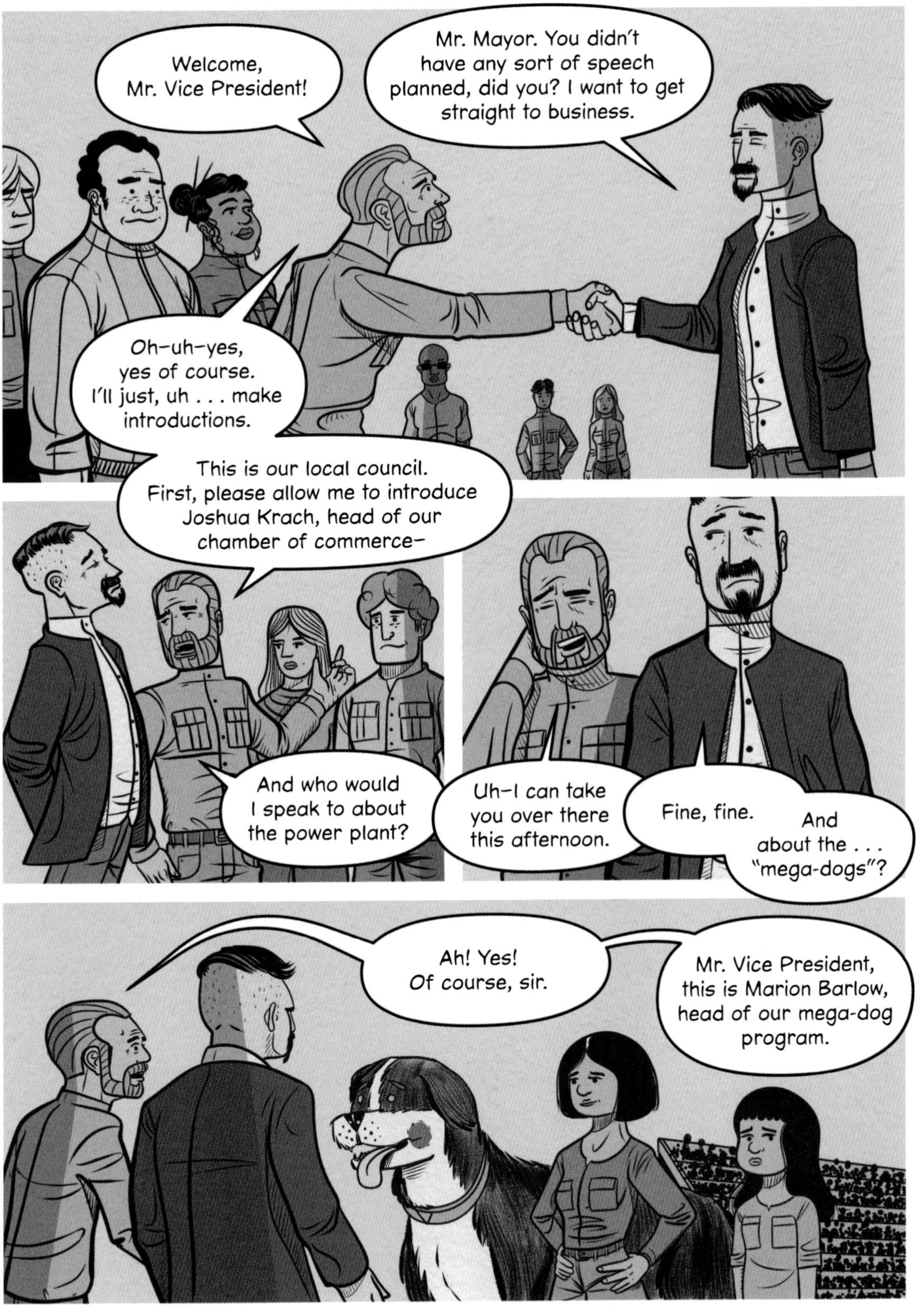
Welcome, Mr. Vice President!
Mr. Mayor. You didn't have any sort of speech planned, did you? I want to get straight to business.
Oh–uh–yes, yes of course. I'll just, uh . . . make introductions.
This is our local council. First, please allow me to introduce Joshua Krach, head of our chamber of commerce–
And who would I speak to about the power plant?
Uh–I can take you over there this afternoon.
Fine, fine.
And about the . . . "mega-dogs"?
Ah! Yes! Of course, sir.
Mr. Vice President, this is Marion Barlow, head of our mega-dog program.

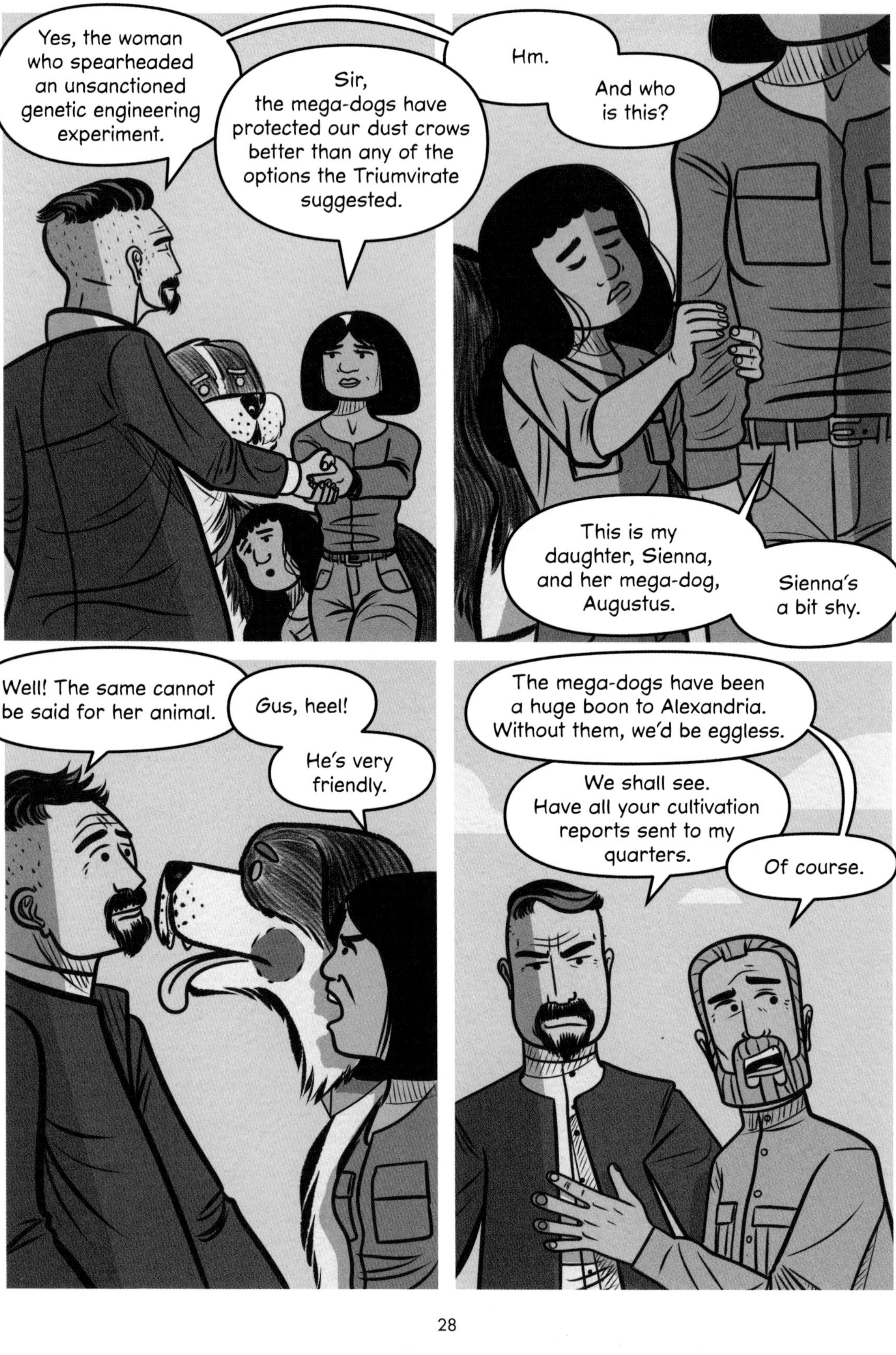
Yes, the woman who spearheaded an unsanctioned genetic engineering experiment.
Sir, the mega-dogs have protected our dust crows better than any of the options the Triumvirate suggested.
Hm.
And who is this?
This is my daughter, Sienna, and her mega-dog, Augustus.
Sienna's a bit shy.
Well! The same cannot be said for her animal.
Gus, heel!
He's very friendly.
The mega-dogs have been a huge boon to Alexandria. Without them, we'd be eggless.
We shall see. Have all your cultivation reports sent to my quarters.
Of course.

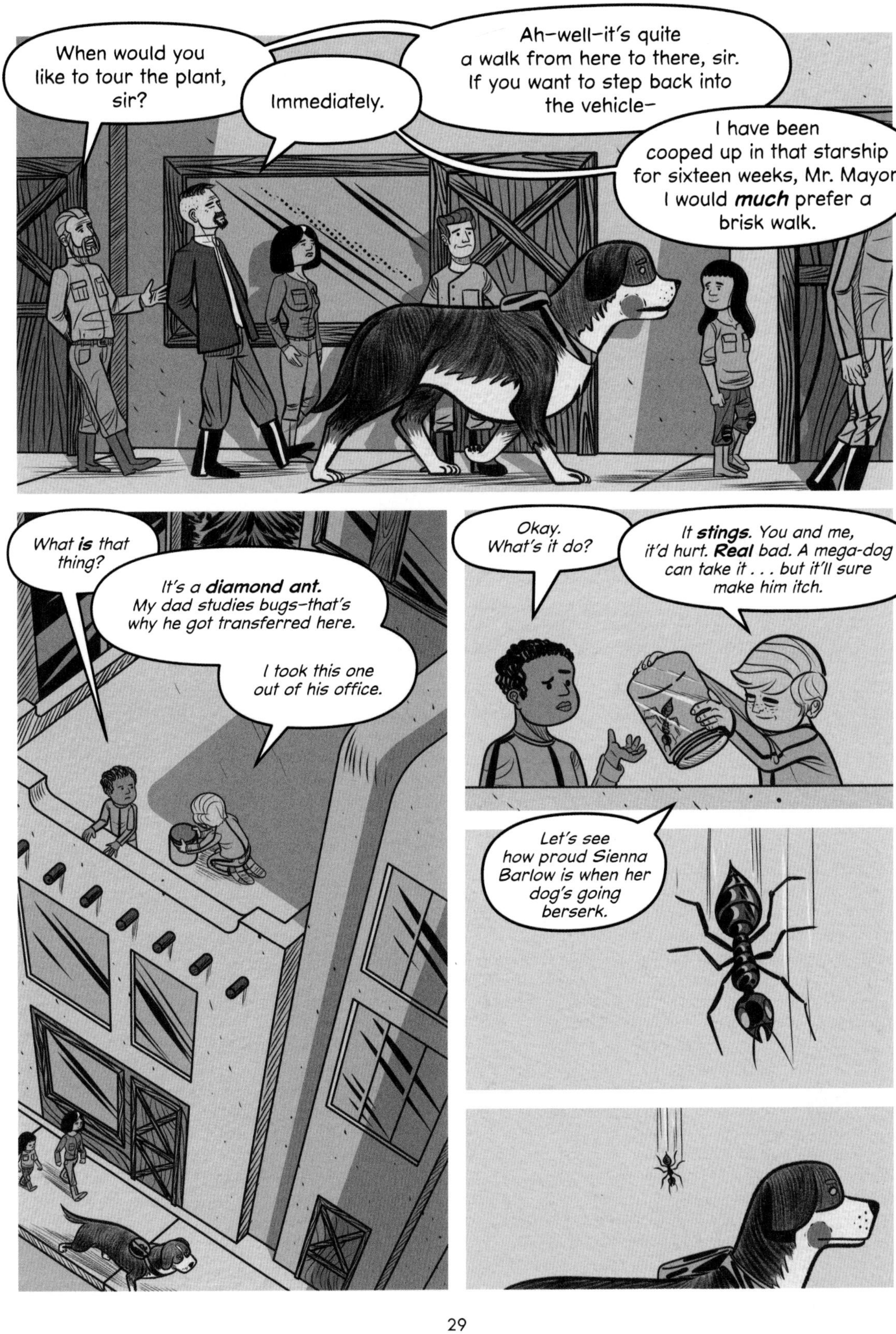
When would you like to tour the plant, sir?
Immediately.
Ah—well—it's quite a walk from here to there, sir. If you want to step back into the vehicle—
I have been cooped up in that starship for sixteen weeks, Mr. Mayor. I would **much** prefer a brisk walk.
*What **is** that thing?*
*It's a **diamond ant.** My dad studies bugs—that's why he got transferred here.*
I took this one out of his office.
Okay. What's it do?
*It **stings**. You and me, it'd hurt. **Real** bad. A mega-dog can take it . . . but it'll sure make him itch.*
Let's see how proud Sienna Barlow is when her dog's going berserk.

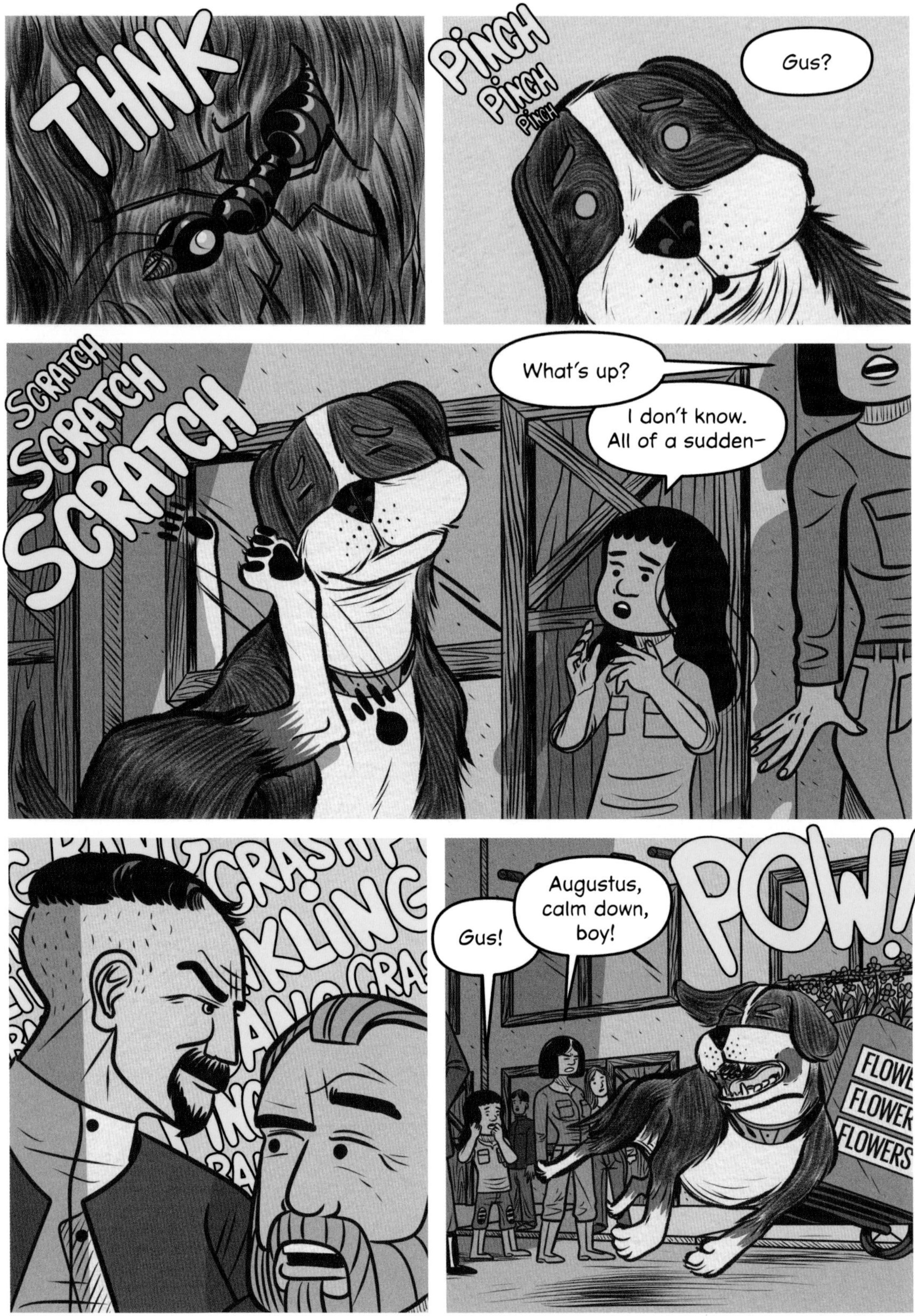
THNK
PINCH
PINCH
PINCH
Gus?
SCRATCH
SCRATCH
SCRATCH
What's up?
I don't know.
All of a sudden–
CRASH
KLING
Gus!
Augustus, calm down, boy!
POW!
FLOWERS
FLOWERS
FLOWERS

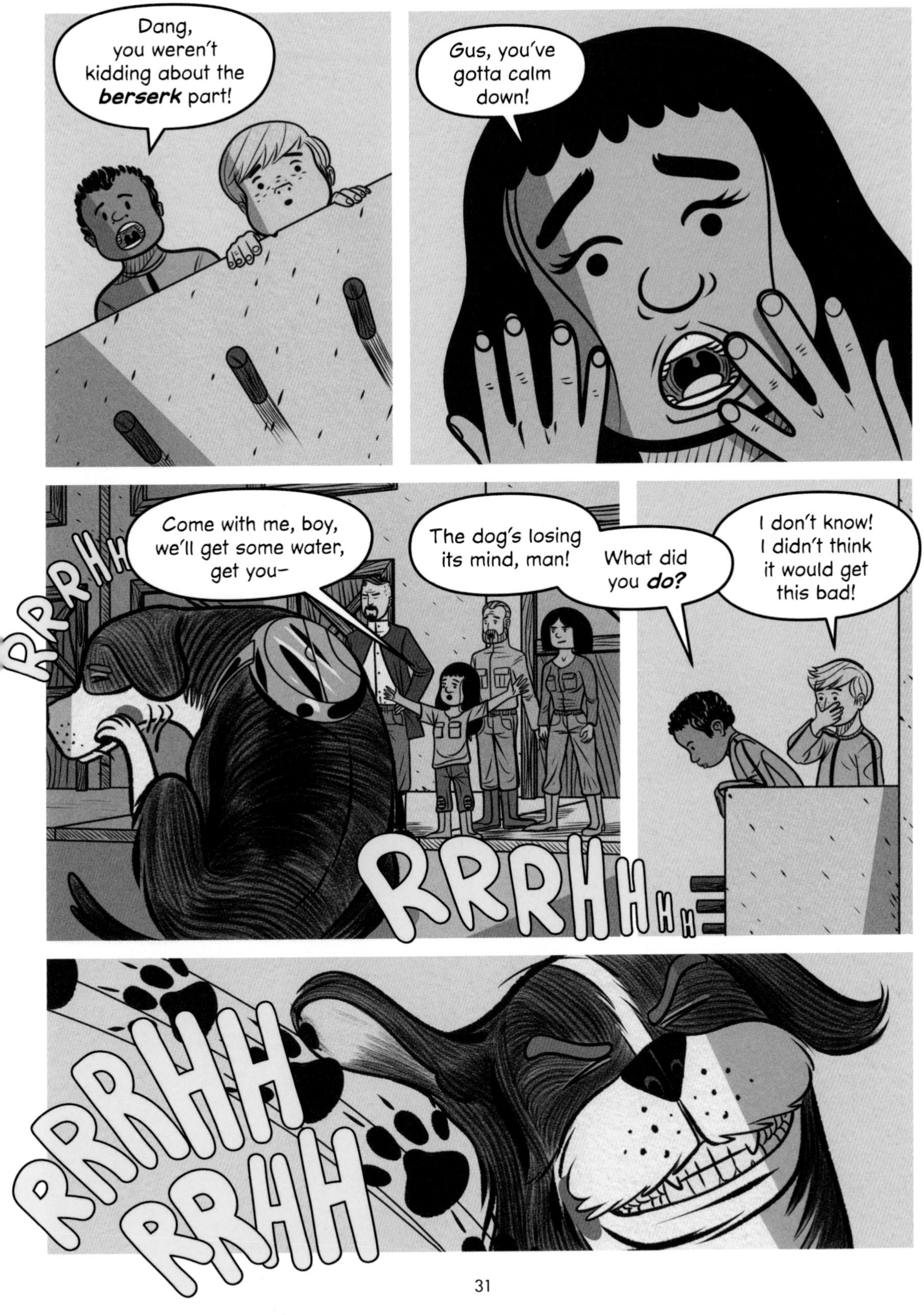
Dang, you weren't kidding about the **berserk** part!
Gus, you've gotta calm down!
RRRHH
Come with me, boy, we'll get some water, get you–
The dog's losing its mind, man!
What did you **do?**
I don't know! I didn't think it would get this bad!
RRRHHHHH
RRHH RRAH

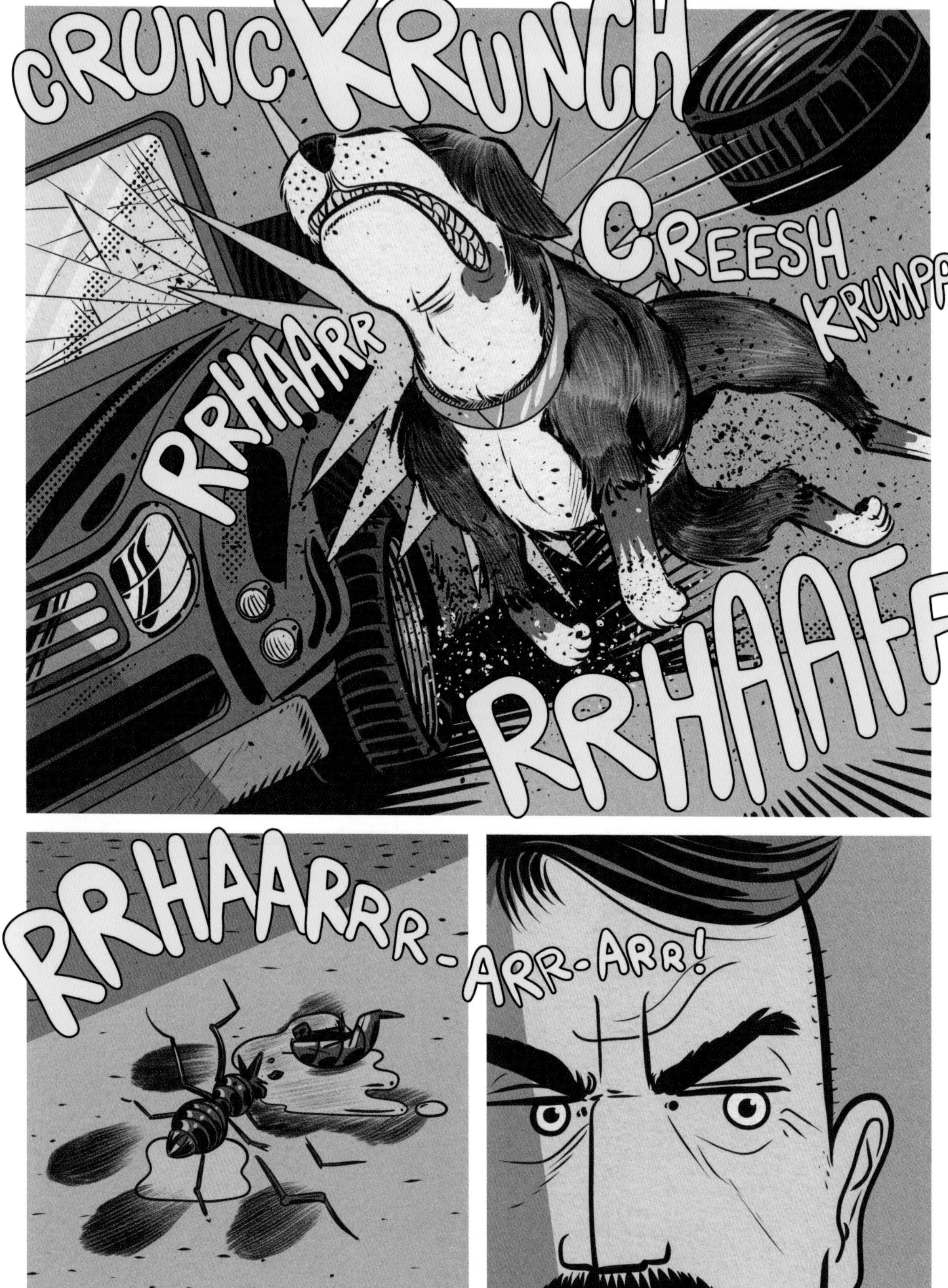
CRUNCKRUNCH
CREESH
KRUMPP
RRHAARR
RRHAAFF
RRHAARRR-ARR-ARR!

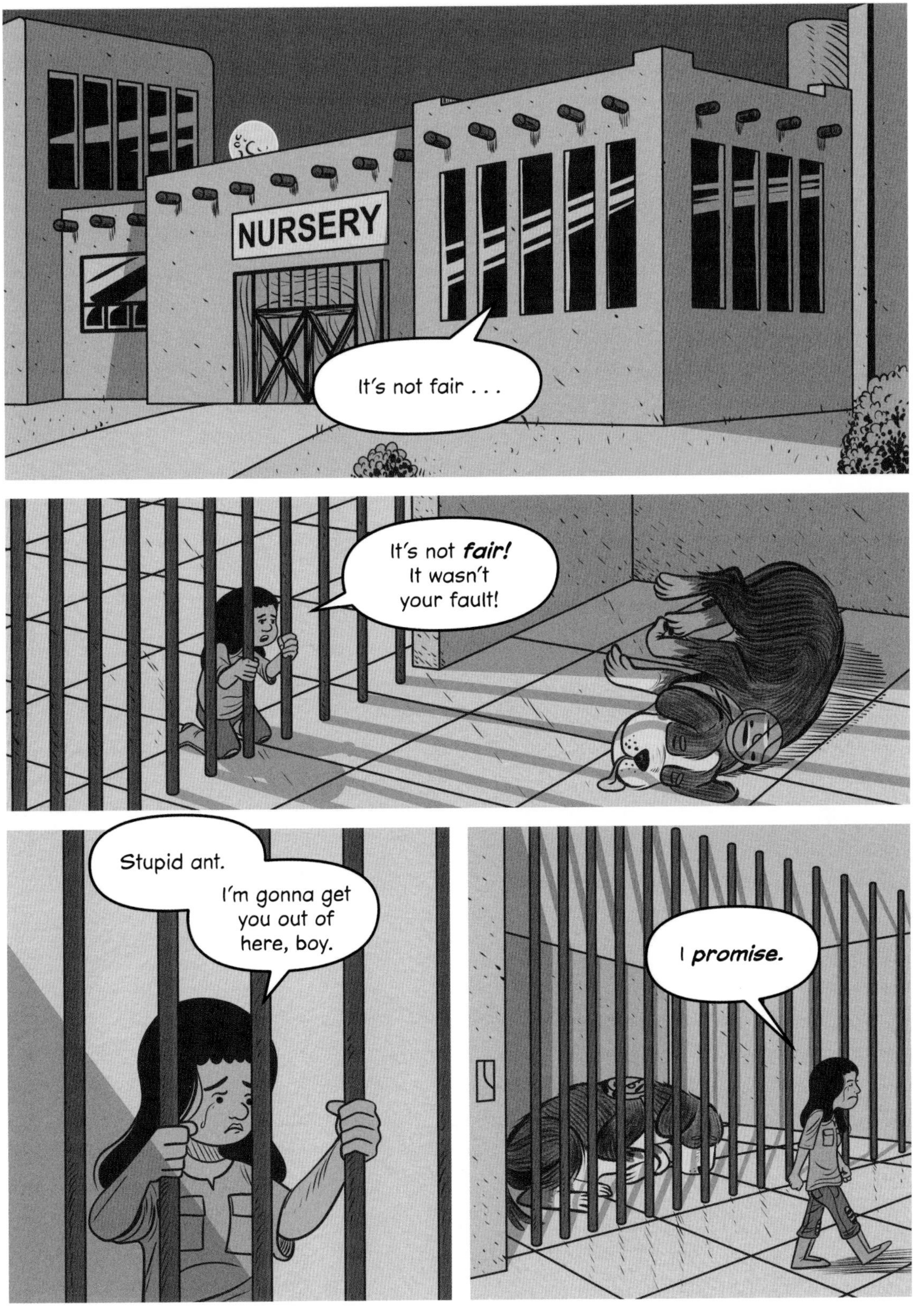
NURSERY
It's not fair . . .
It's not **fair!** It wasn't your fault!
Stupid ant.
I'm gonna get you out of here, boy.
I **promise.**

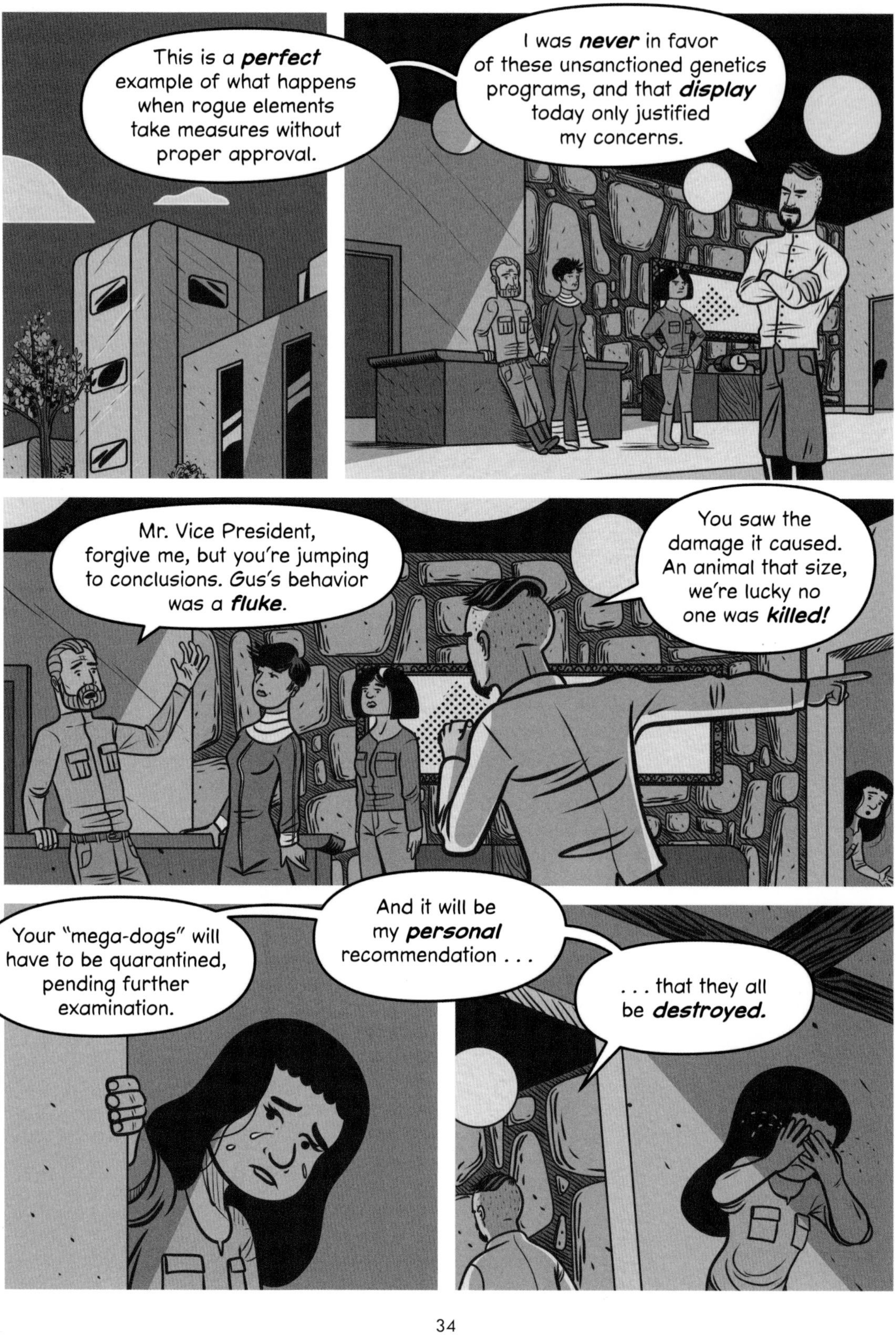
This is a perfect example of what happens when rogue elements take measures without proper approval.
I was never in favor of these unsanctioned genetics programs, and that display today only justified my concerns.
Mr. Vice President, forgive me, but you're jumping to conclusions. Gus's behavior was a fluke.
You saw the damage it caused. An animal that size, we're lucky no one was killed!
Your "mega-dogs" will have to be quarantined, pending further examination.
And it will be my personal recommendation . . .
. . . that they all be destroyed.

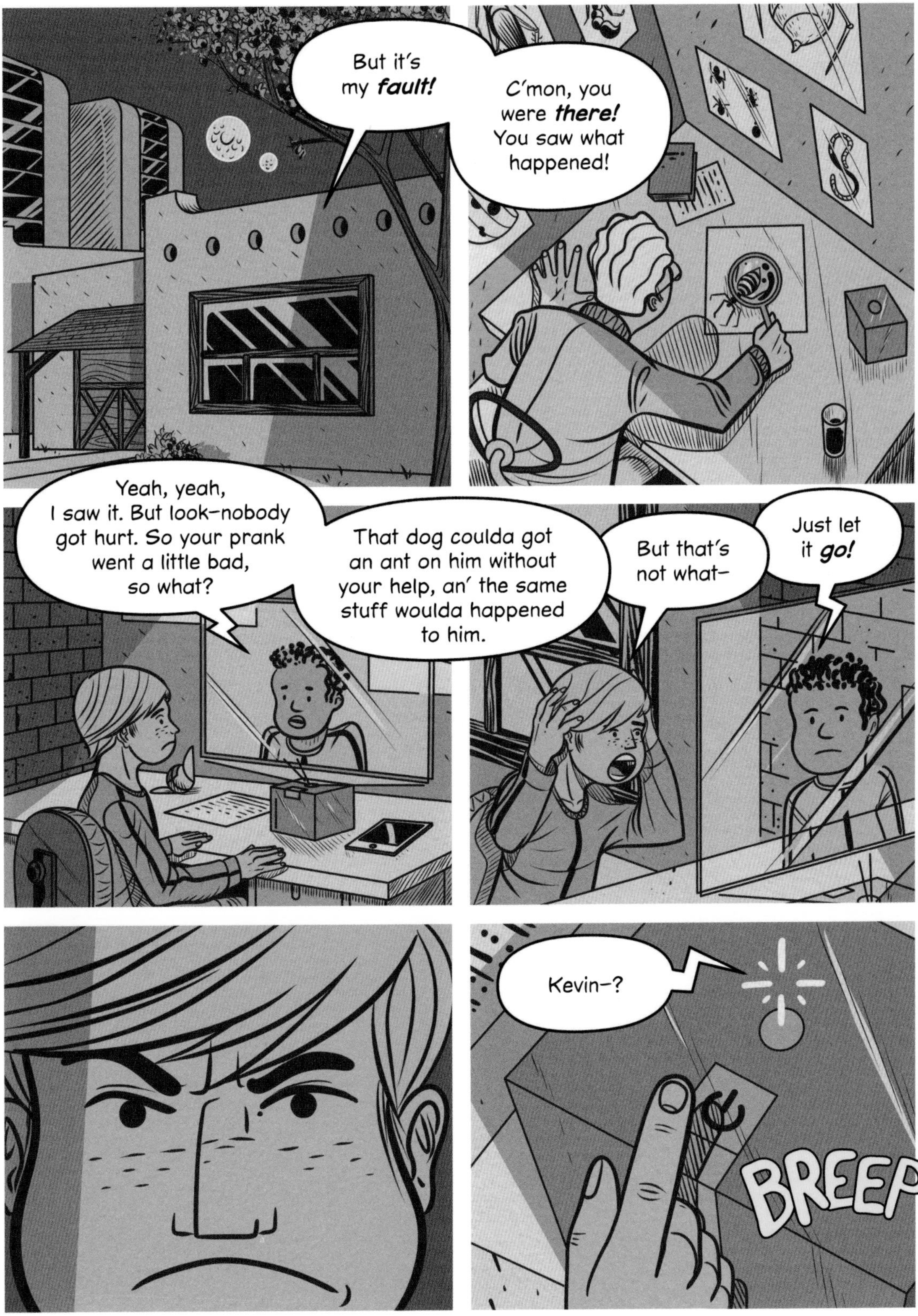
But it's my ***fault!***
C'mon, you were ***there!*** You saw what happened!
Yeah, yeah, I saw it. But look–nobody got hurt. So your prank went a little bad, so what?
That dog coulda got an ant on him without your help, an' the same stuff woulda happened to him.
But that's not what–
Just let it ***go!***
Kevin–?
BREEP

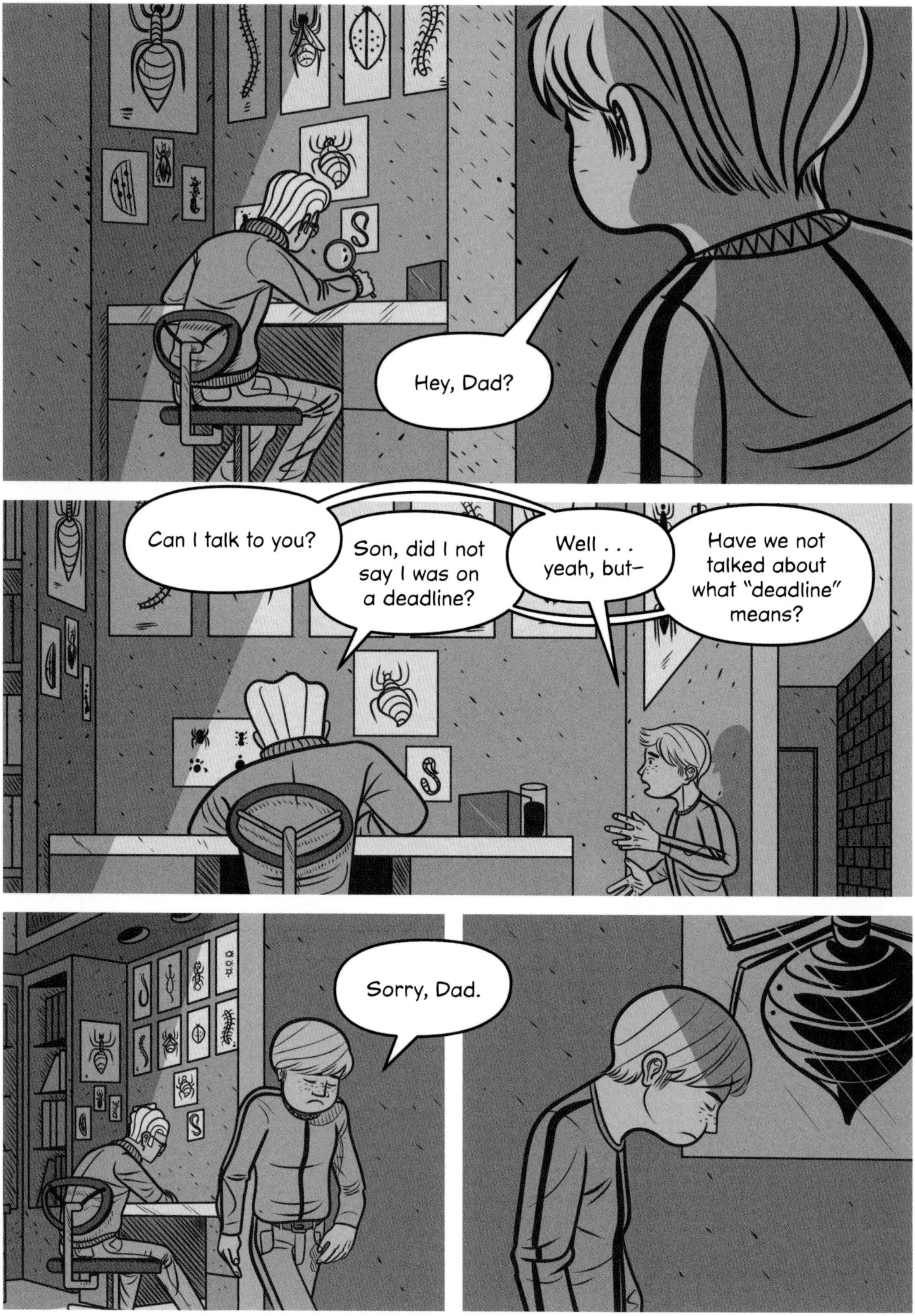

Hey, Dad?
Can I talk to you?
Son, did I not say I was on a deadline?
Well . . . yeah, but–
Have we not talked about what "deadline" means?
Sorry, Dad.

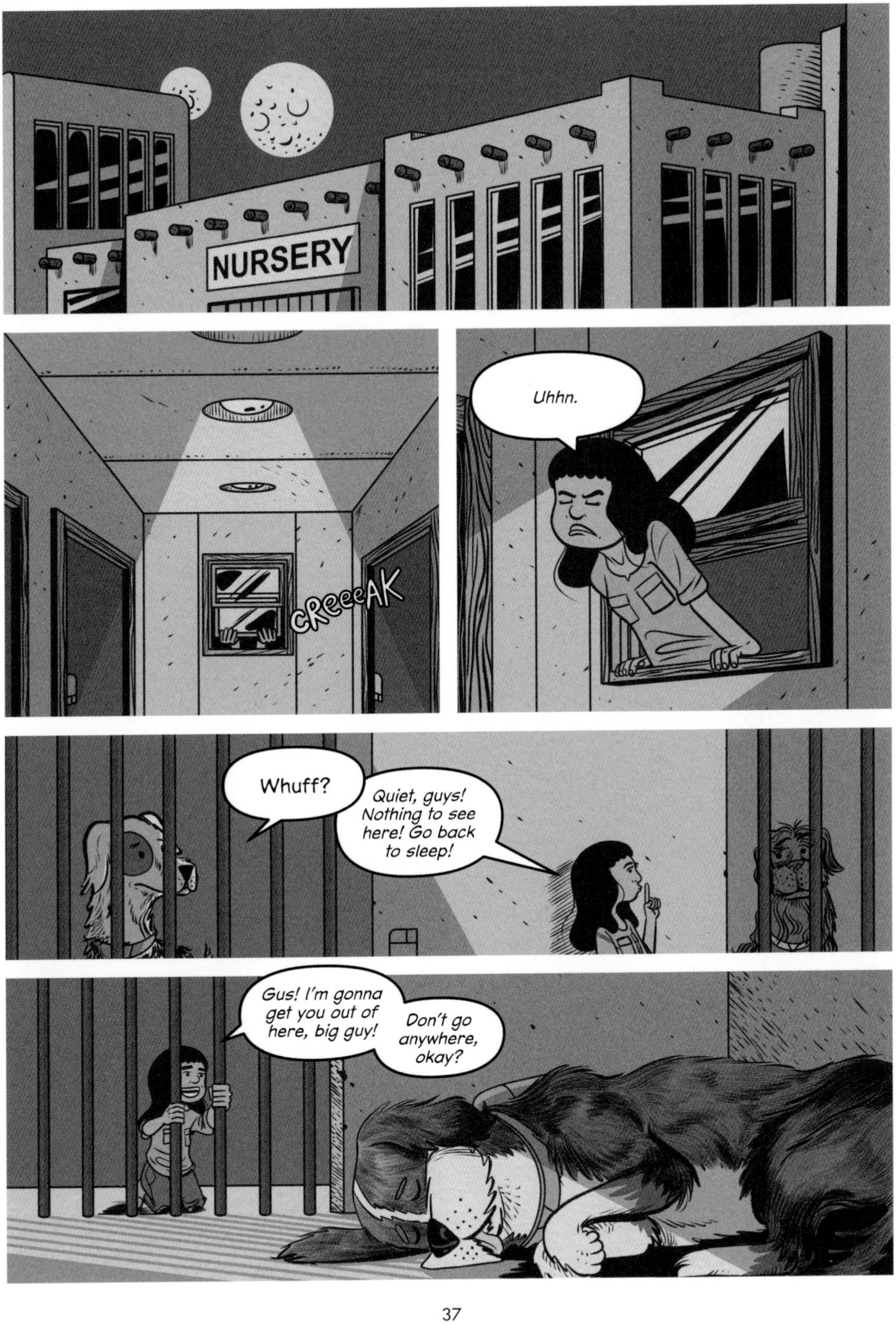
NURSERY
CREEEAK
Uhhn.
Whuff?
Quiet, guys! Nothing to see here! Go back to sleep!
Gus! I'm gonna get you out of here, big guy!
Don't go anywhere, okay?

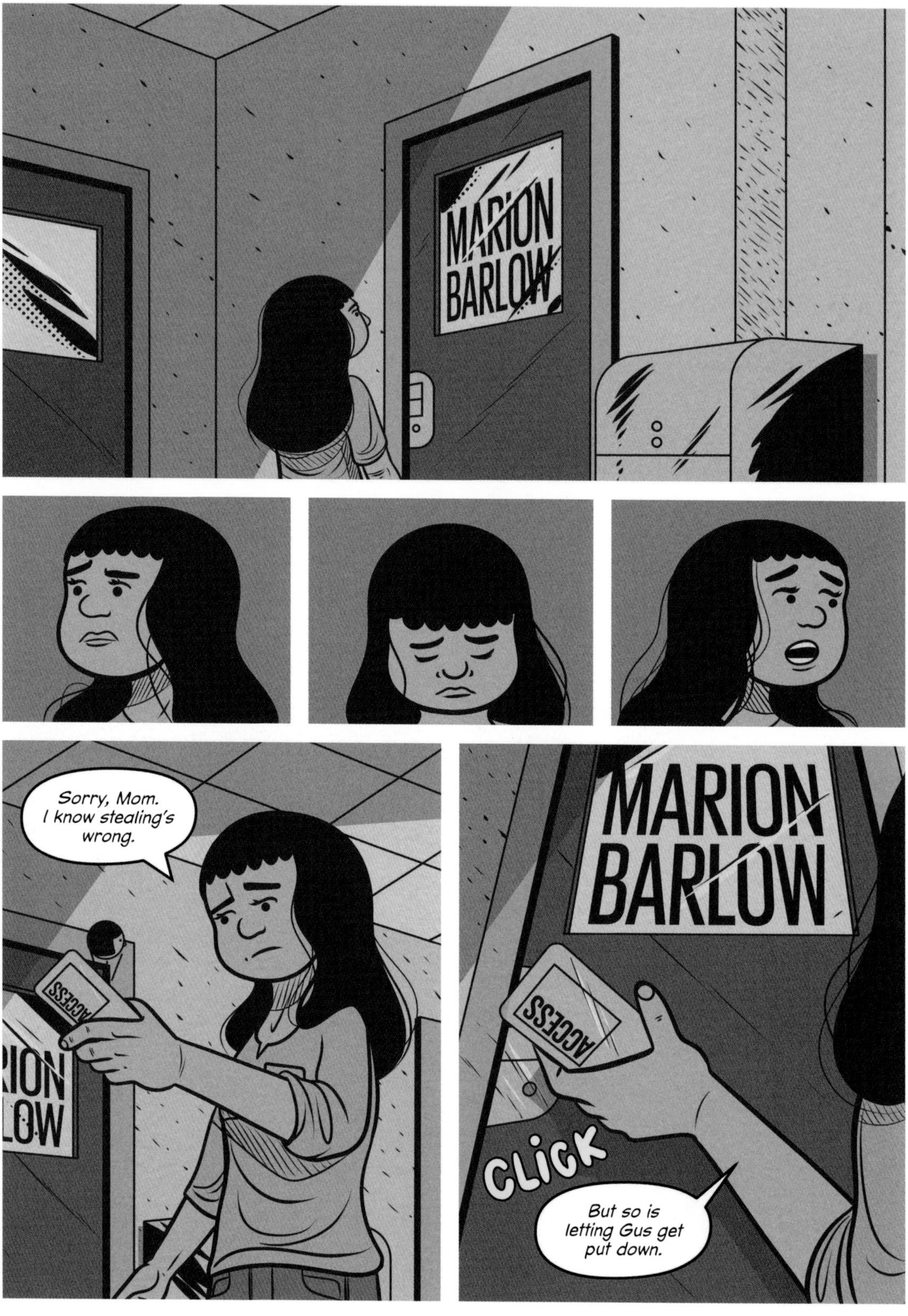
MARION BARLOW
Sorry, Mom. I know stealing's wrong.
ACCESS
MARION BARLOW
CLICK
But so is letting Gus get put down.

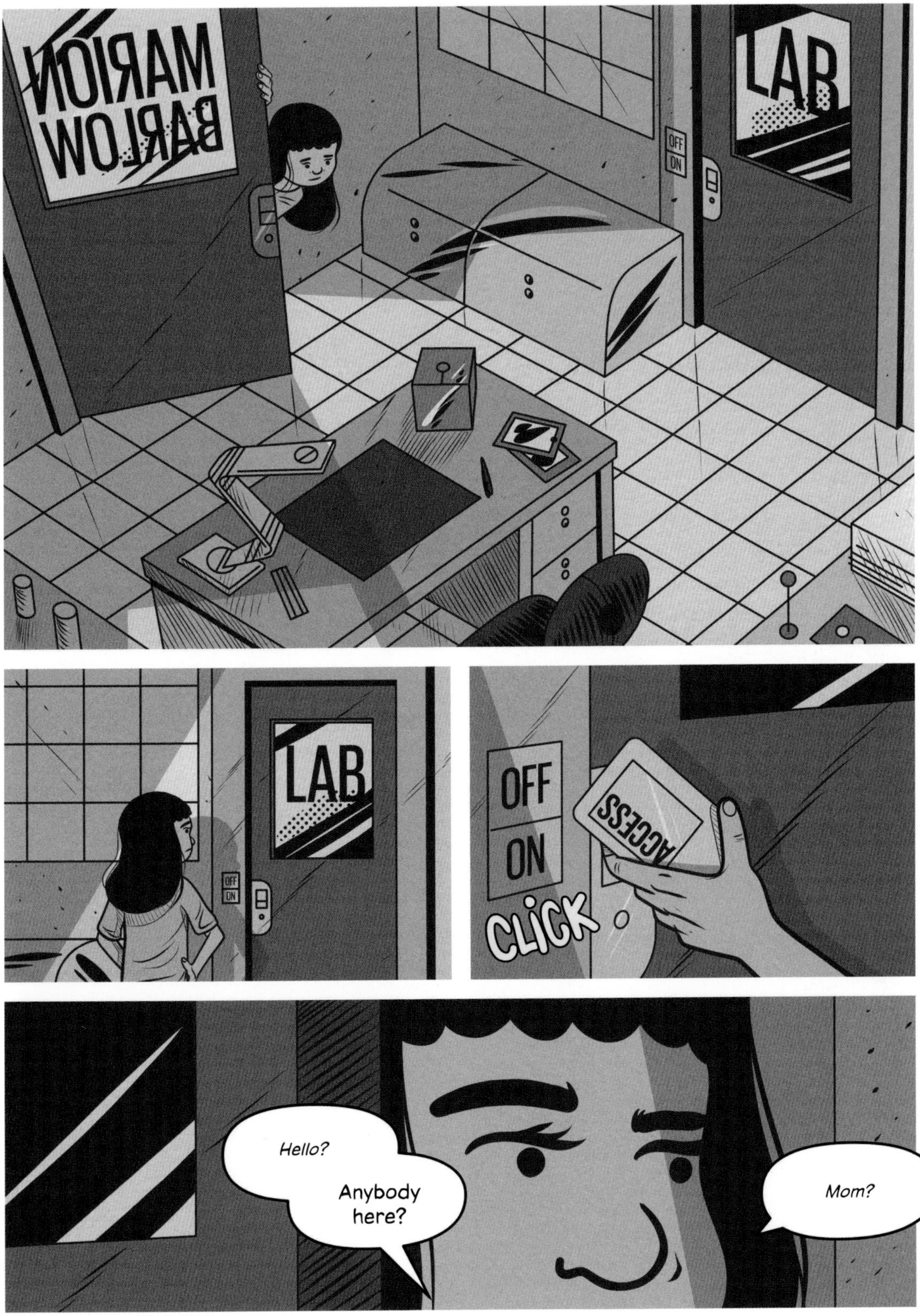
MARION BARLOW
LAB
OFF
ON
LAB
OFF
ON
ACCESS
CLICK
Hello?
Anybody here?
Mom?

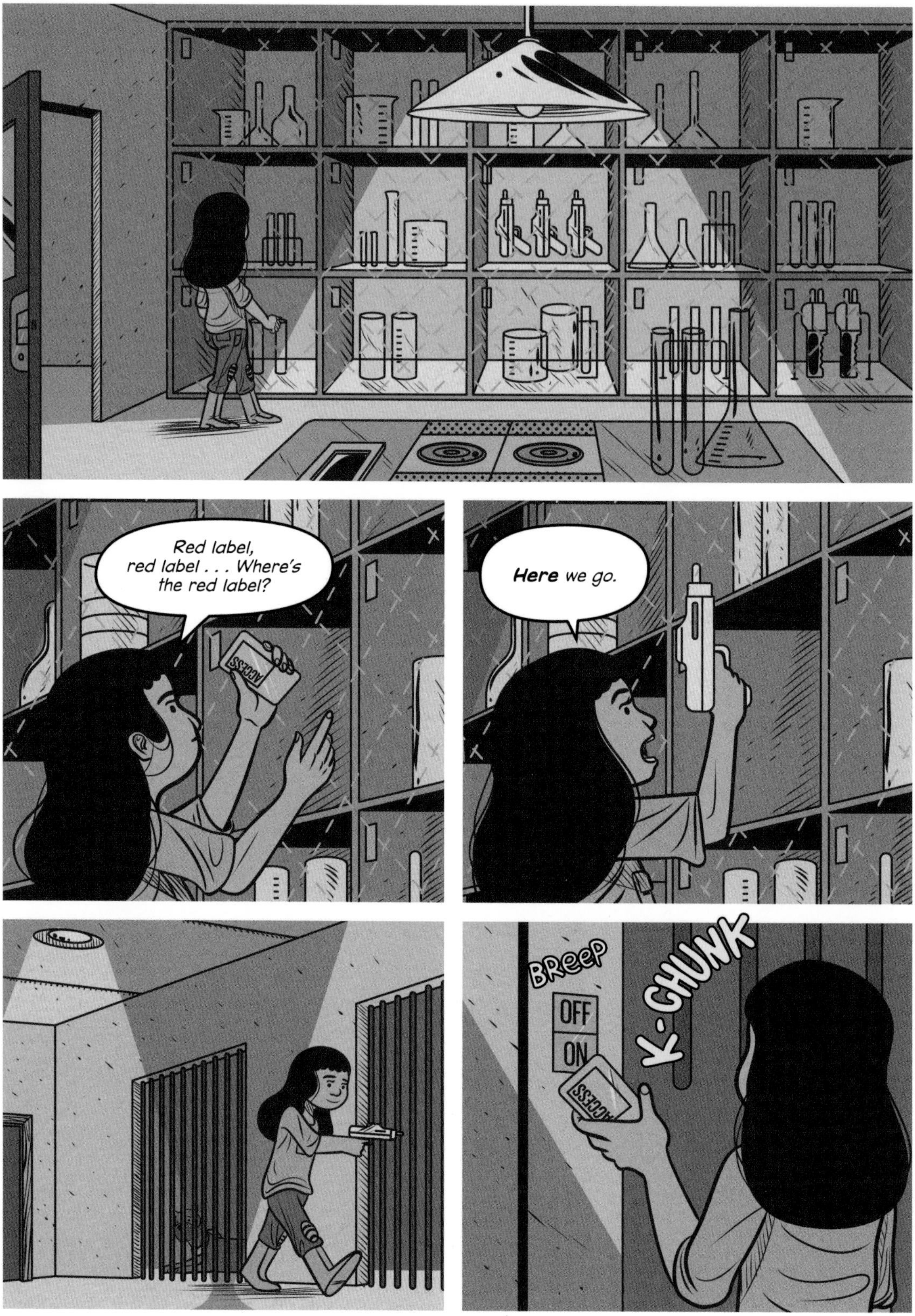
Red label, red label . . . Where's the red label?
ACCESS
Here we go.
BREEP
K-CHUNK
OFF
ON
ACCESS

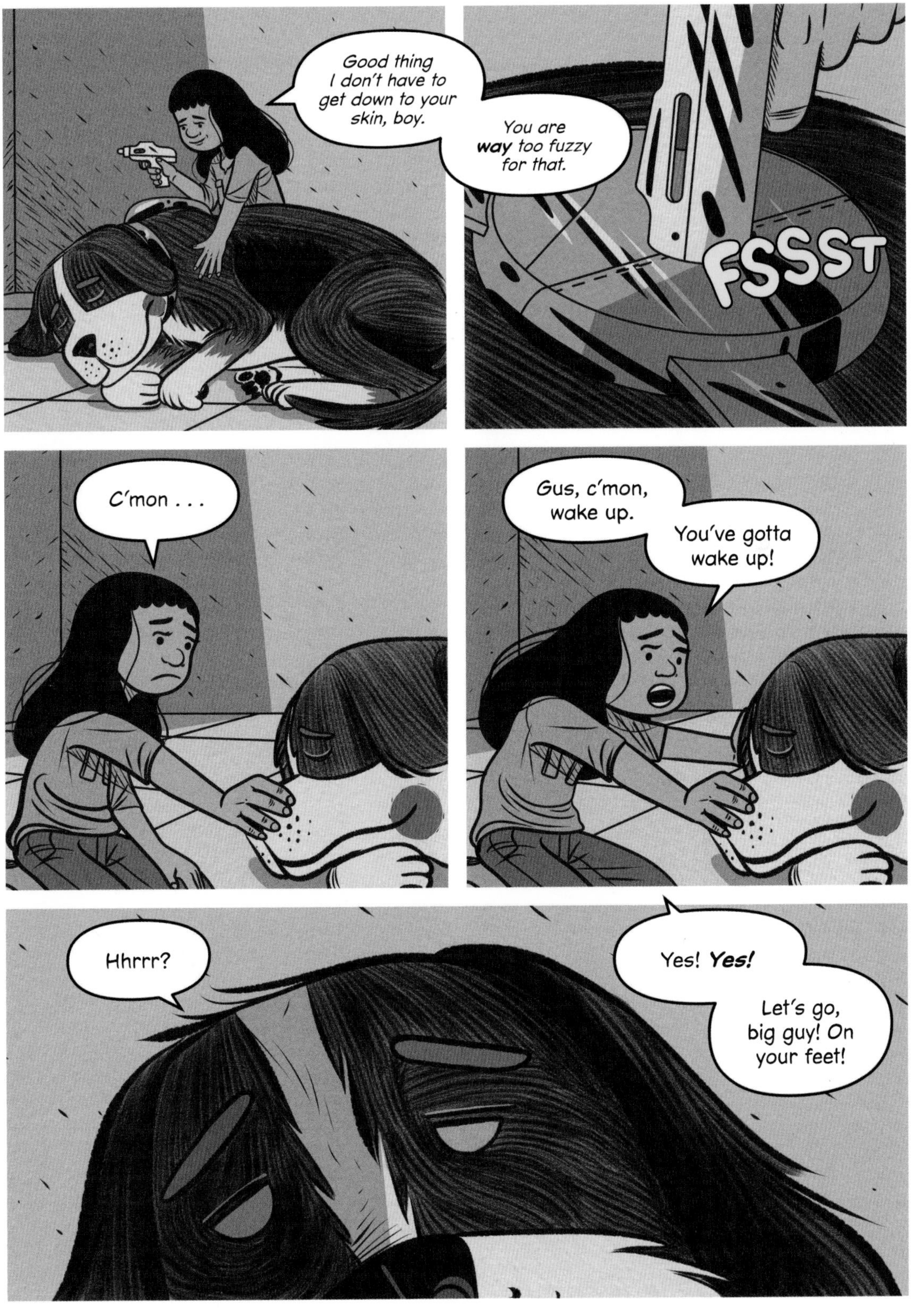
Good thing I don't have to get down to your skin, boy.
You are **way** too fuzzy for that.
FSSST
C'mon . . .
Gus, c'mon, wake up.
You've gotta wake up!
Hhrrr?
Yes! ***Yes!***
Let's go, big guy! On your feet!

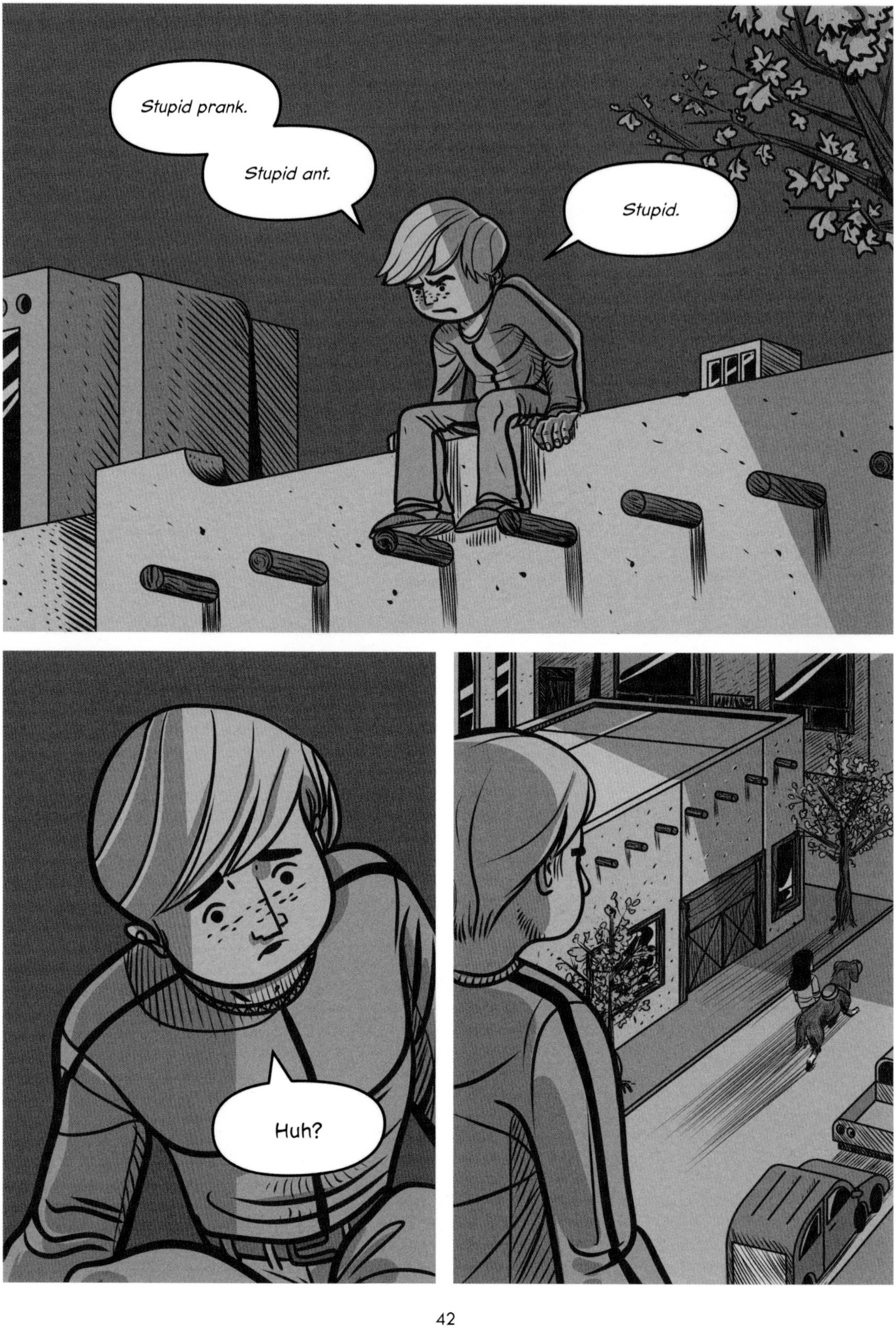
Stupid prank.
Stupid ant.
Stupid.
Huh?

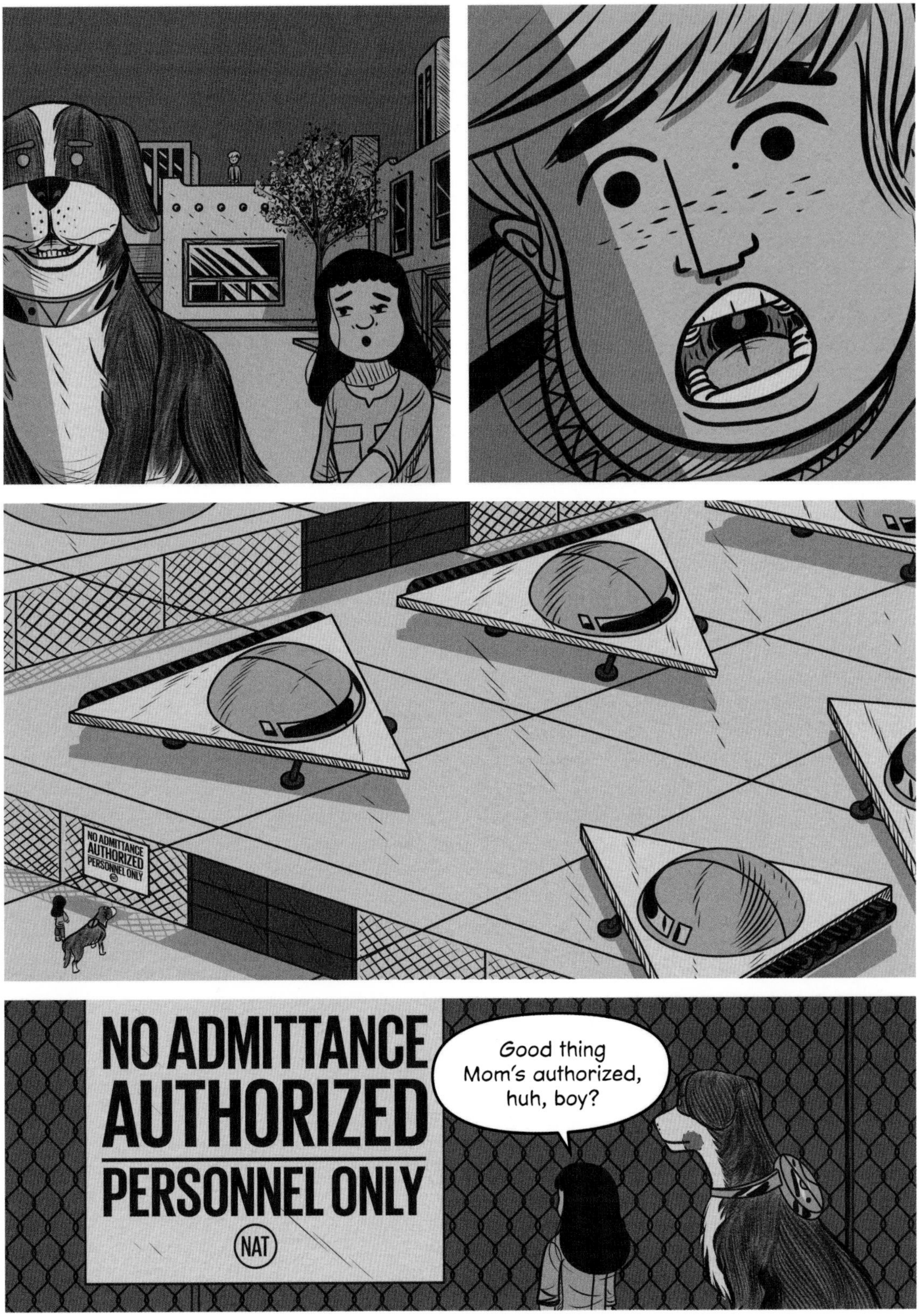
NO ADMITTANCE
AUTHORIZED
PERSONNEL ONLY
NAT
Good thing Mom's authorized, huh, boy?

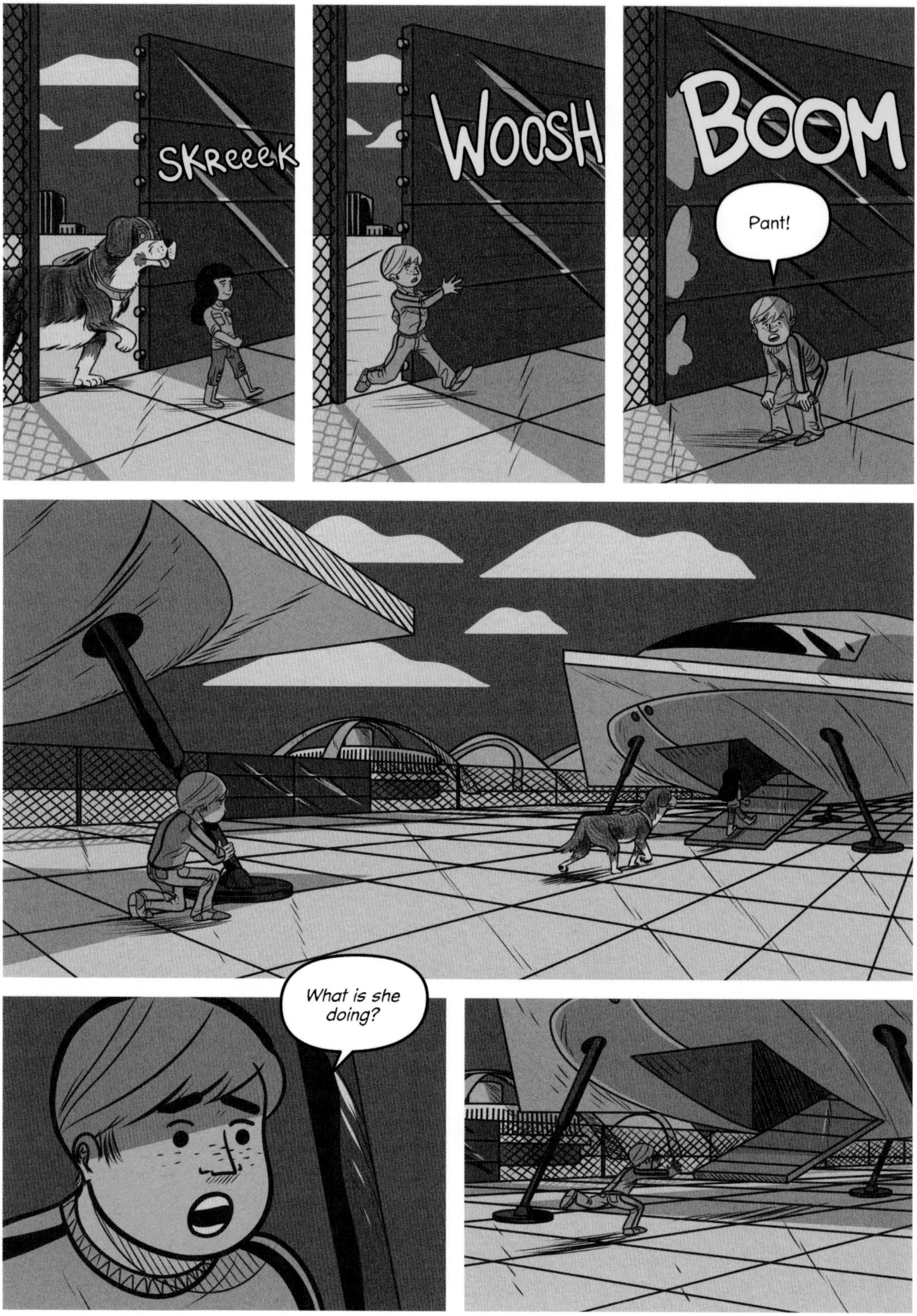
SKReeeK
WOOSH
BOOM
Pant!
What is she doing?

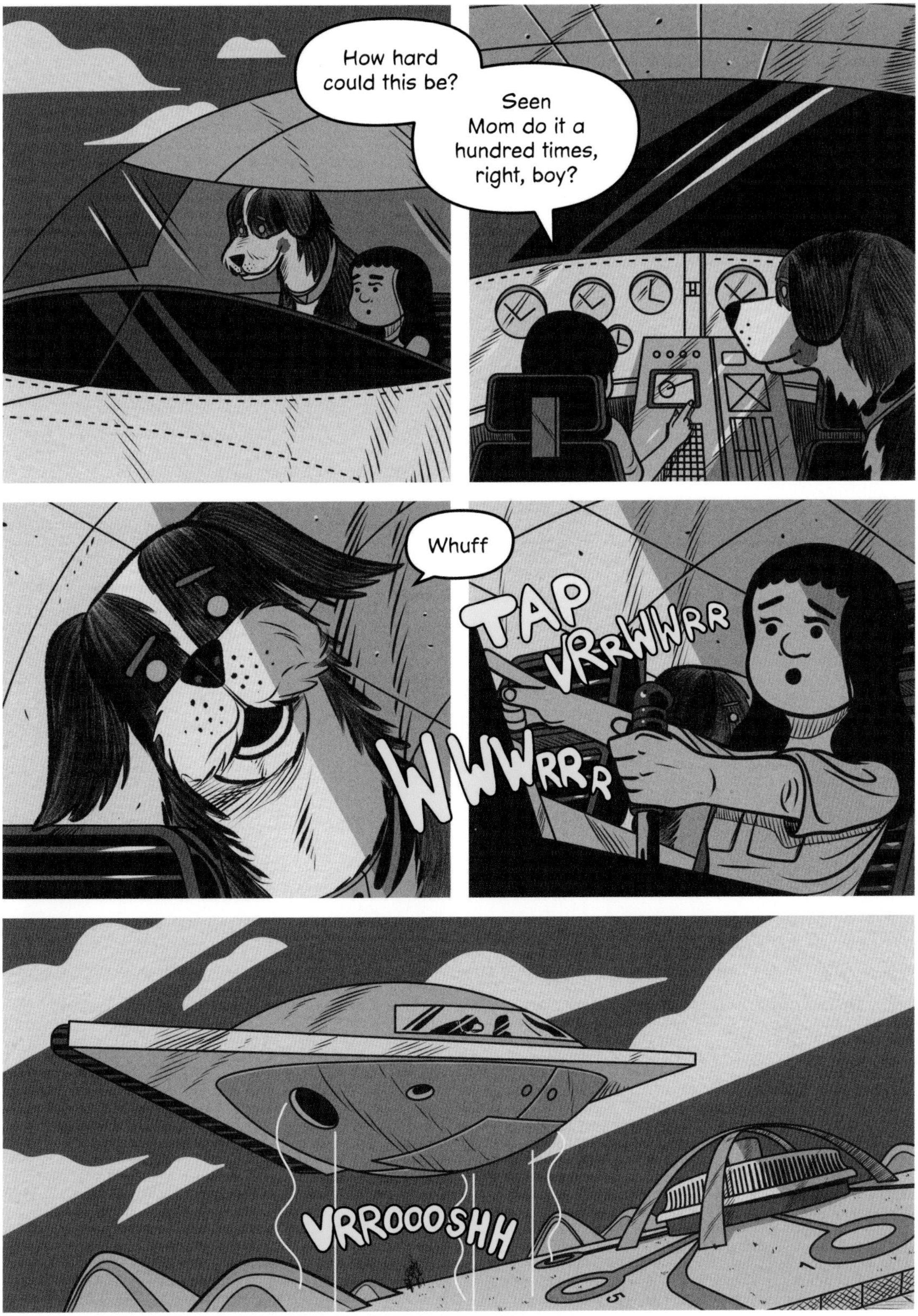
How hard could this be?
Seen Mom do it a hundred times, right, boy?
Whuff
TAP
VRRWWRR
WWWRRR
VRROOOSHH

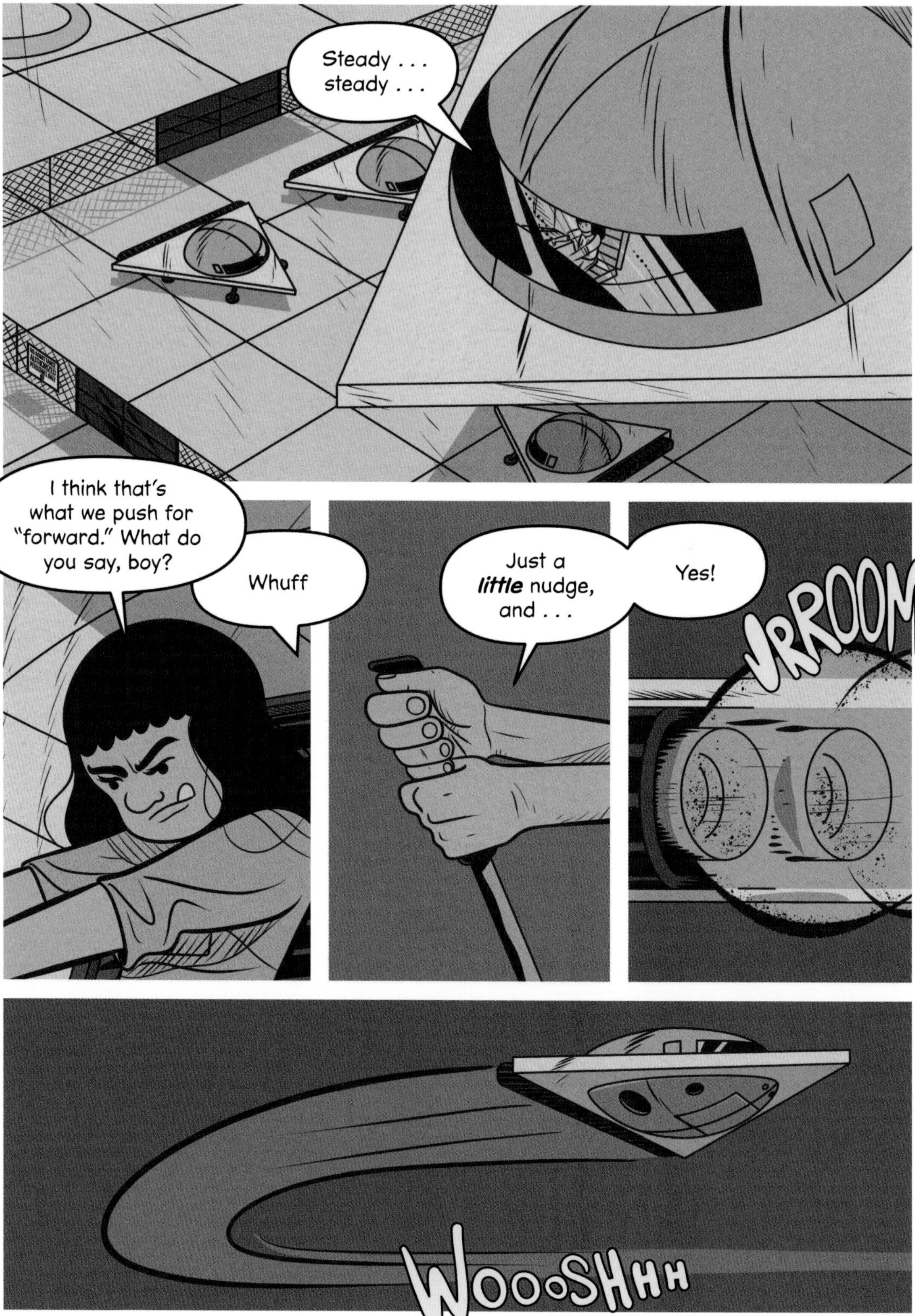
Steady . . . steady . . .
I think that's what we push for "forward." What do you say, boy?
Whuff
Just a *little* nudge, and . . .
Yes!
VRROOM
WOOOSHHH

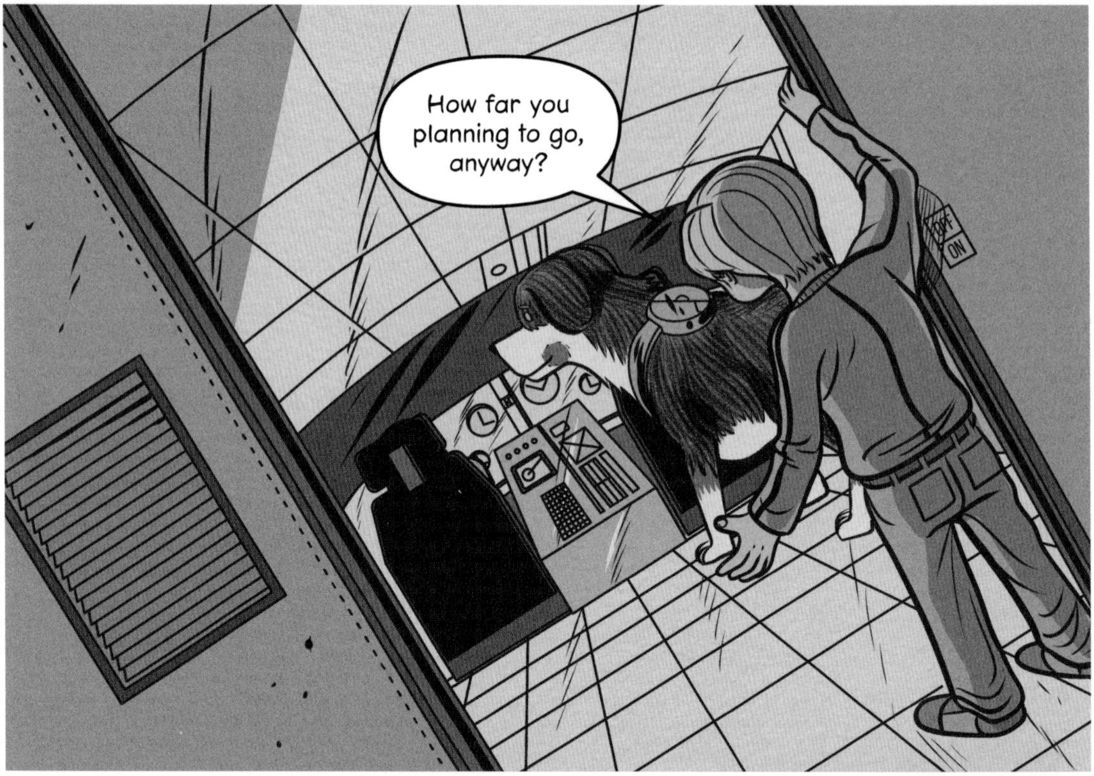
How far you planning to go, anyway?
OFF
ON

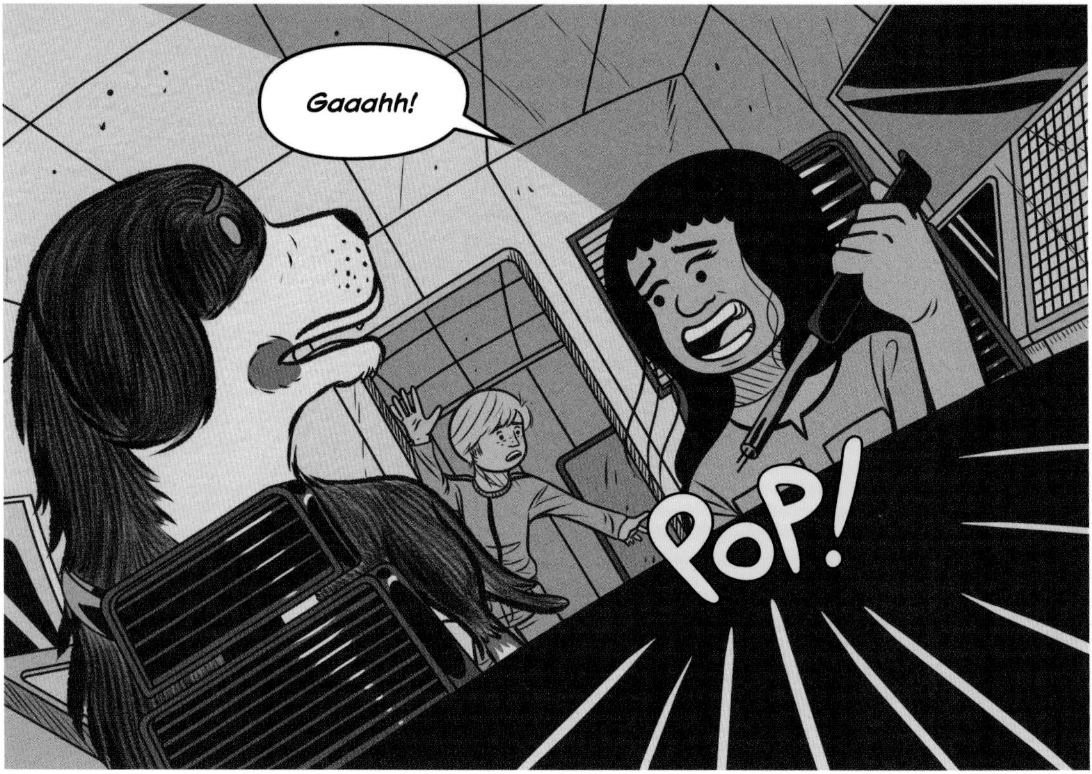
Gaaahh!
POP!

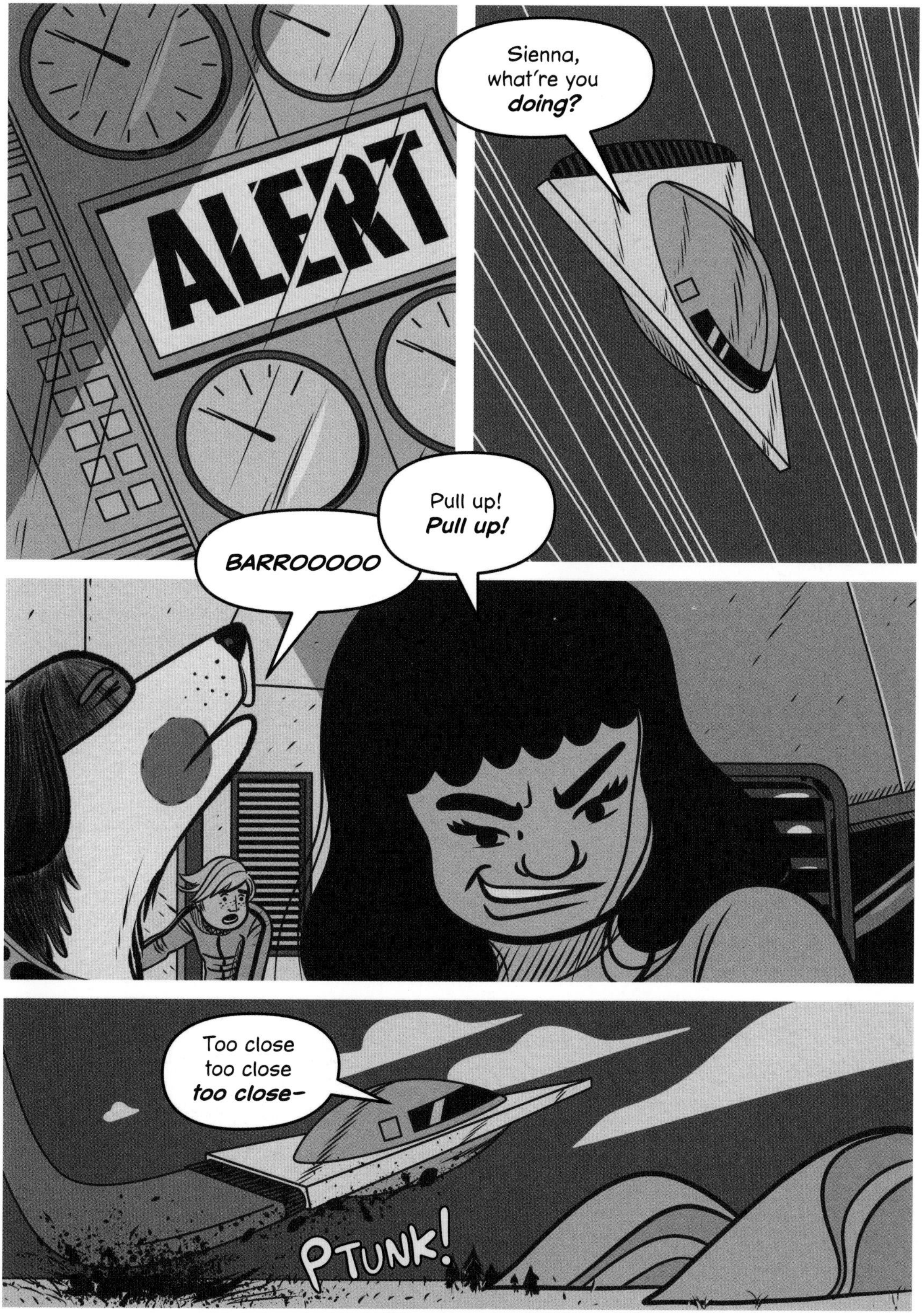
ALERT
Sienna, what're you *doing?*
Pull up! ***Pull up!***
BARROOOOO
Too close too close ***too close-***
PTUNK!

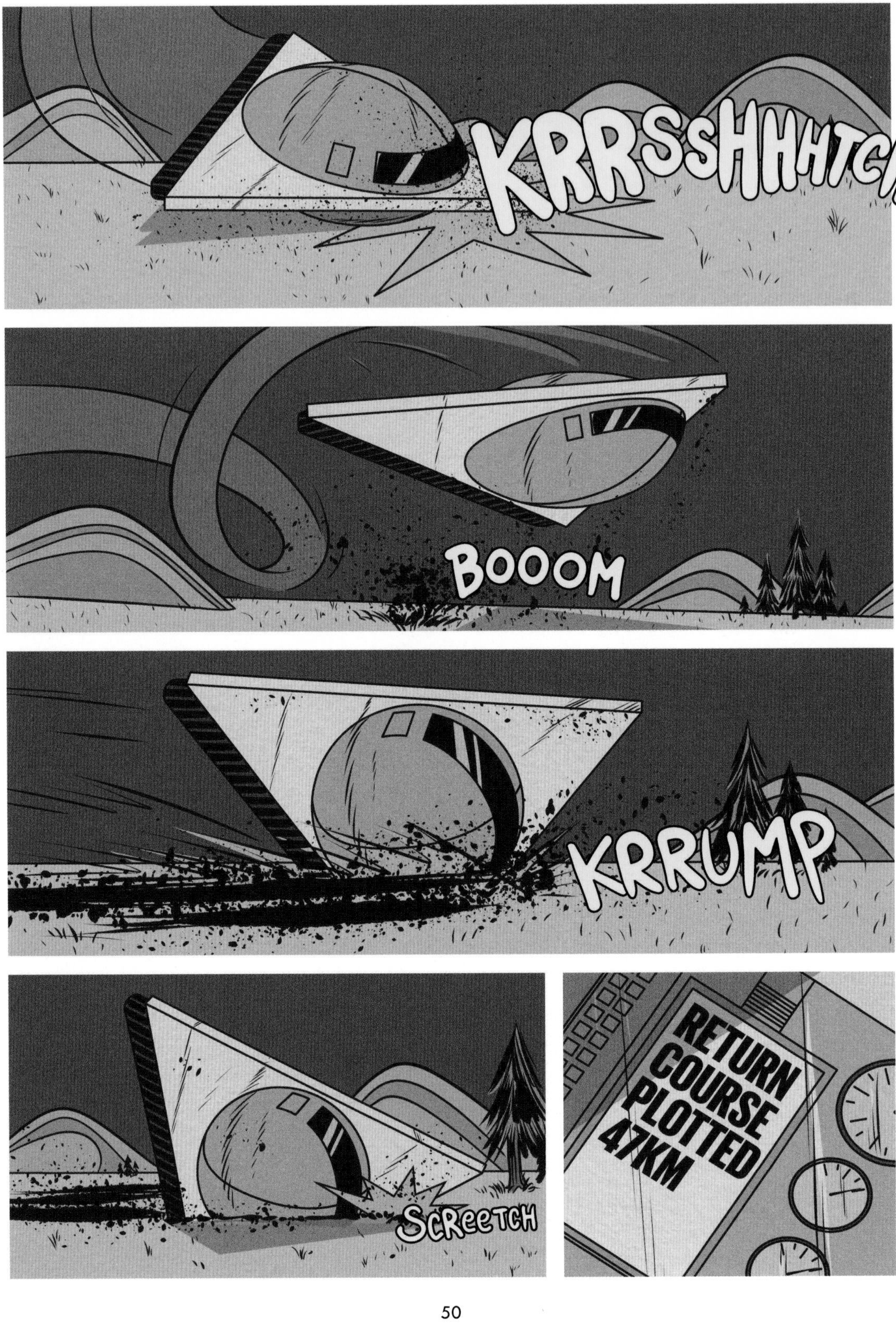
KRRSSHHHTCH
BOOOM
KRRUMP
SCREETCH
RETURN COURSE PLOTTED 47KM

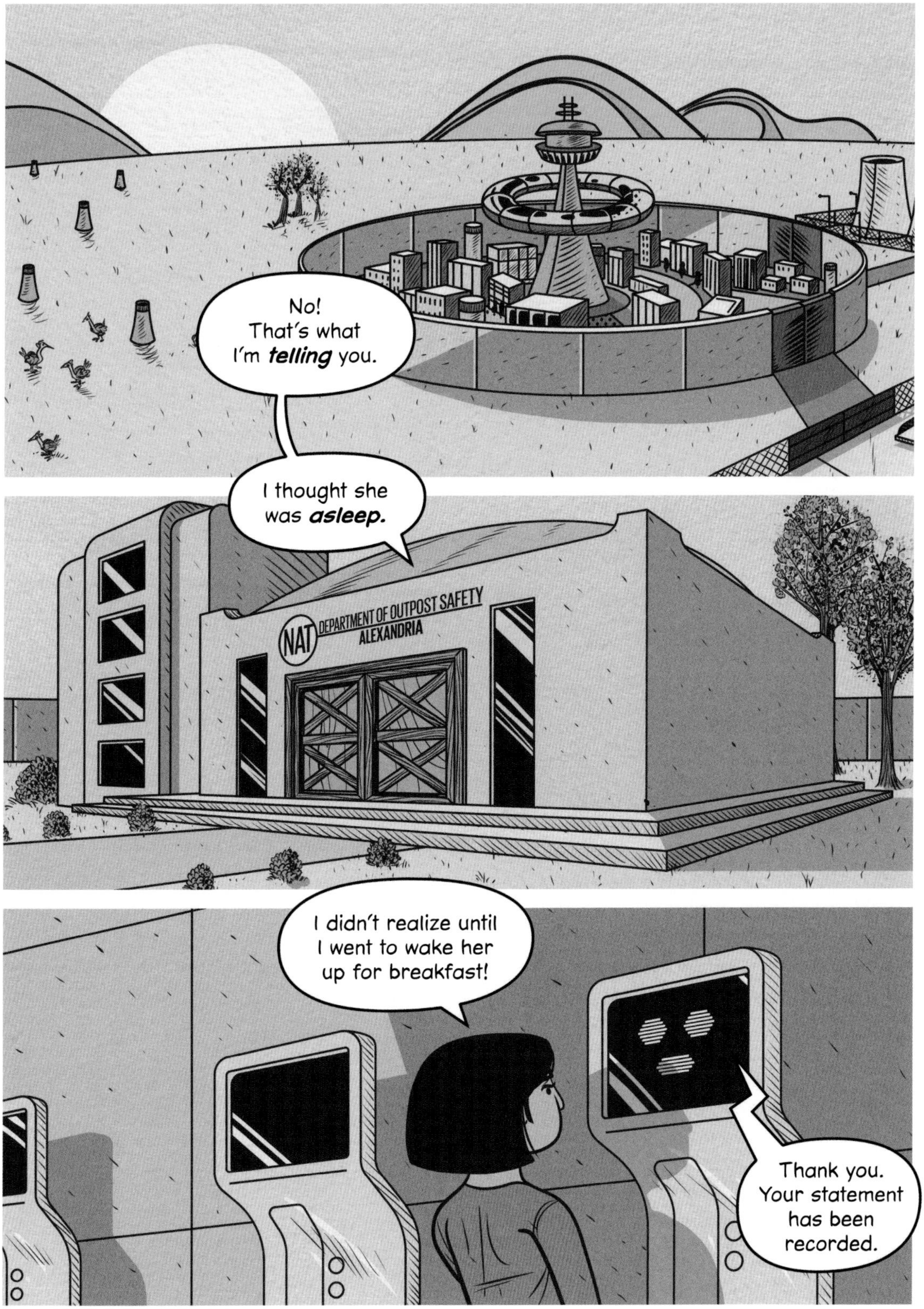
No! That's what I'm ***telling*** you.
I thought she was ***asleep.***
NAT DEPARTMENT OF OUTPOST SAFETY ALEXANDRIA
I didn't realize until I went to wake her up for breakfast!
Thank you. Your statement has been recorded.

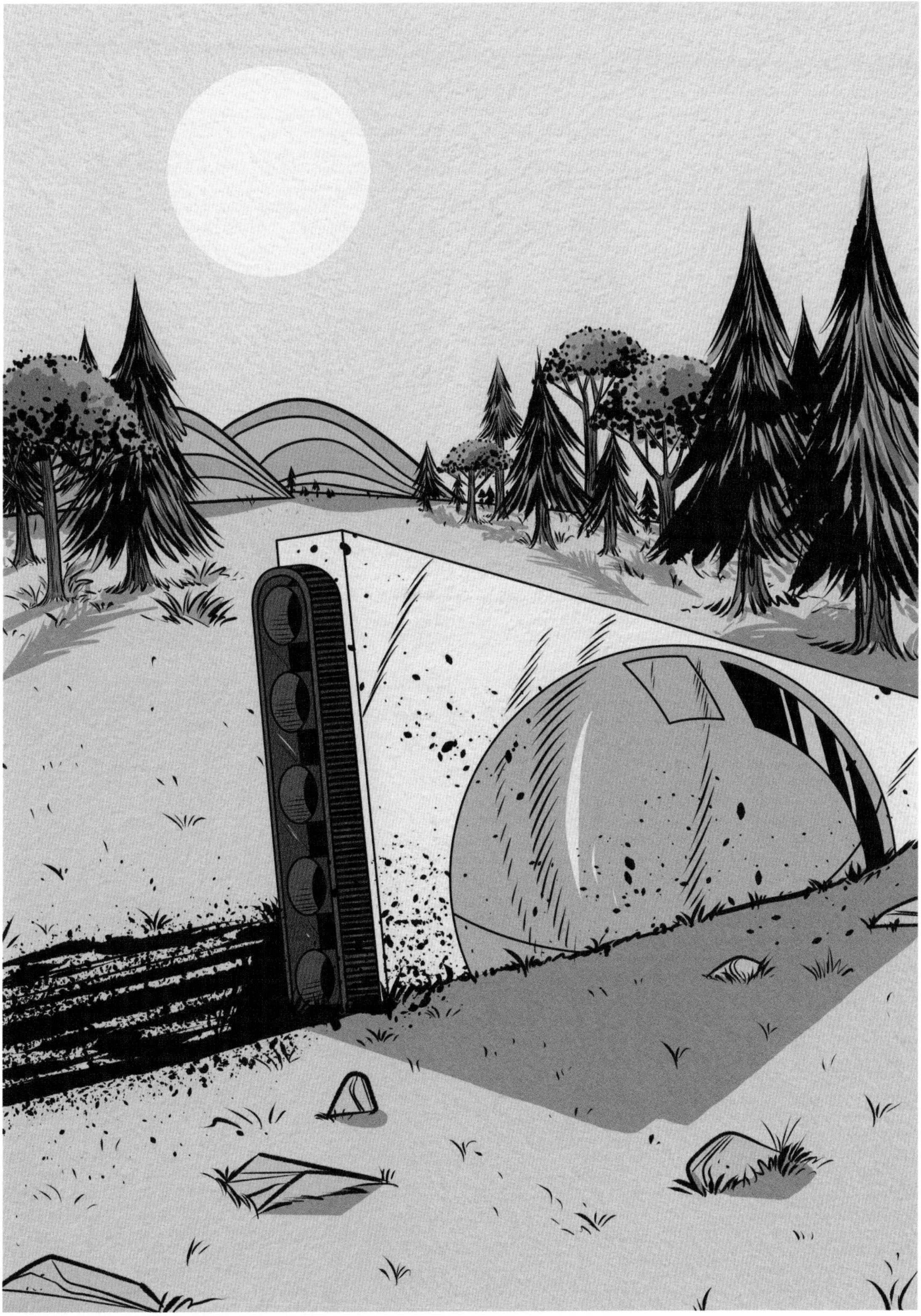

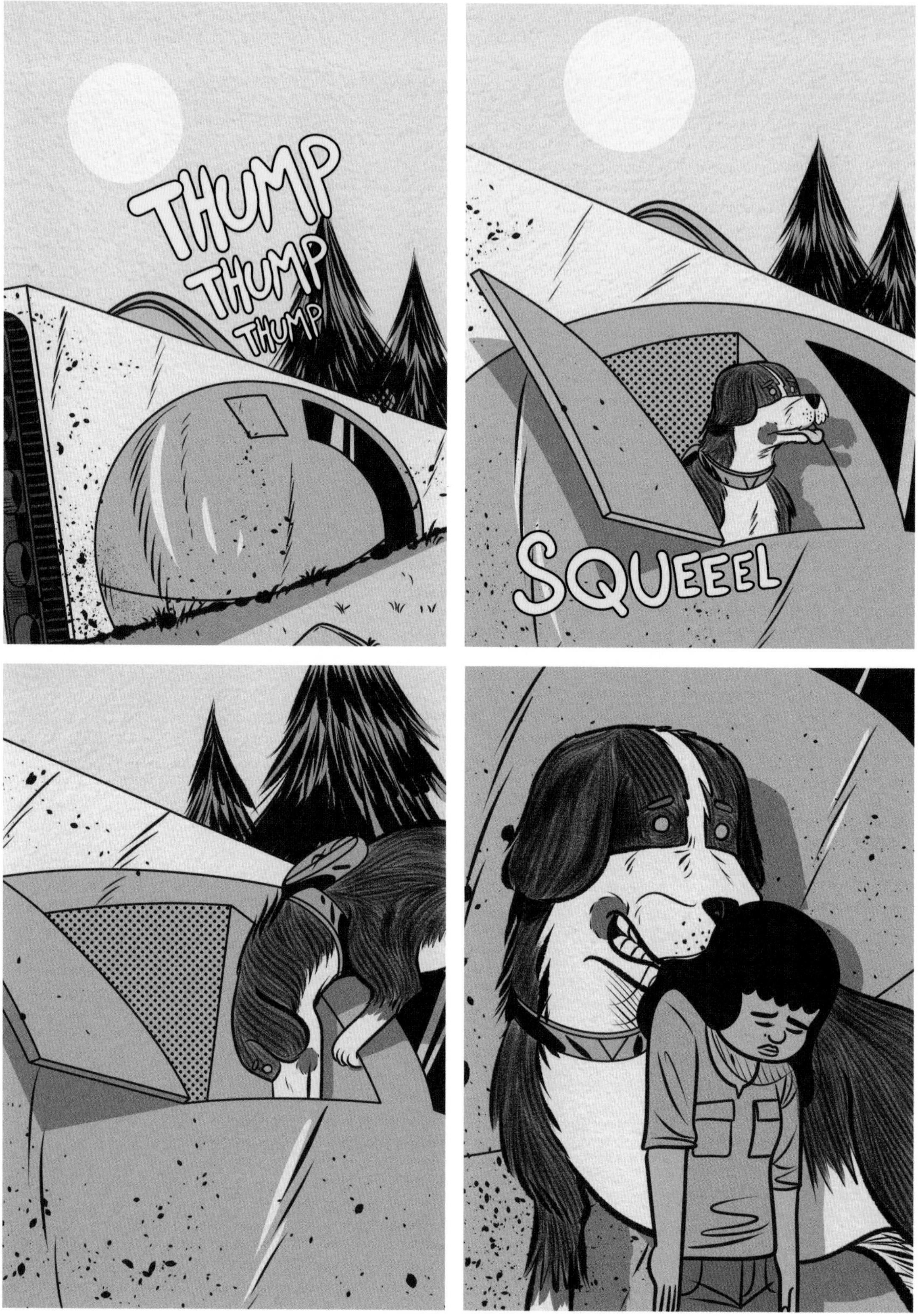
THUMP
THUMP
THUMP
SQUEEEL

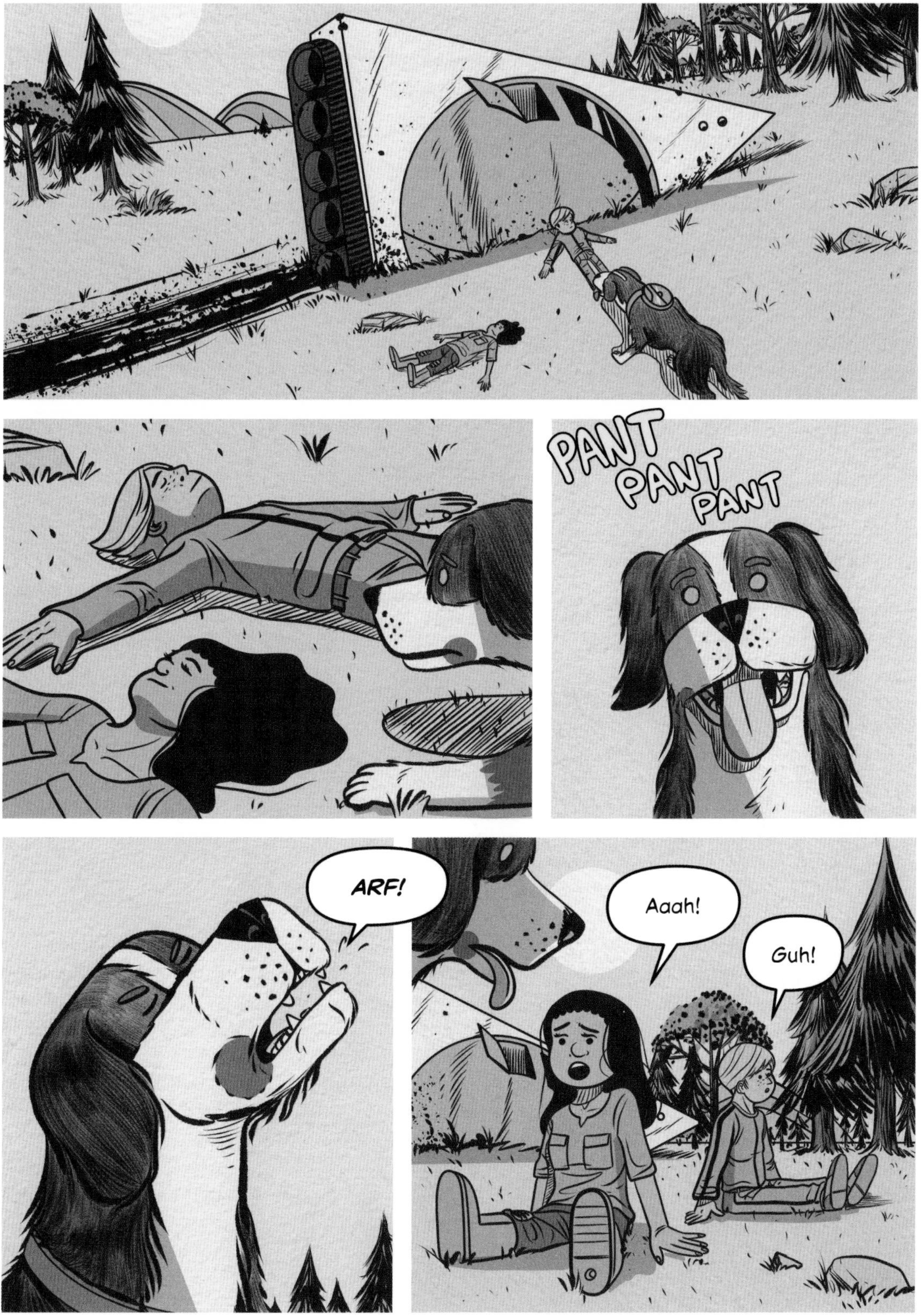
PANT
PANT
PANT
ARF!
Aaah!
Guh!

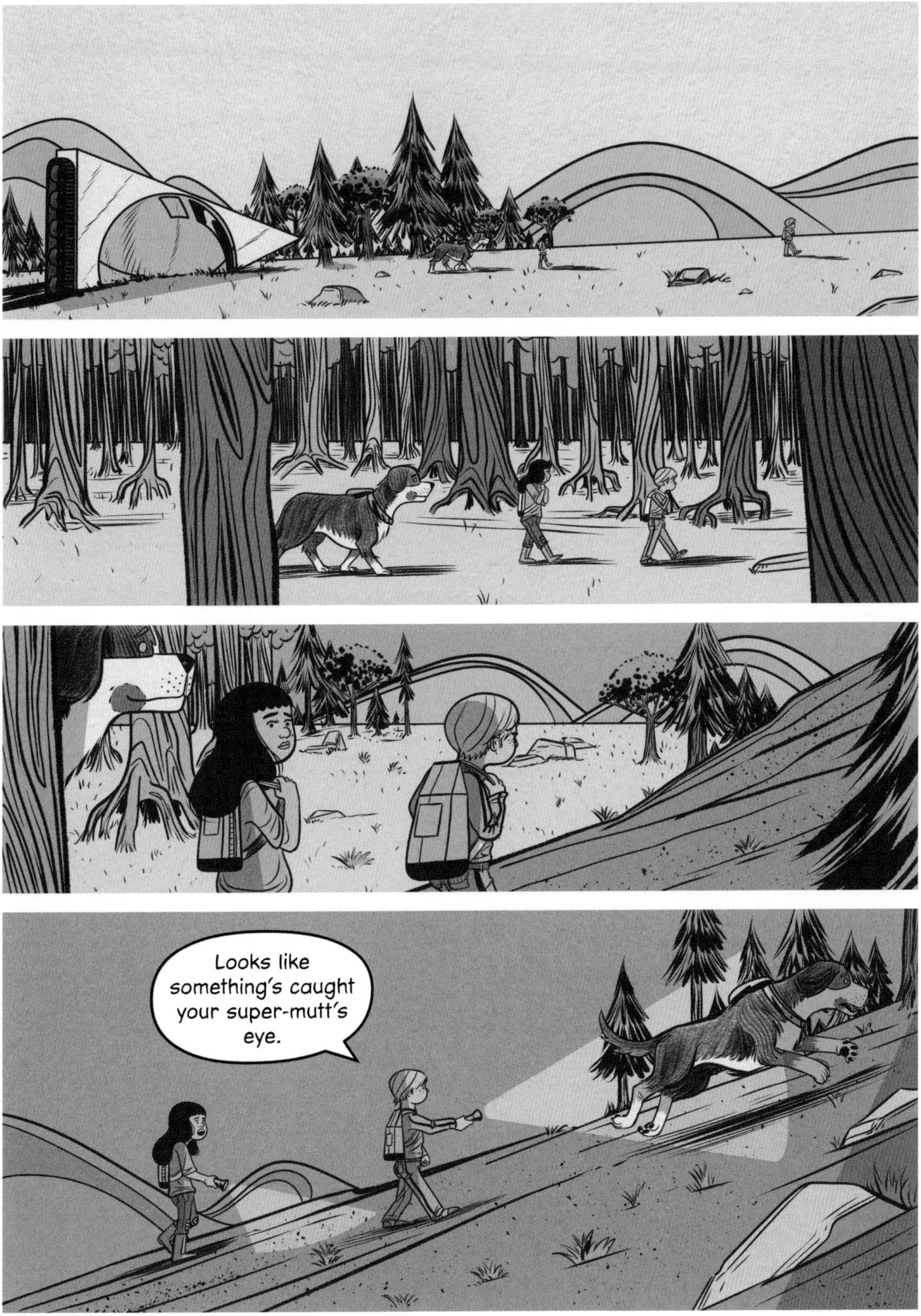
Looks like something's caught your super-mutt's eye.

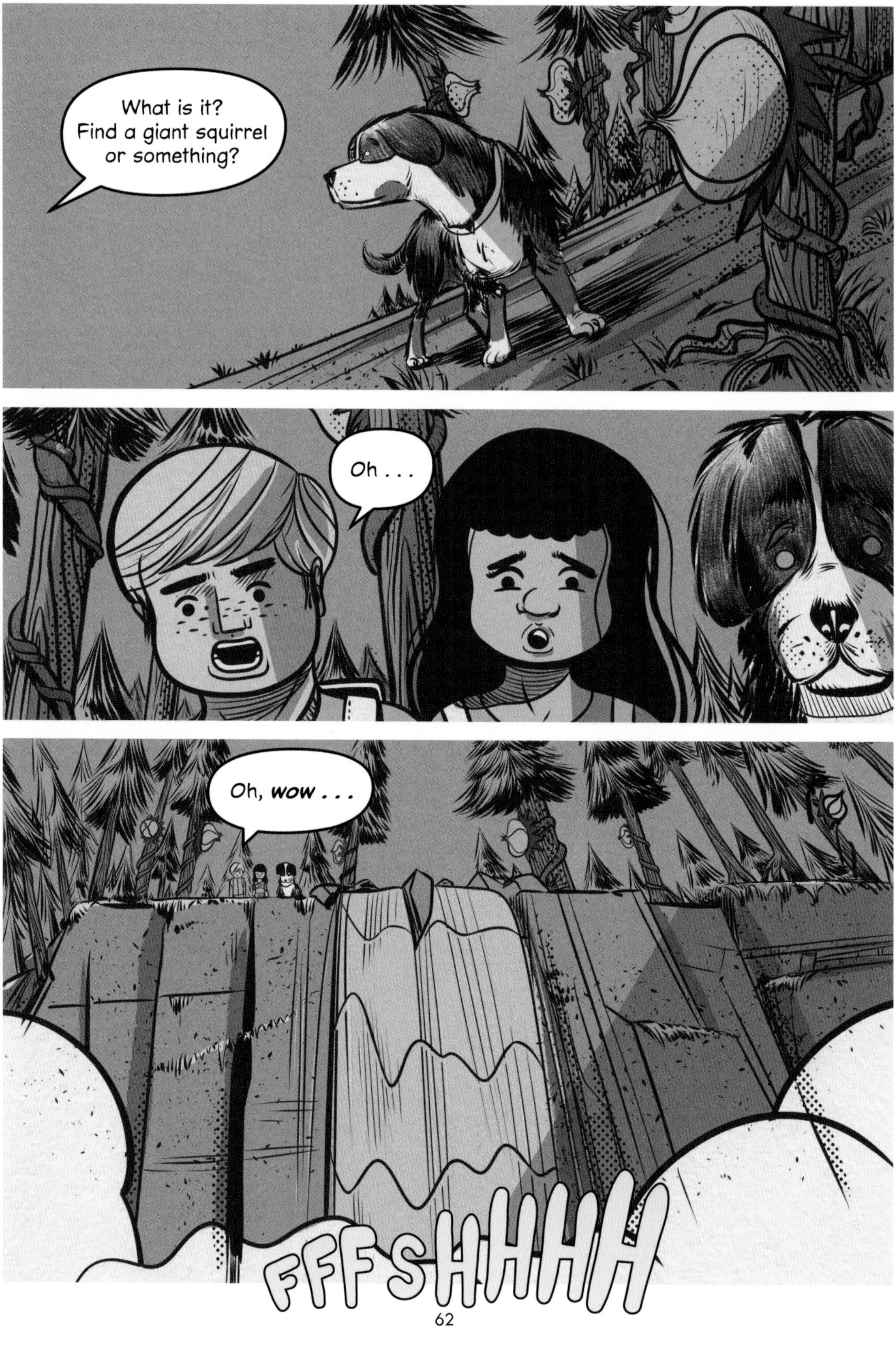
What is it? Find a giant squirrel or something?
Oh . . .
Oh, *wow* . . .
FFFSHHHH

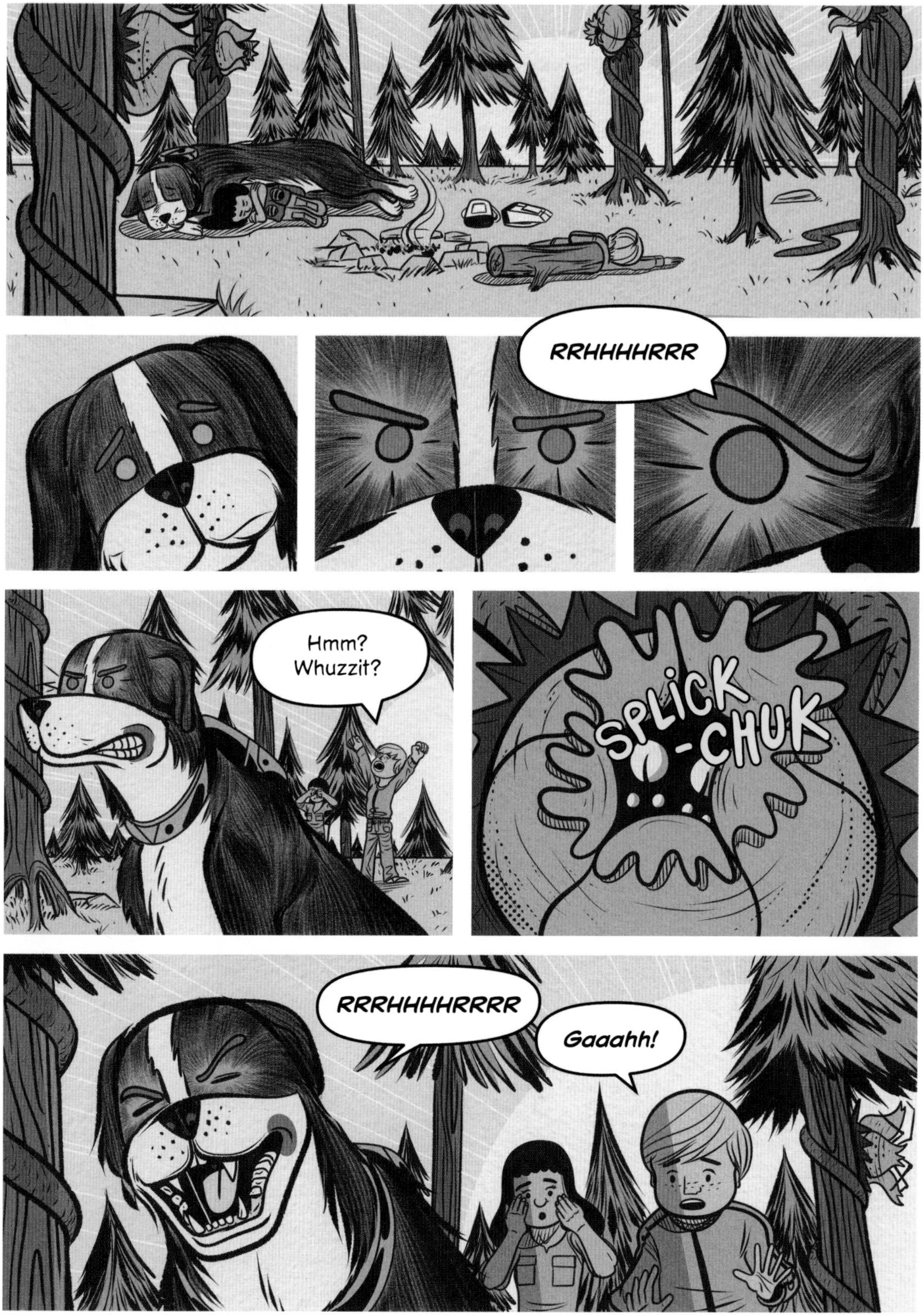
RRHHHHRRR
Hmm? Whuzzit?
SPLICK -CHUK
RRRHHHHRRRR
Gaaahh!

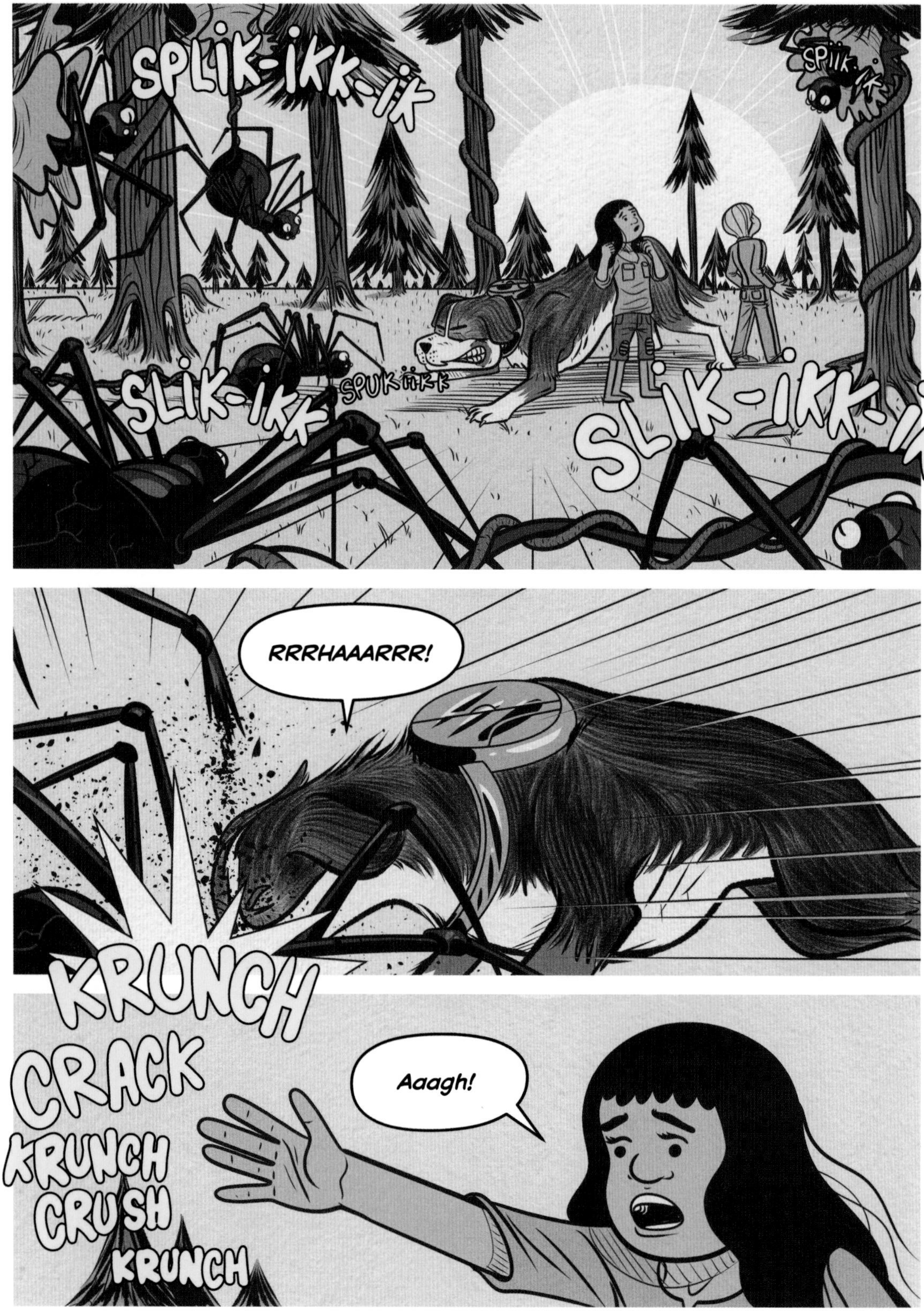

SPLIK-IKK-IK
SPLIK-IK
SLIK-IKK
SPUK IIKK
SLIK-IKK-IK
RRRHAAARRR!
KRUNCH
CRACK
KRUNCH
CRUSH
KRUNCH
Aaagh!

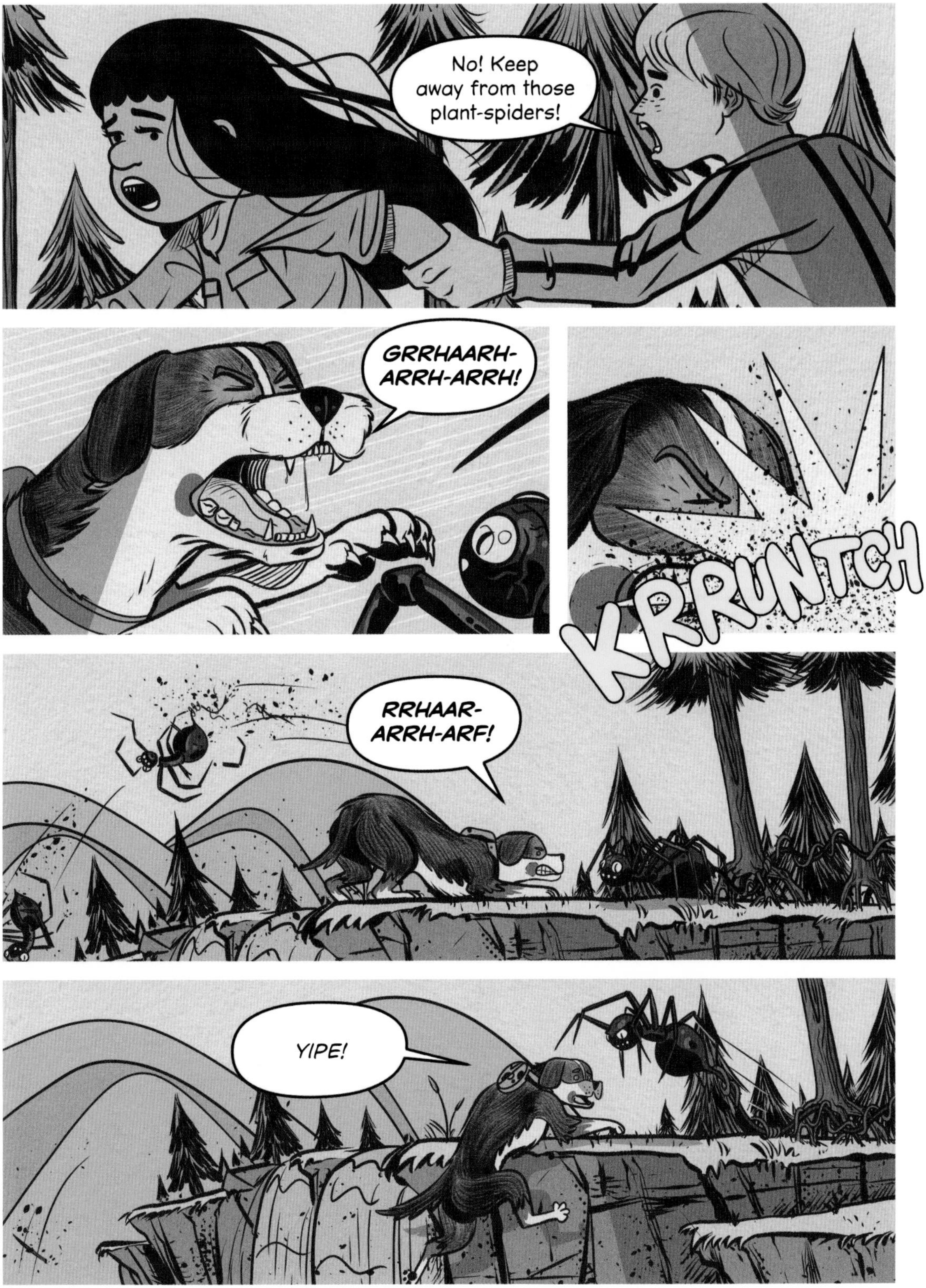
No! Keep away from those plant-spiders!
GRRHAARH-ARRH-ARRH!
KRRUNTCH
RRHAAR-ARRH-ARF!
YIPE!

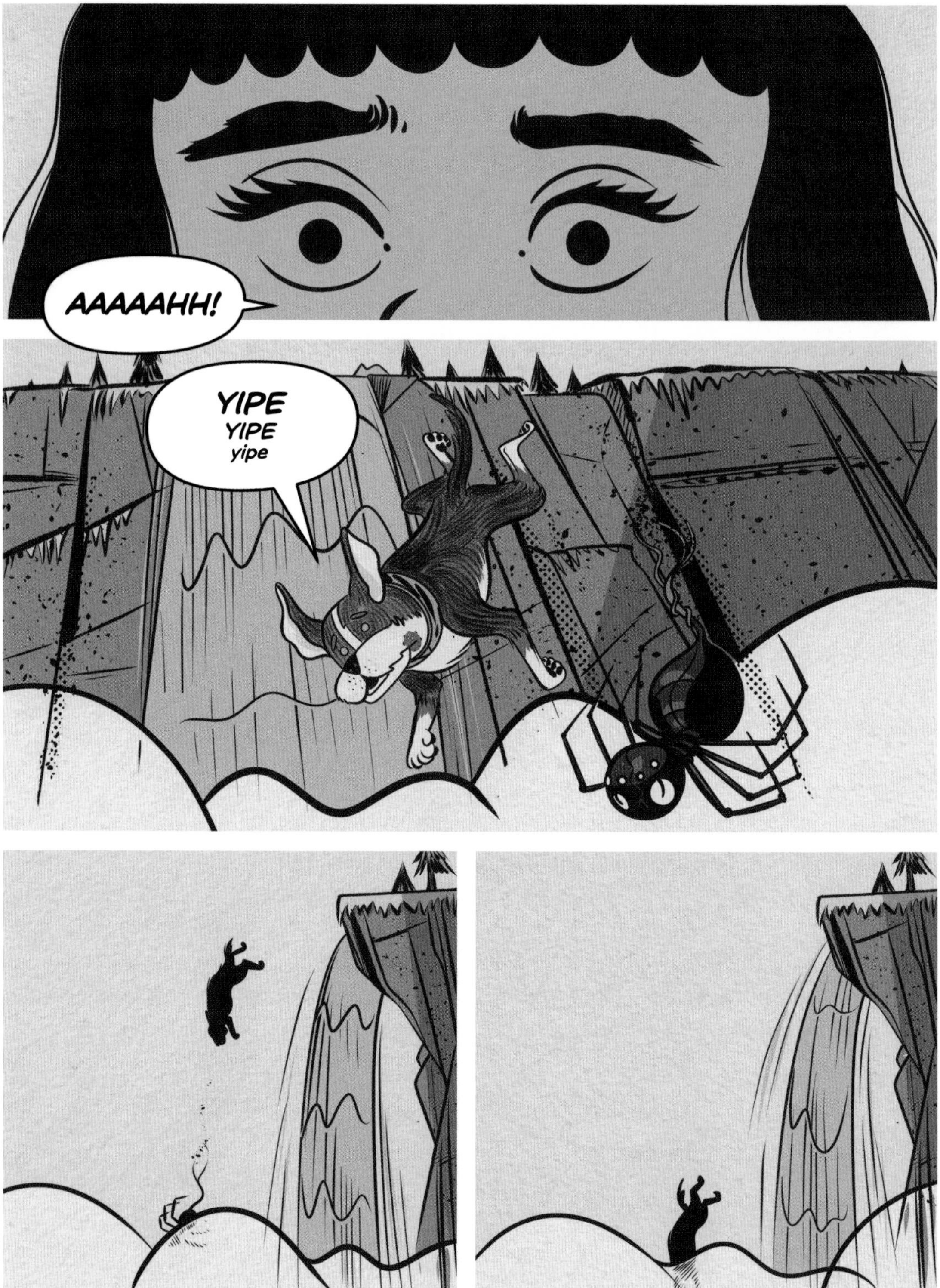
AAAAAHH!
YIPE
YIPE
yipe

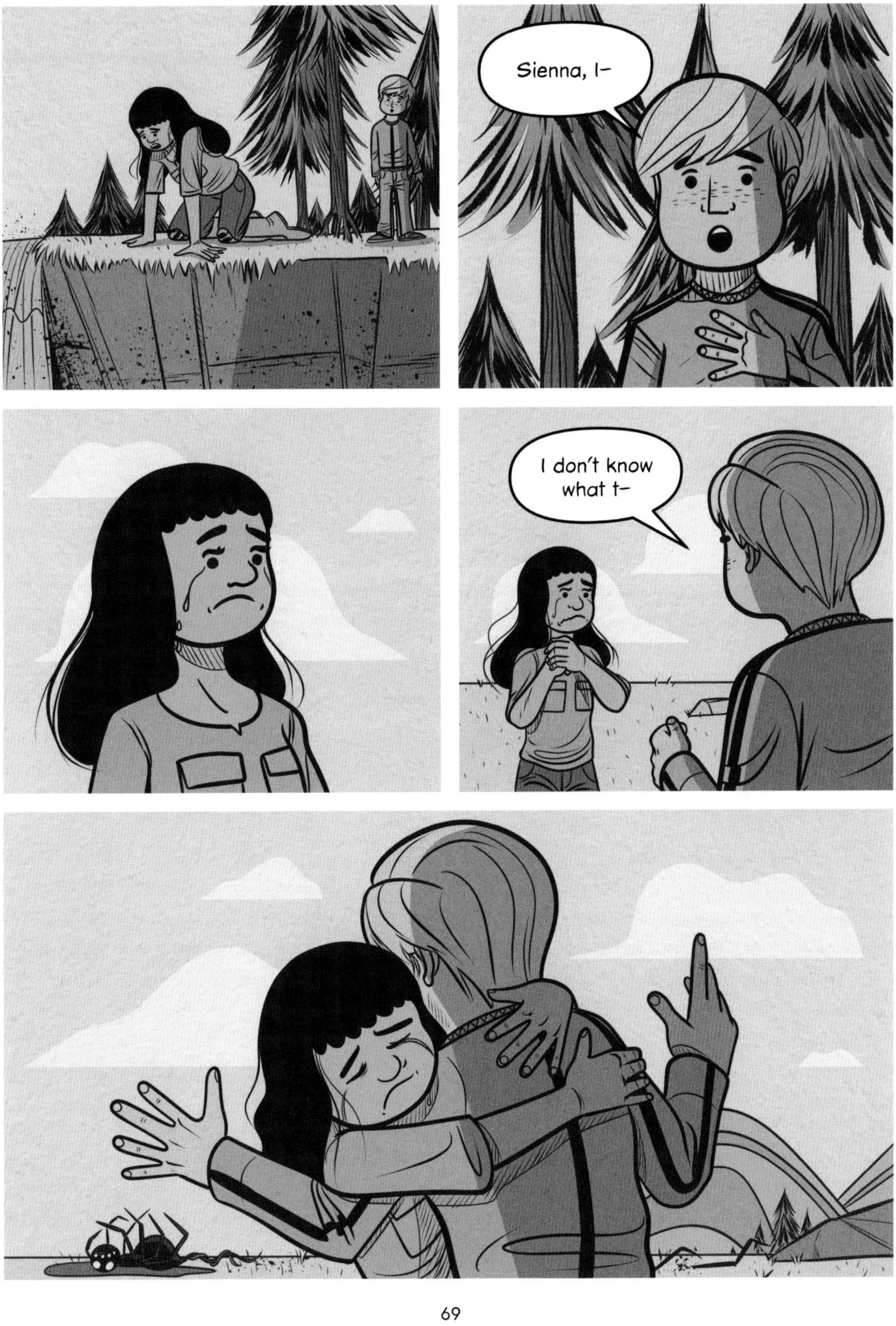
Sienna, I-
I don't know what t-

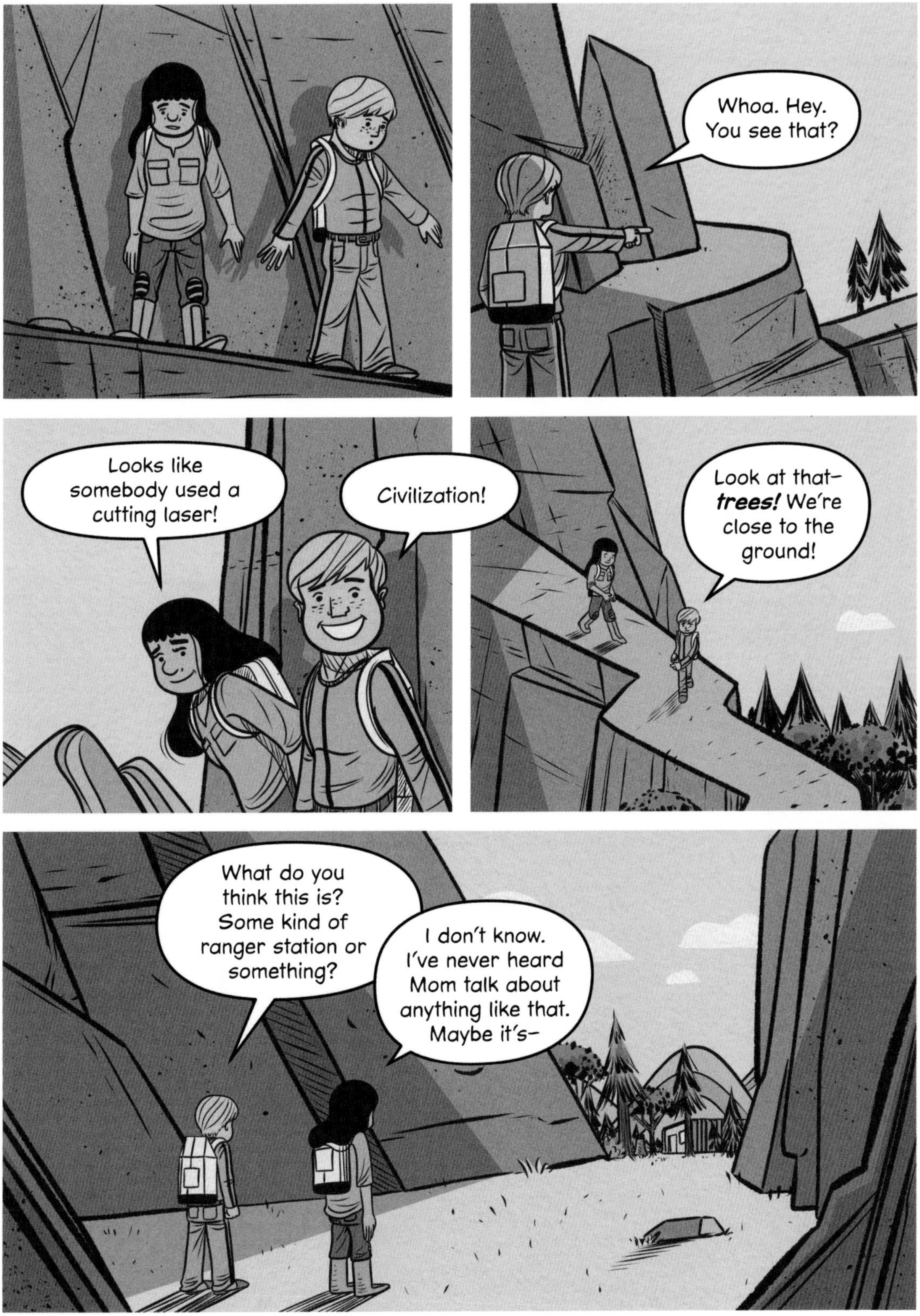
Whoa. Hey. You see that?
Looks like somebody used a cutting laser!
Civilization!
Look at that- **trees!** We're close to the ground!
What do you think this is? Some kind of ranger station or something?
I don't know. I've never heard Mom talk about anything like that. Maybe it's-

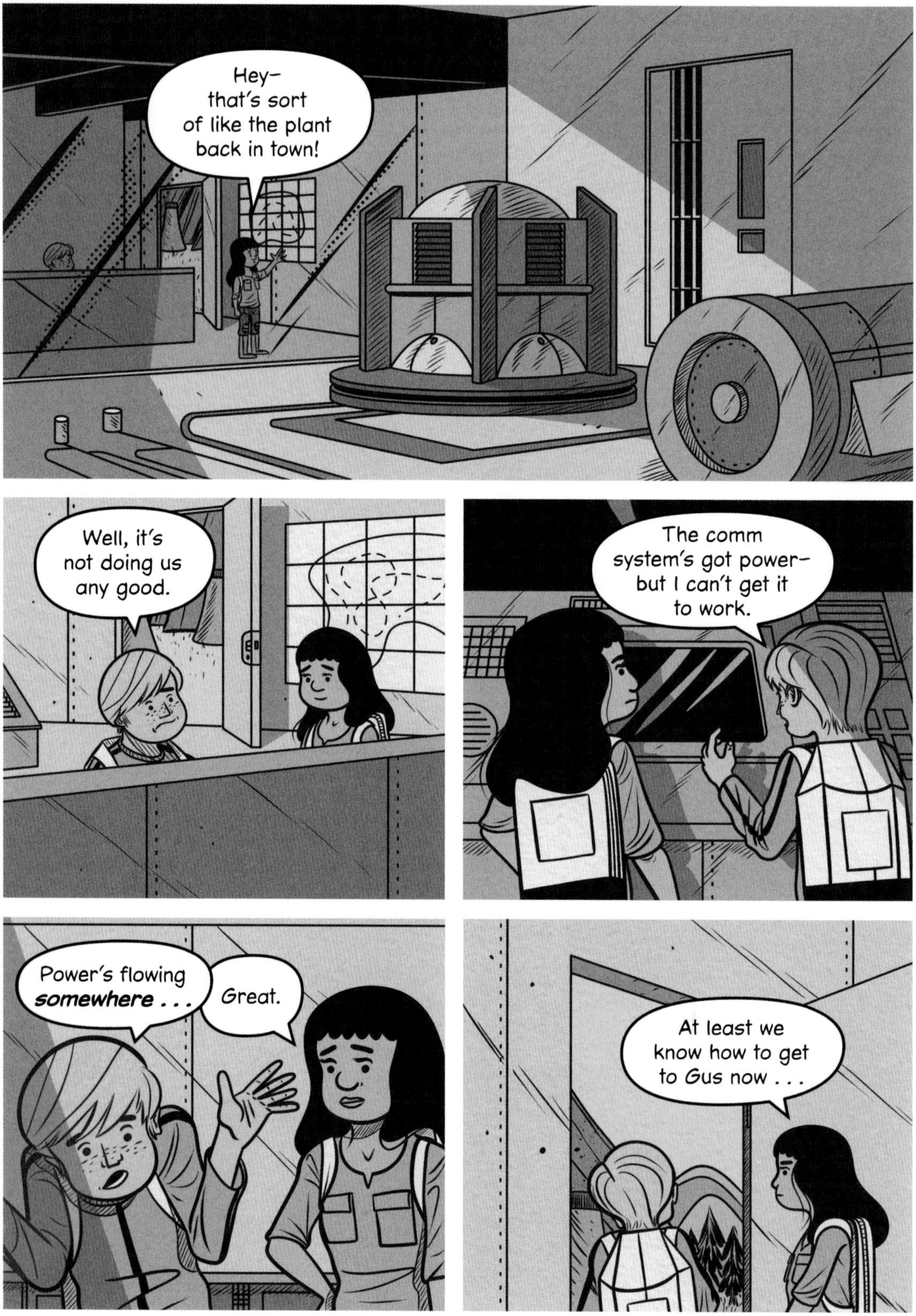
Hey—
that's sort
of like the plant
back in town!
Well, it's
not doing us
any good.
The comm
system's got power-
but I can't get it
to work.
Power's flowing
somewhere . . .
Great.
At least we
know how to get
to Gus now . . .

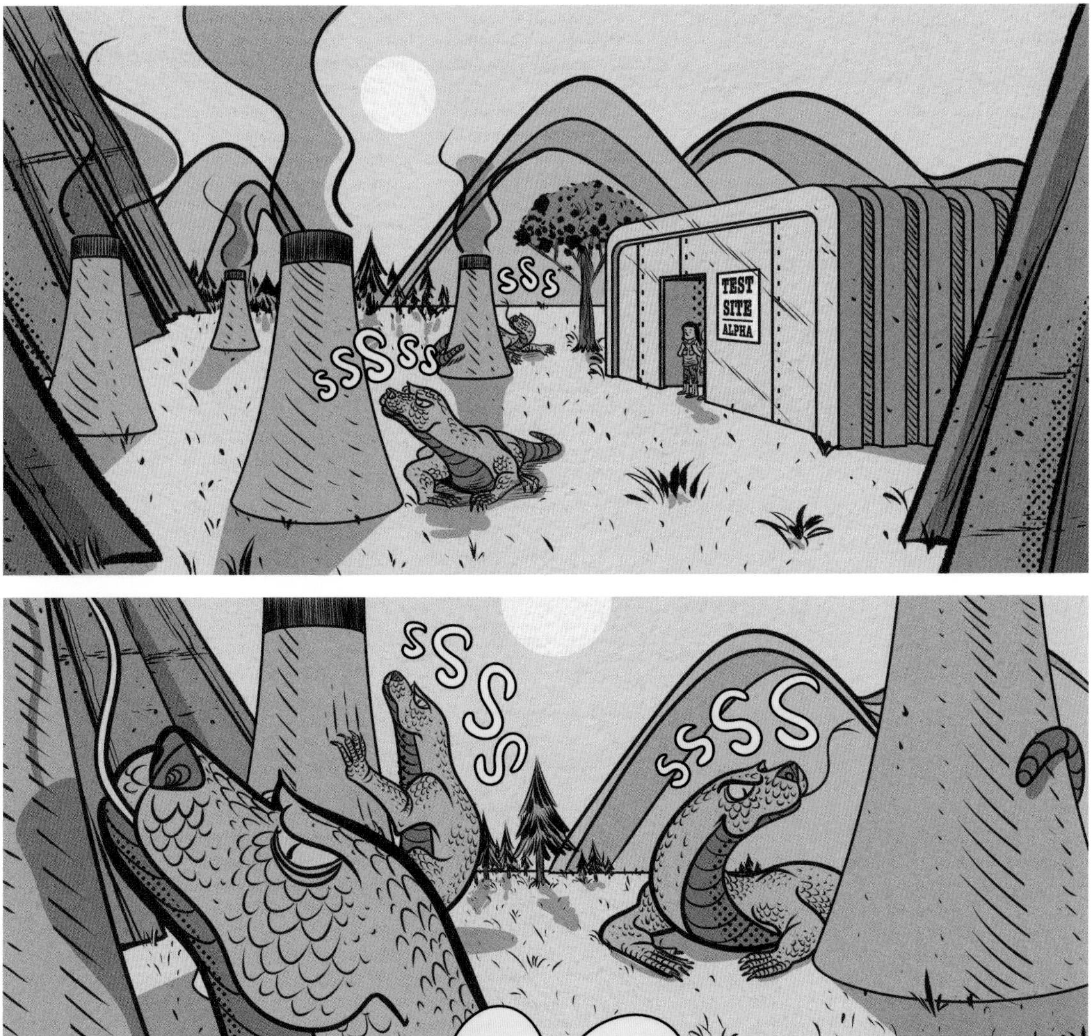
sSs
TEST
SITE
ALPHA
sSSss
sSSSs
sSSSS
sSSSSSssss

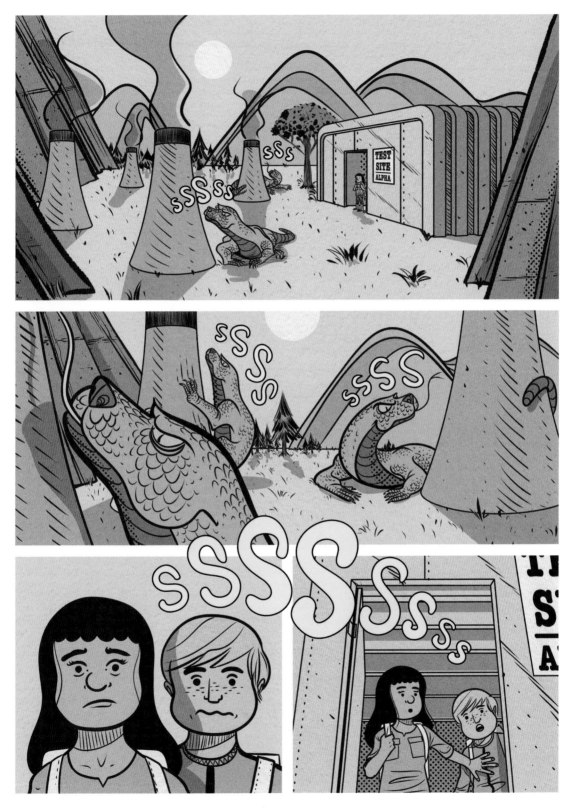

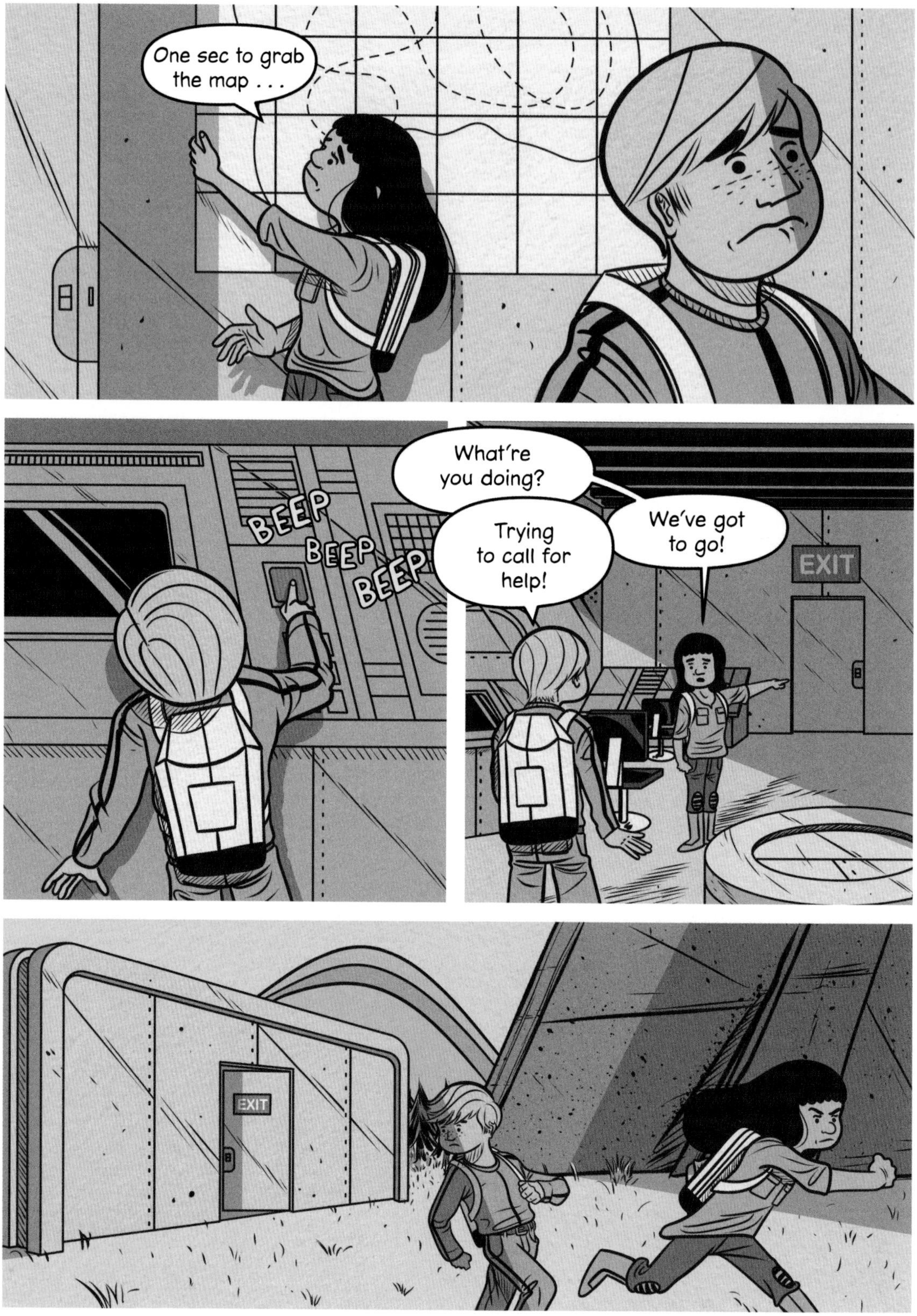
One sec to grab the map . . .
BEEP
BEEP
BEEP
What're you doing?
Trying to call for help!
We've got to go!
EXIT
EXIT

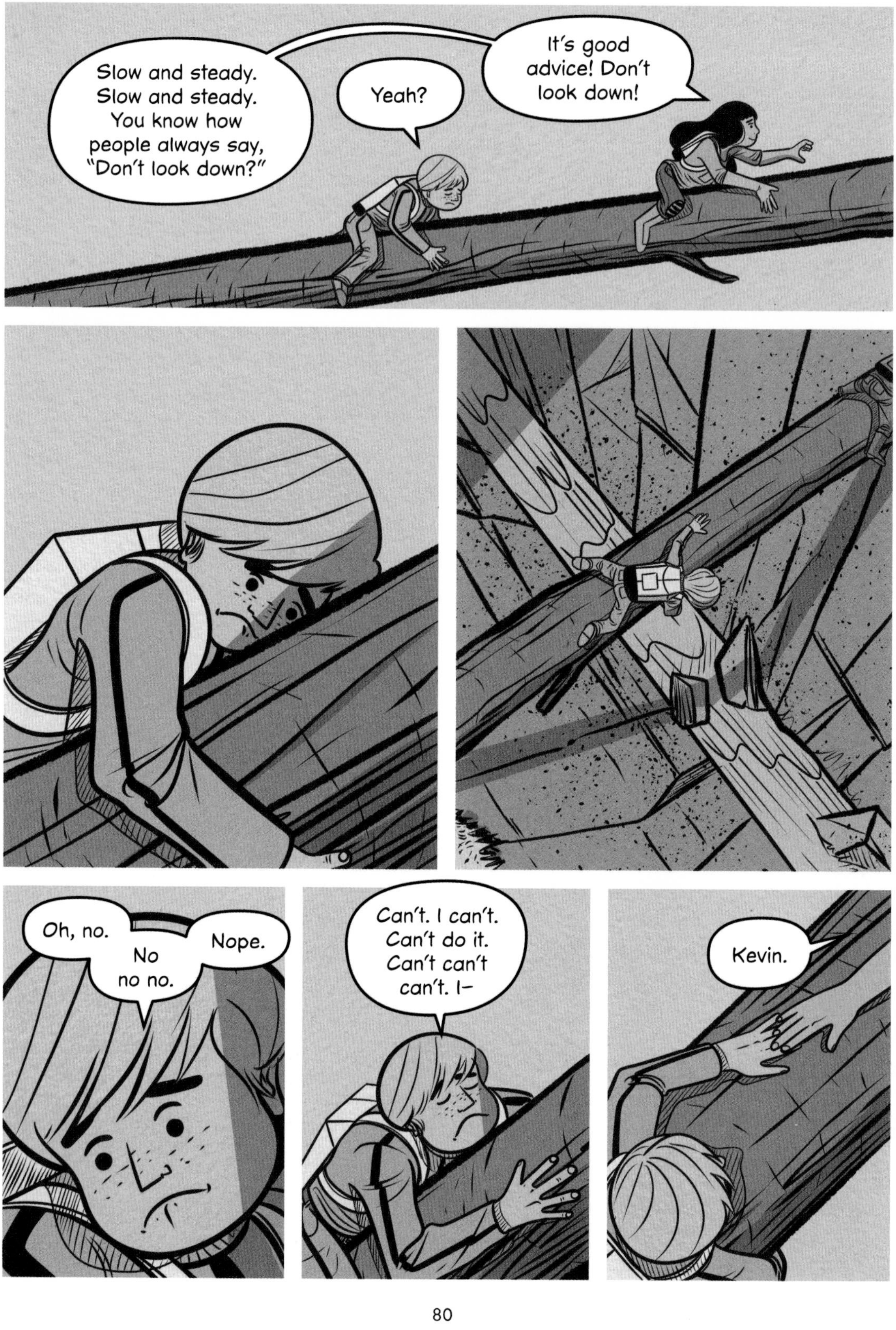
Slow and steady. Slow and steady. You know how people always say, "Don't look down?"
Yeah?
It's good advice! Don't look down!
Oh, no.
No no no.
Nope.
Can't. I can't. Can't do it. Can't can't can't. I–
Kevin.

81

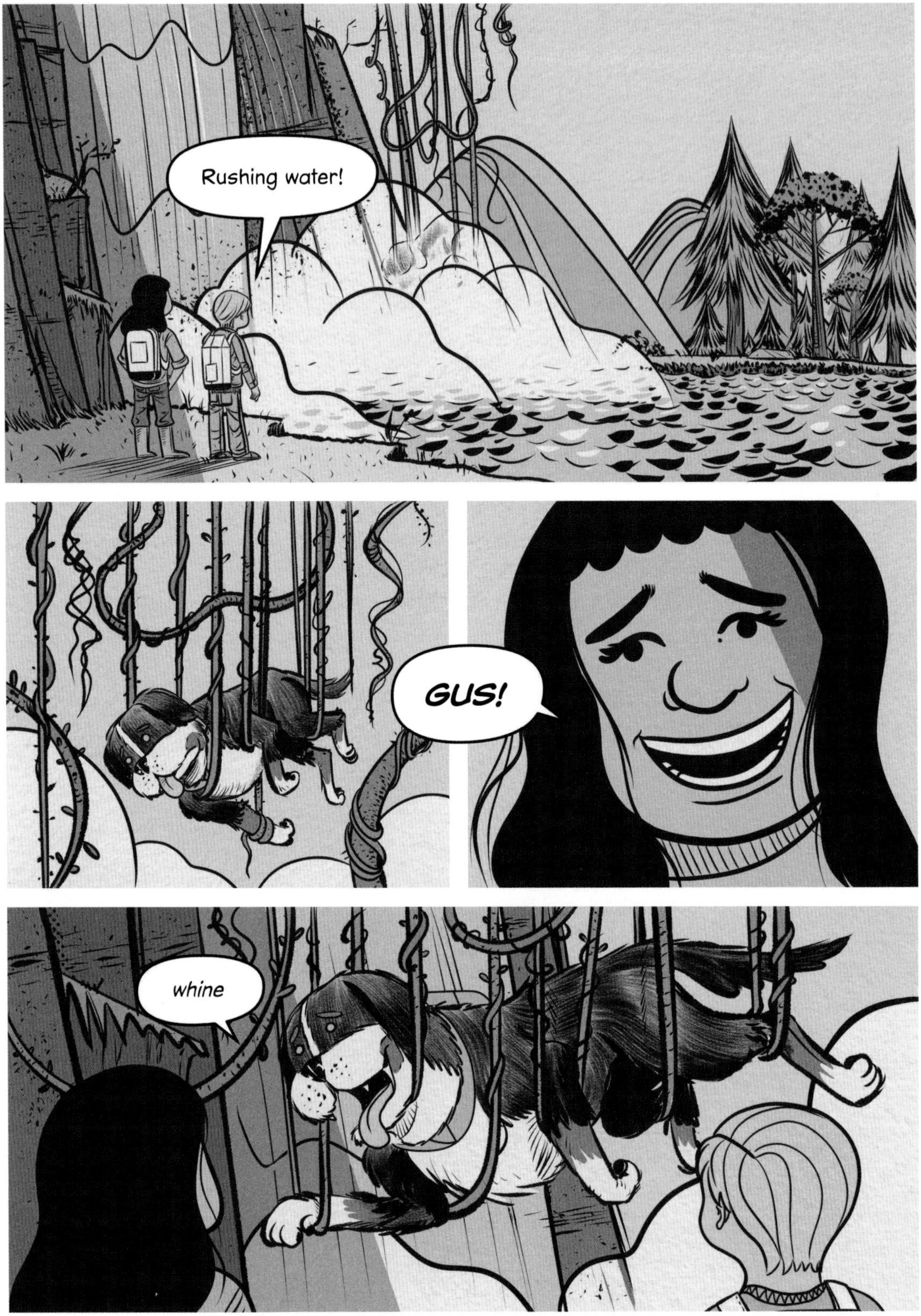

Rushing water!
GUS!
whine

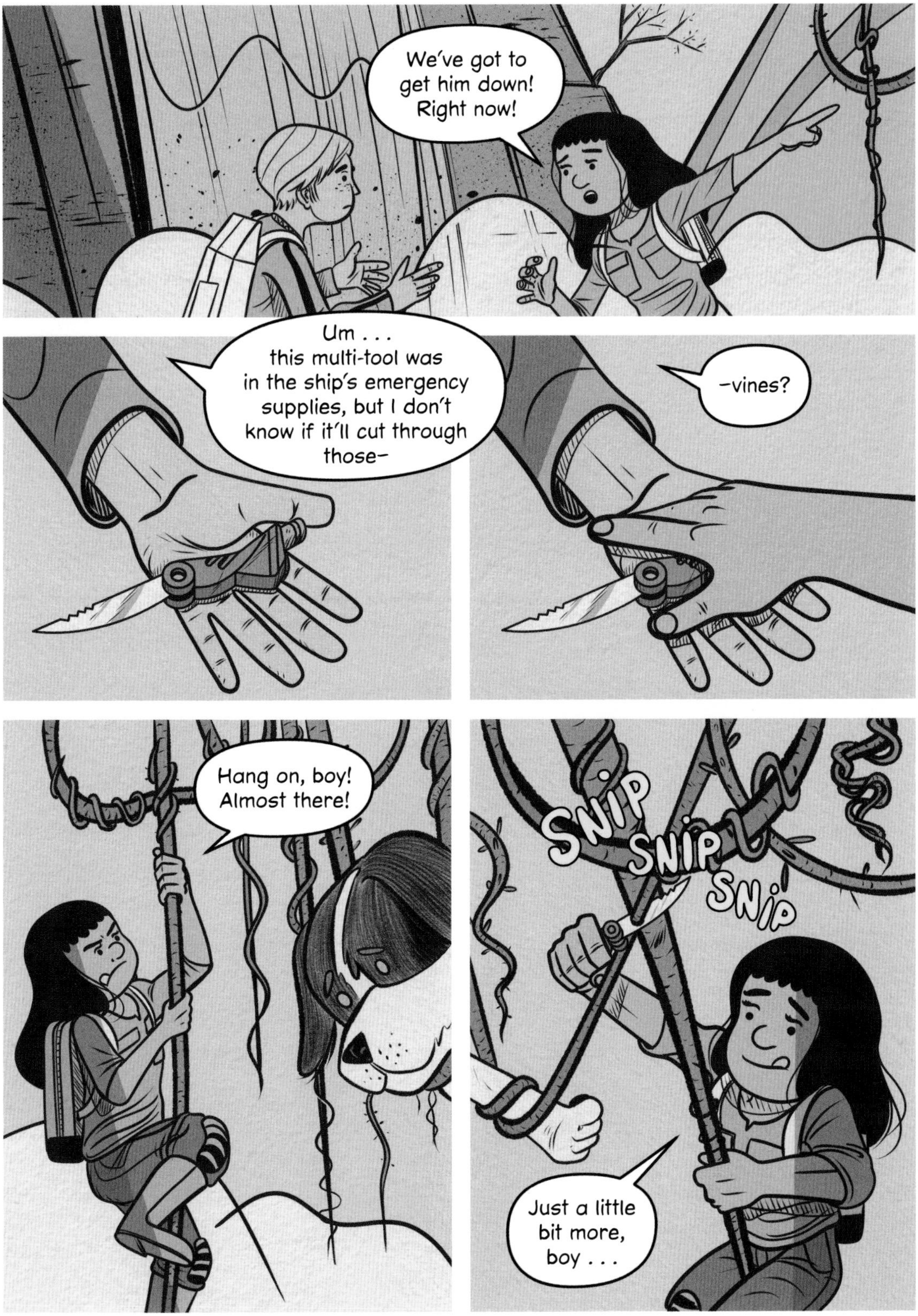
We've got to get him down! Right now!
Um . . . this multi-tool was in the ship's emergency supplies, but I don't know if it'll cut through those–
–vines?
Hang on, boy! Almost there!
SNIP SNIP SNIP
Just a little bit more, boy . . .

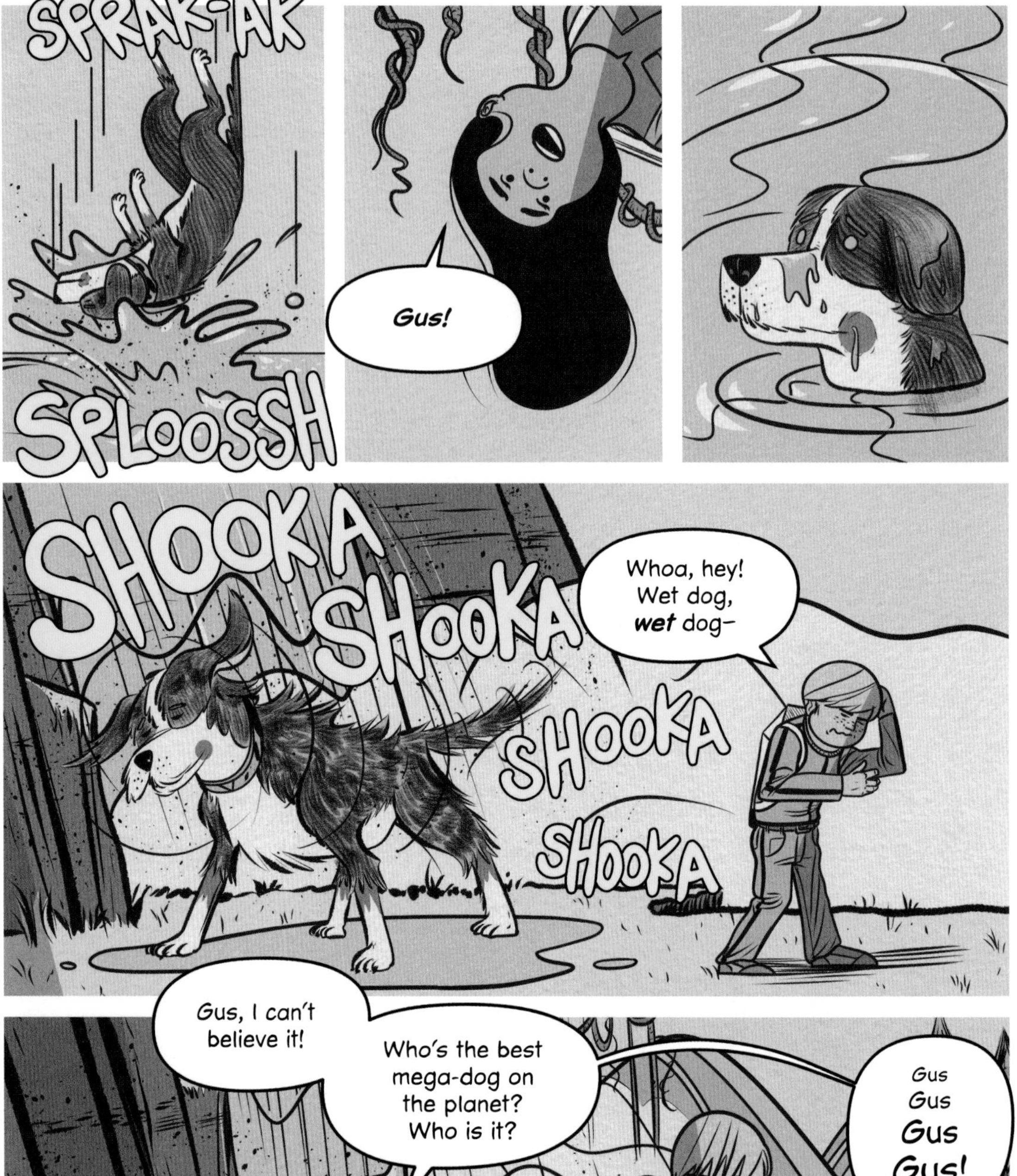
SPRAK-AK
SPLOOSSH
Gus!
SHOOKA
SHOOKA
Whoa, hey! Wet dog, **wet** dog–
SHOOKA
SHOOKA
Gus, I can't believe it!
Who's the best mega-dog on the planet? Who is it?
Gus Gus Gus Gus!

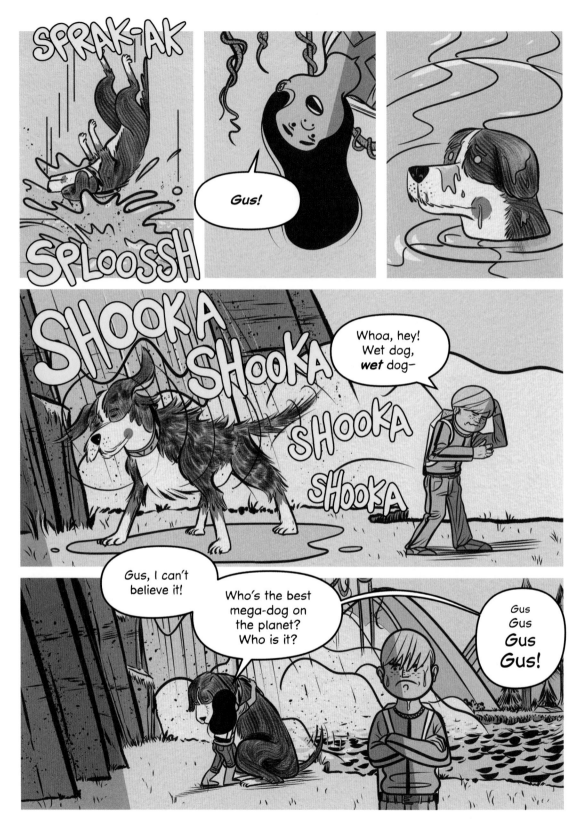

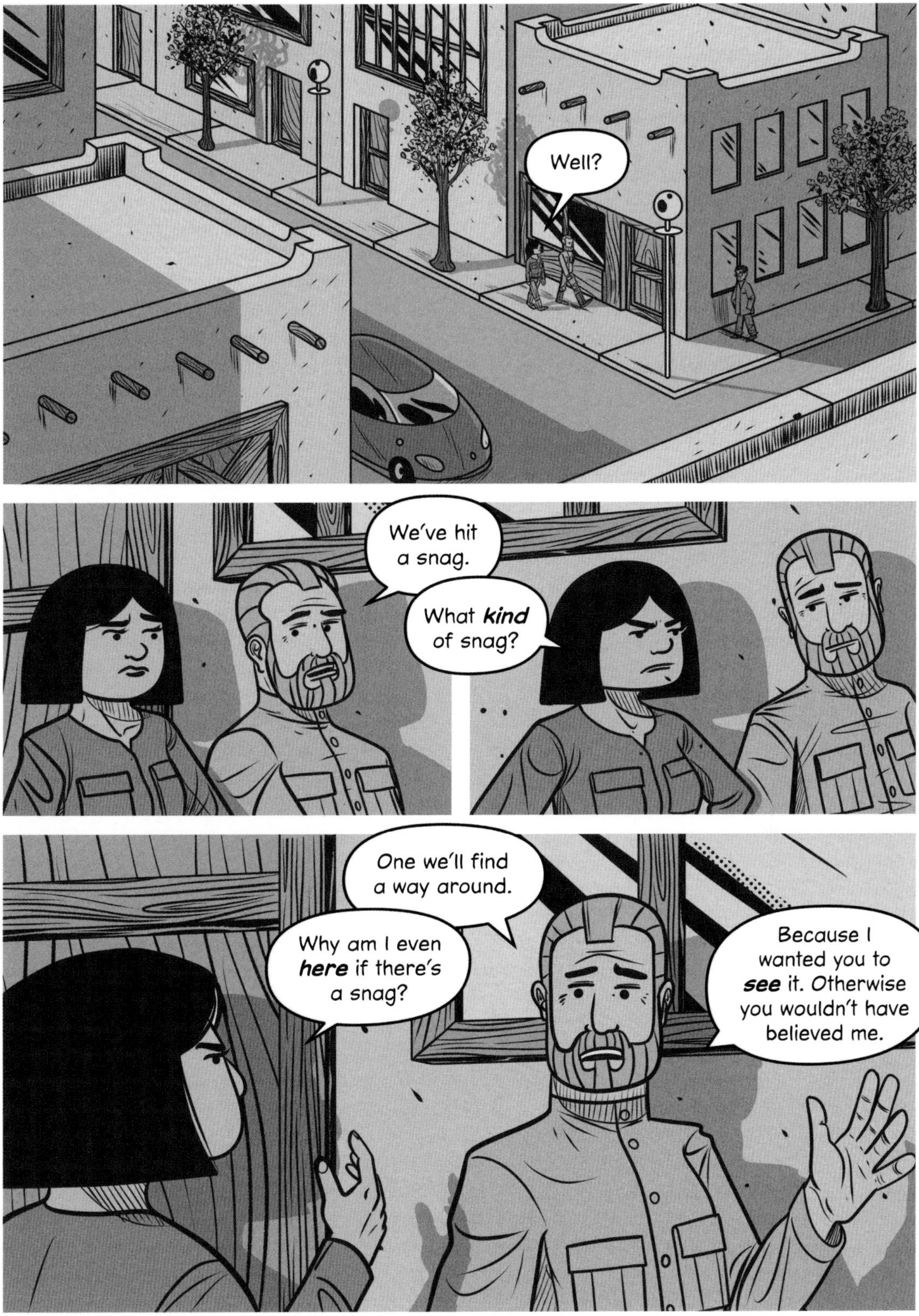
Well?
We've hit a snag.
What *kind* of snag?
One we'll find a way around.
Why am I even *here* if there's a snag?
Because I wanted you to *see* it. Otherwise you wouldn't have believed me.

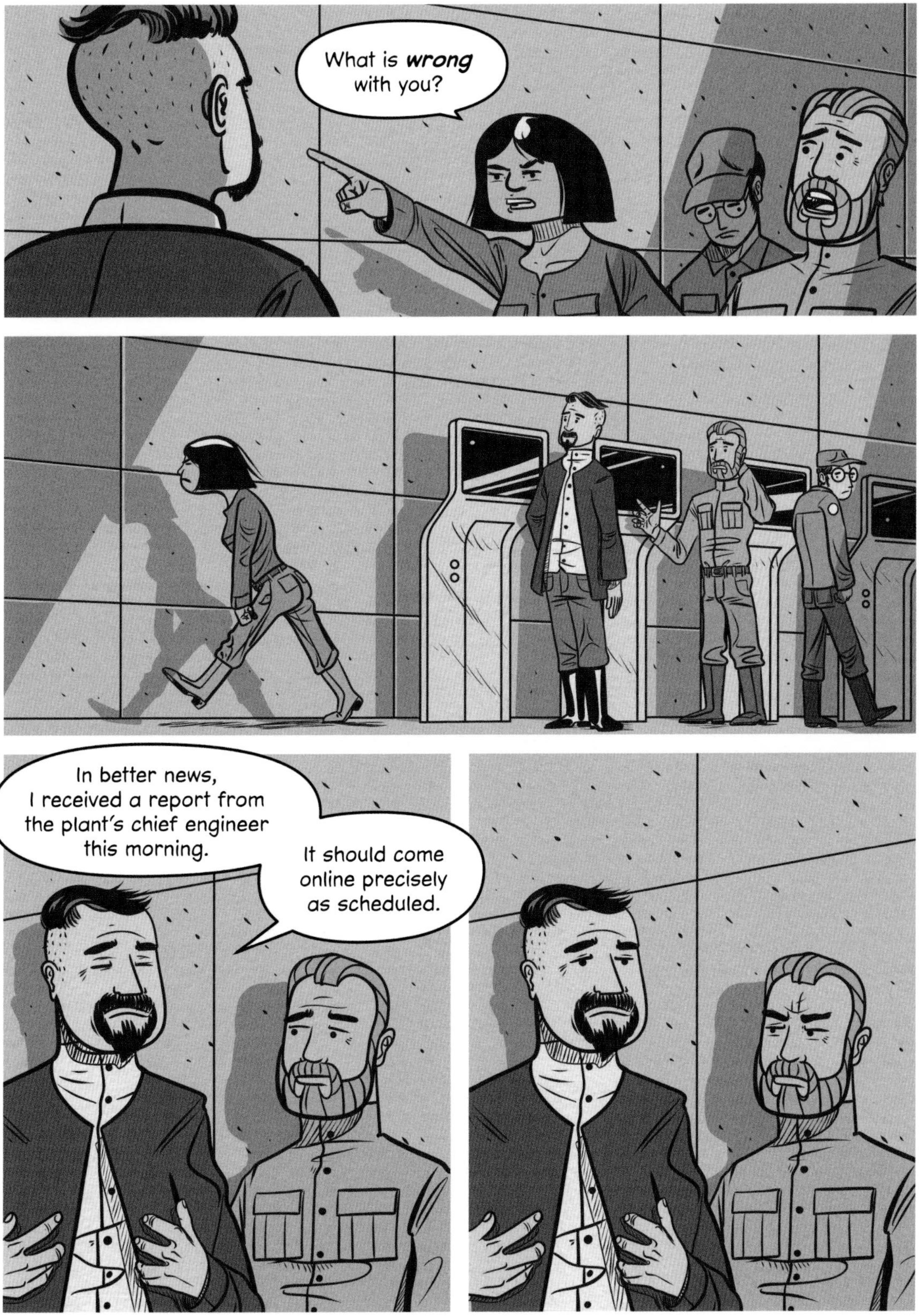
What is ***wrong*** with you?
In better news, I received a report from the plant's chief engineer this morning.
It should come online precisely as scheduled.

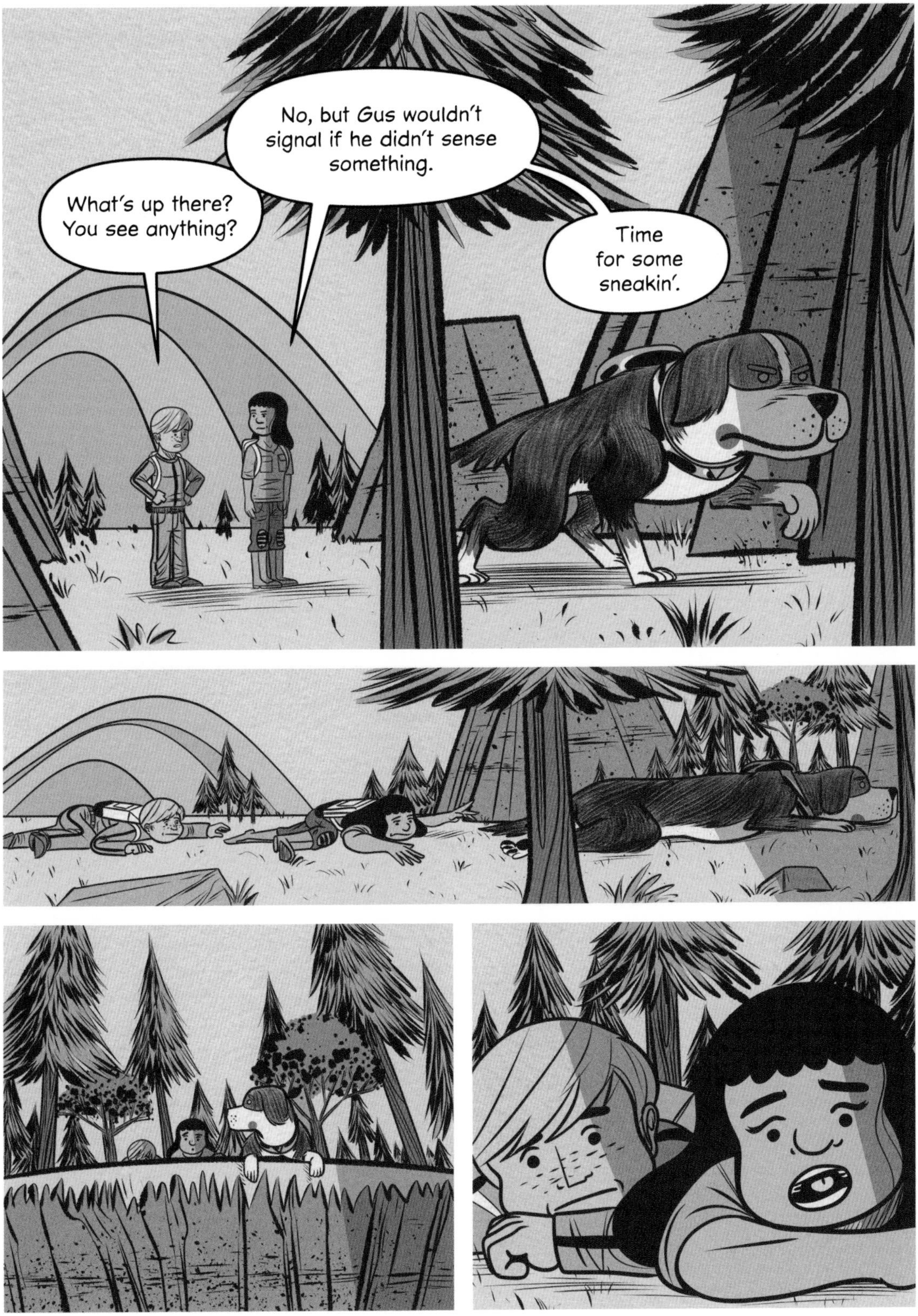
What's up there? You see anything?
No, but Gus wouldn't signal if he didn't sense something.
Time for some sneakin'.

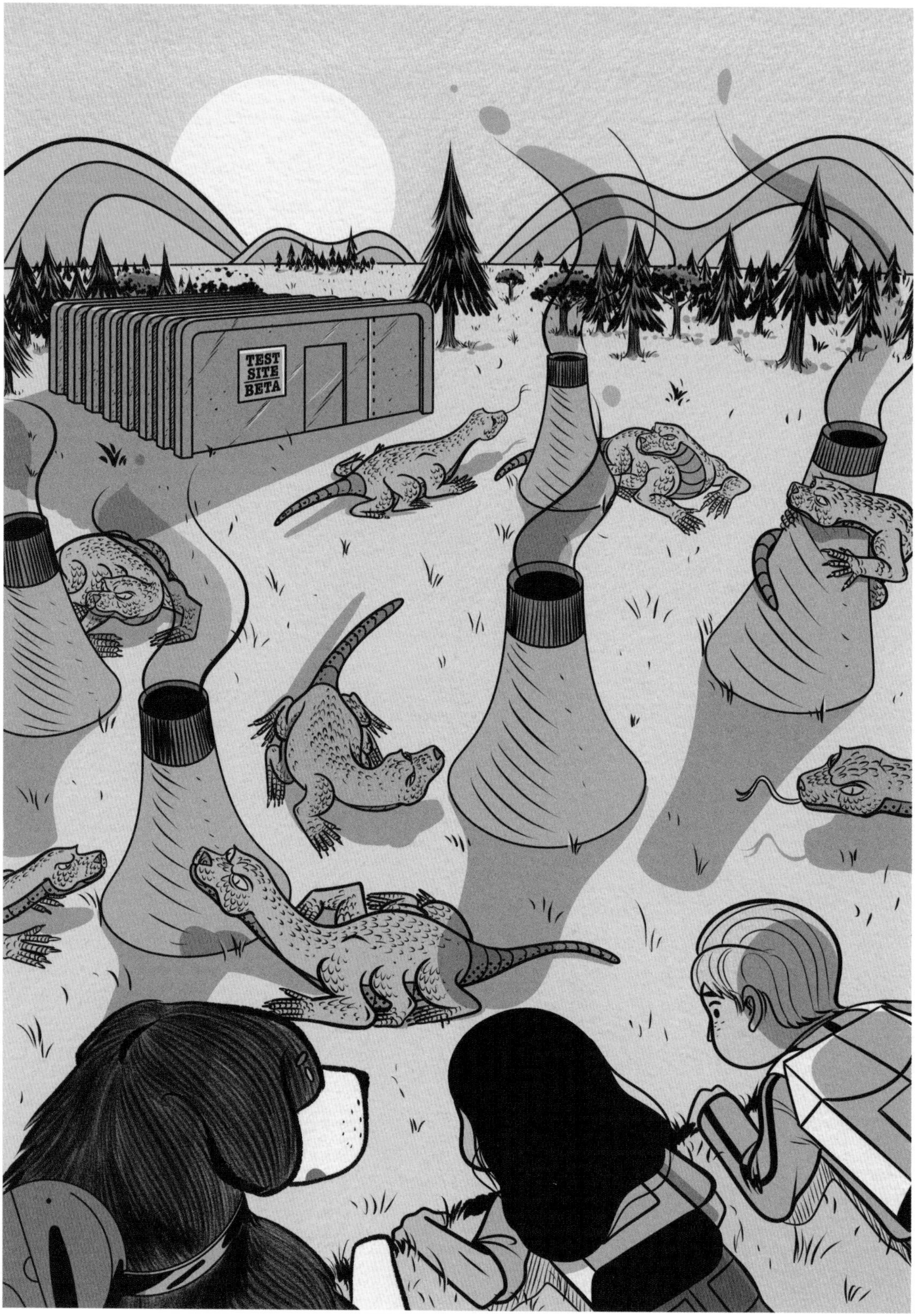
TEST
SITE
BETA

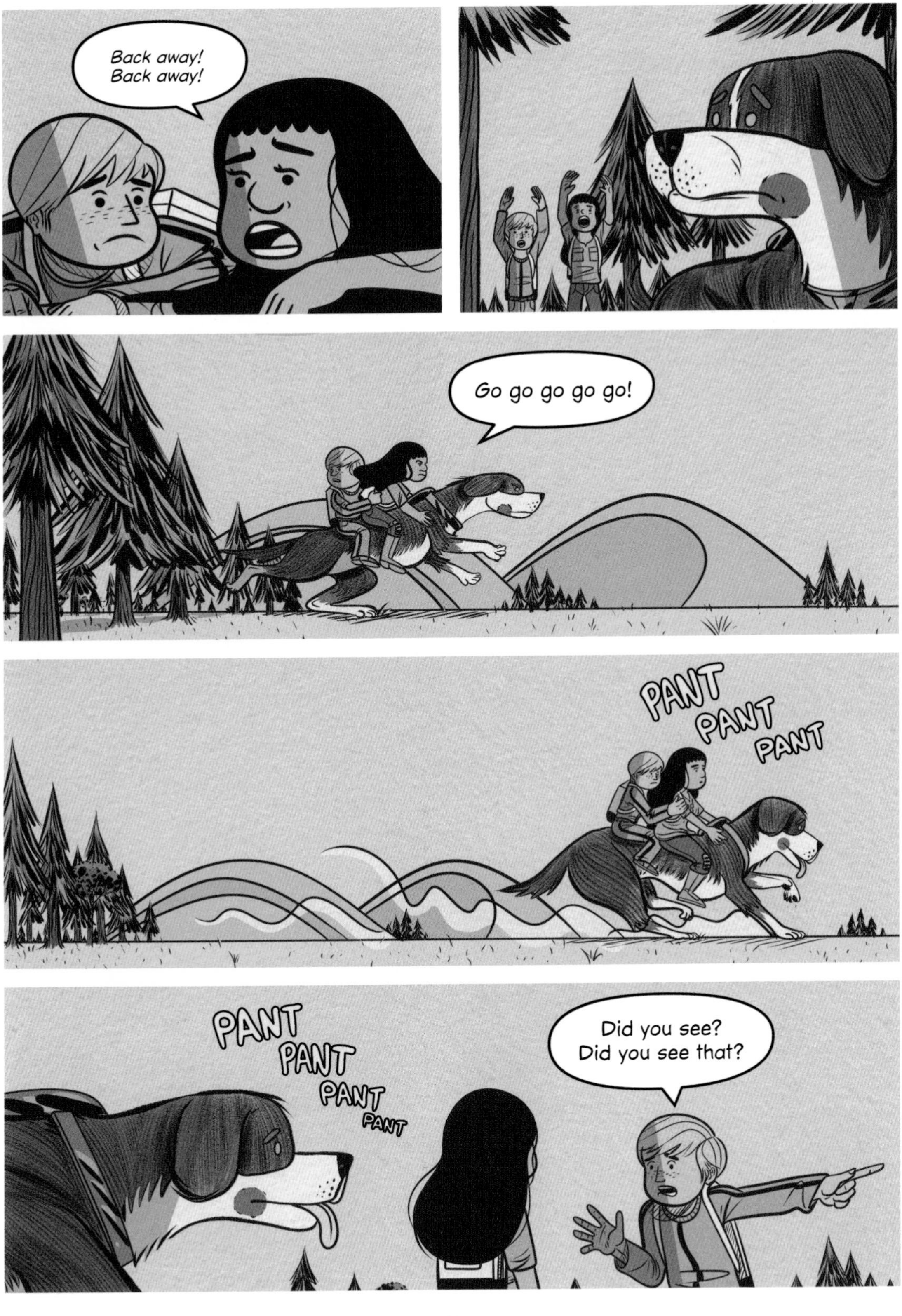

Back away!
Back away!
Go go go go go!
PANT PANT PANT
PANT PANT PANT PANT
Did you see?
Did you see that?

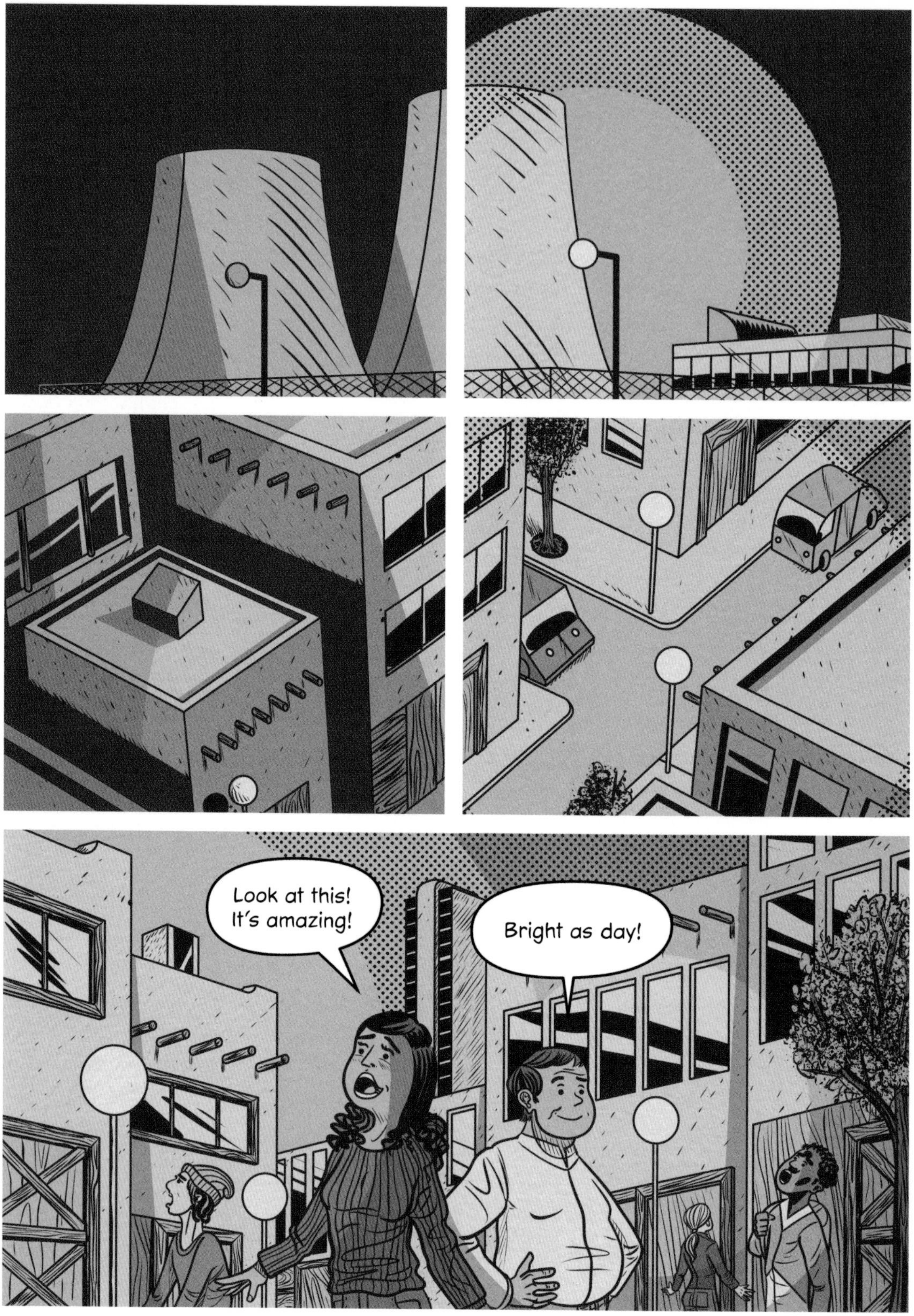
Look at this! It's amazing!
Bright as day!

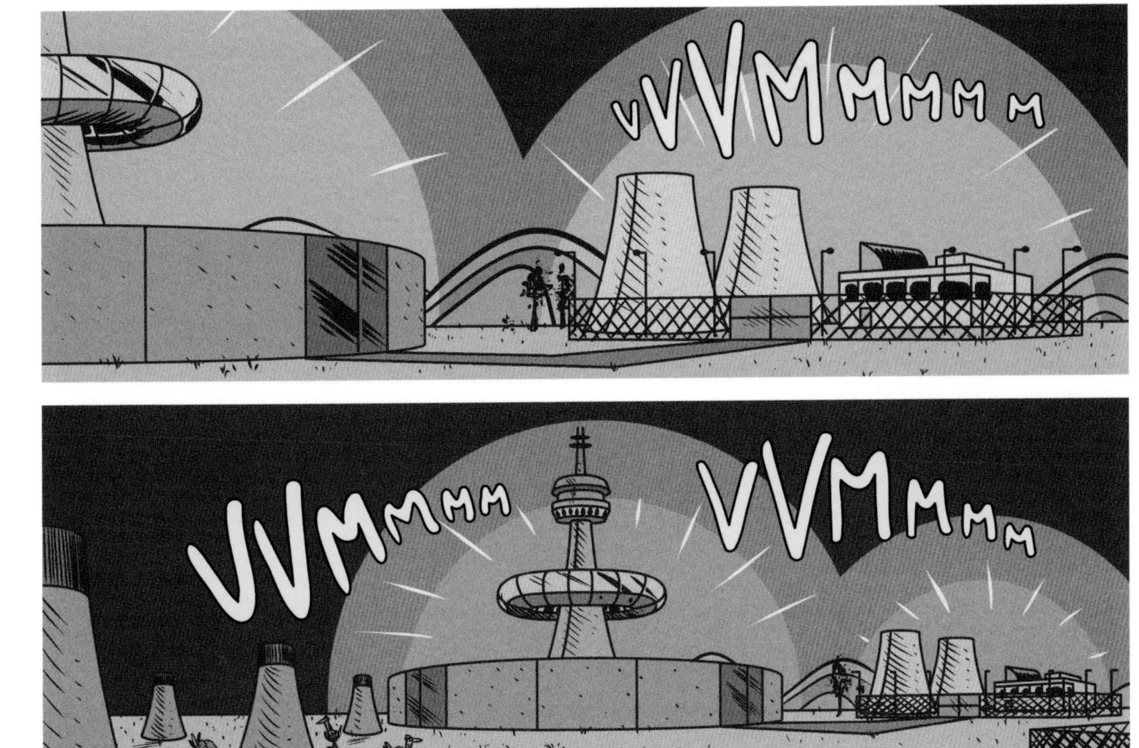
vVVMMMMM
VVMMMM
VVMMMM
VVMMMM
VVMMMM
Ss
sSSSsssSSS

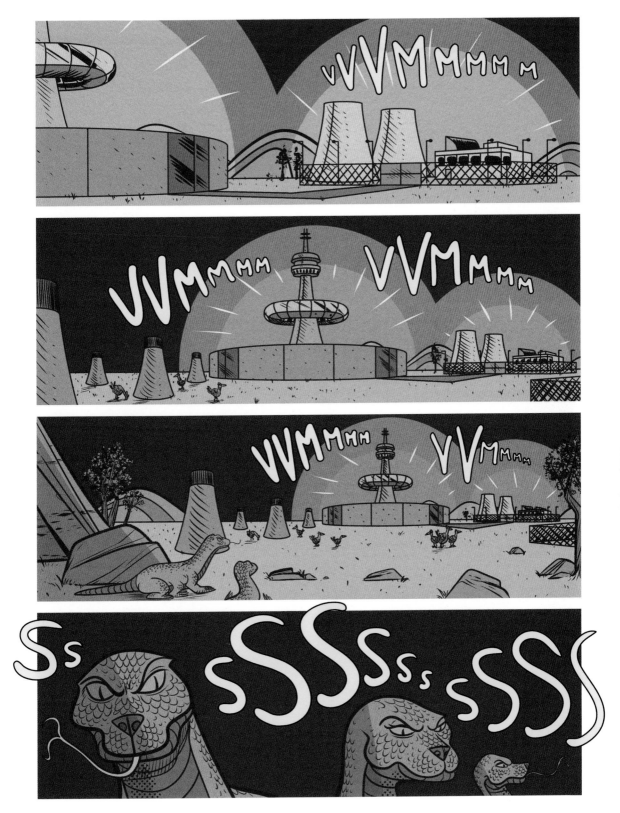

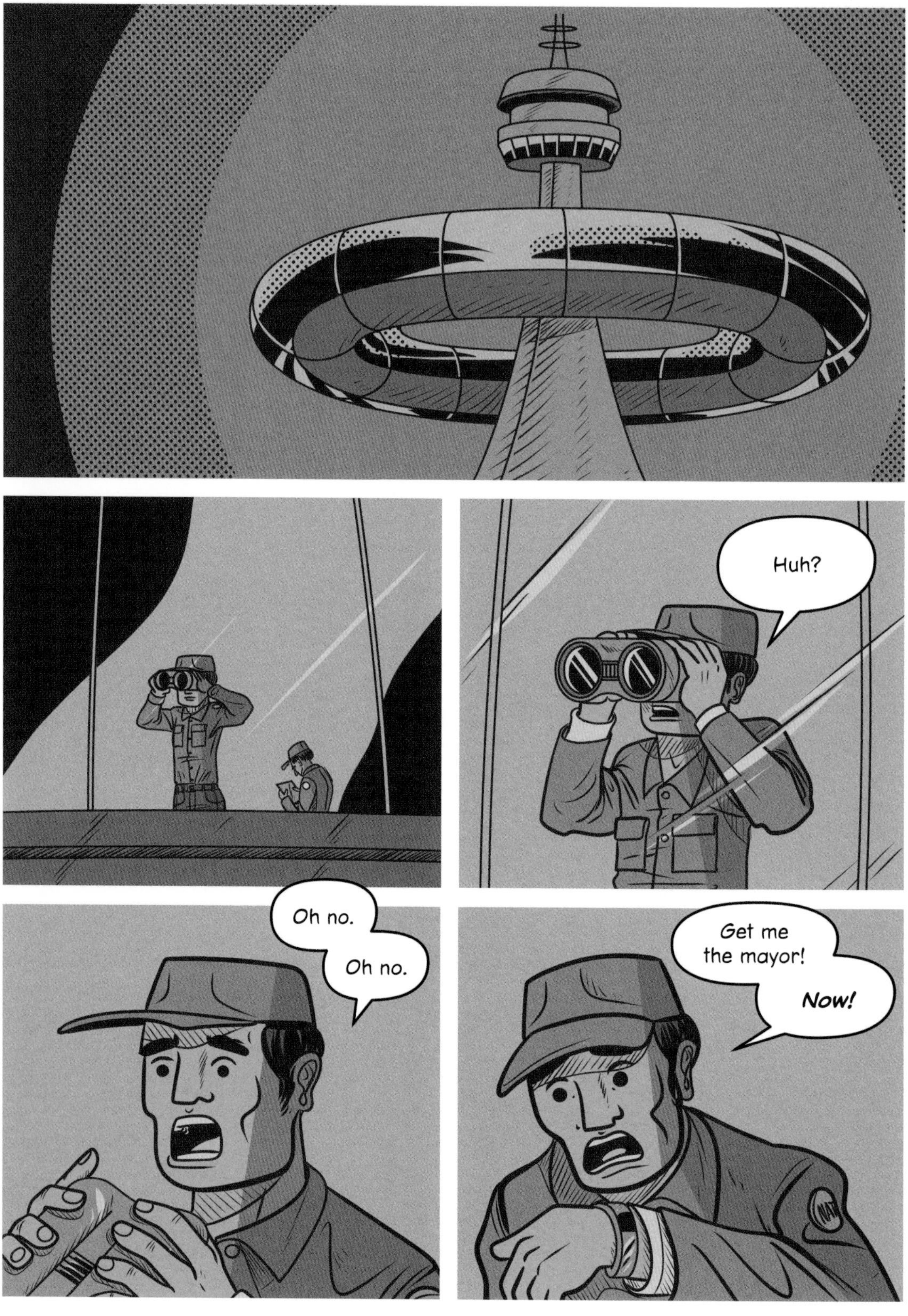
Huh?
Oh no.
Oh no.
Get me the mayor!
Now!

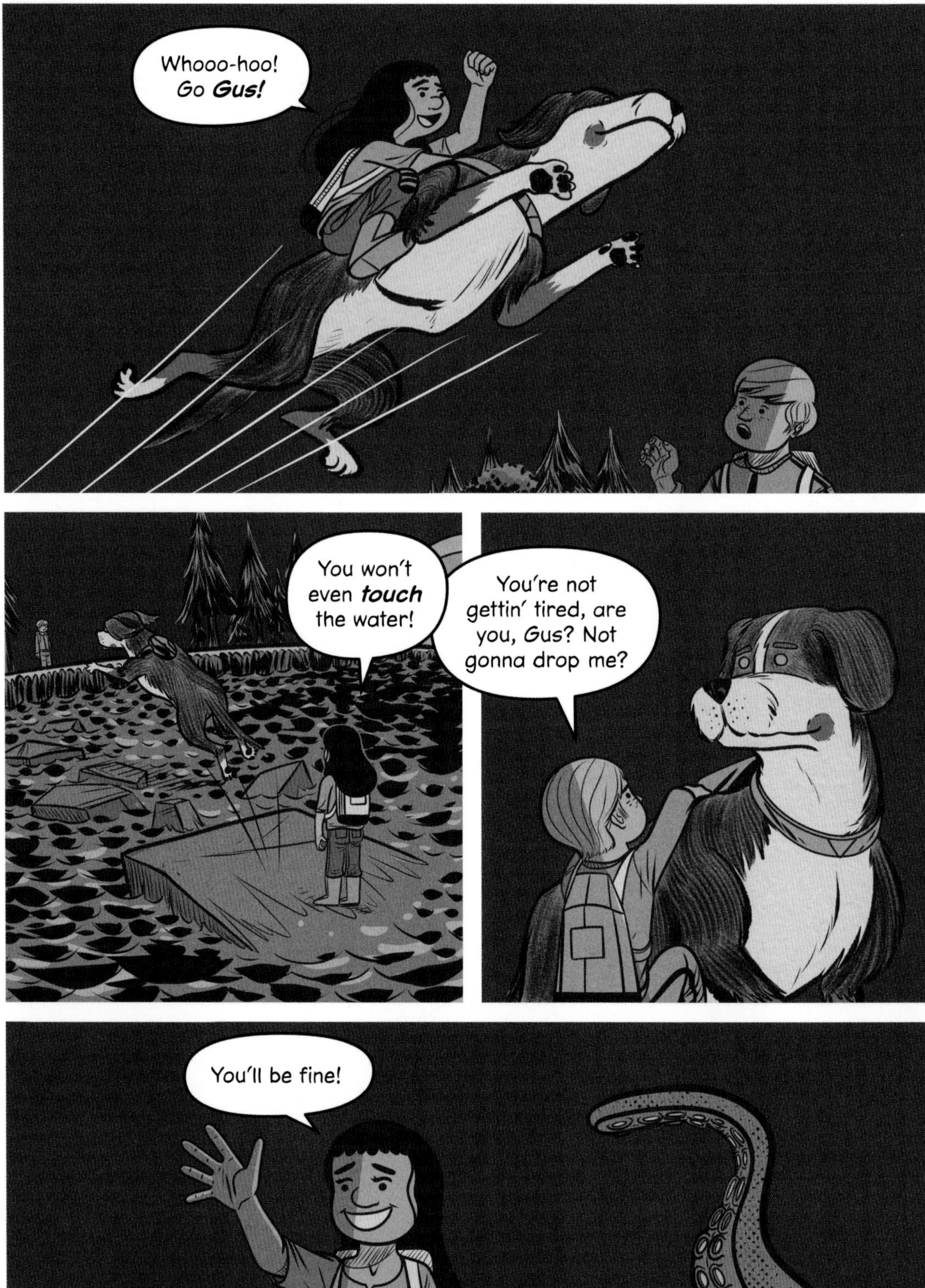
Whooo-hoo! Go **Gus!**
You won't even **touch** the water!
You're not gettin' tired, are you, Gus? Not gonna drop me?
You'll be fine!

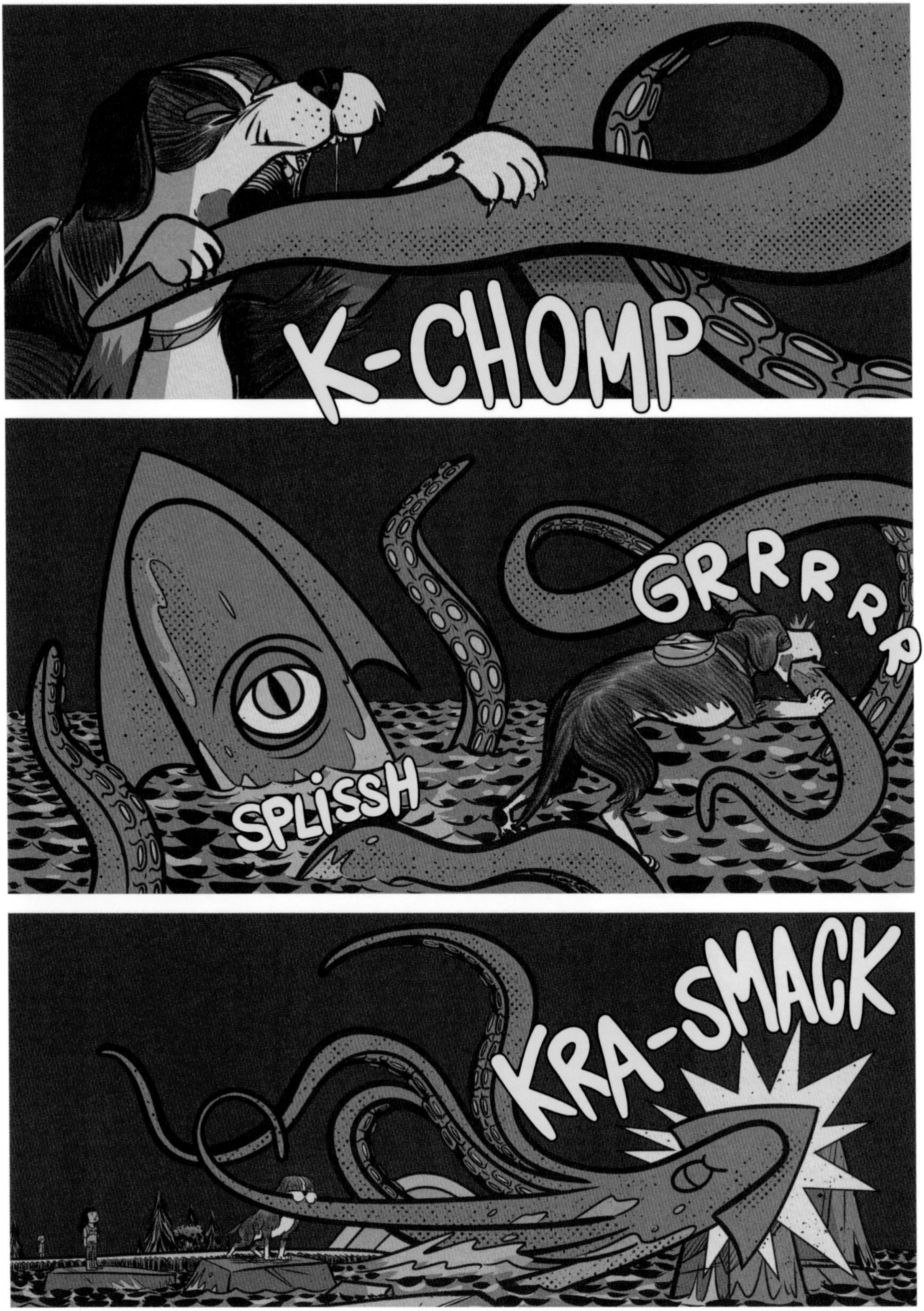
K-CHOMP
GRRRRRR
SPLISSH
KRA-SMACK

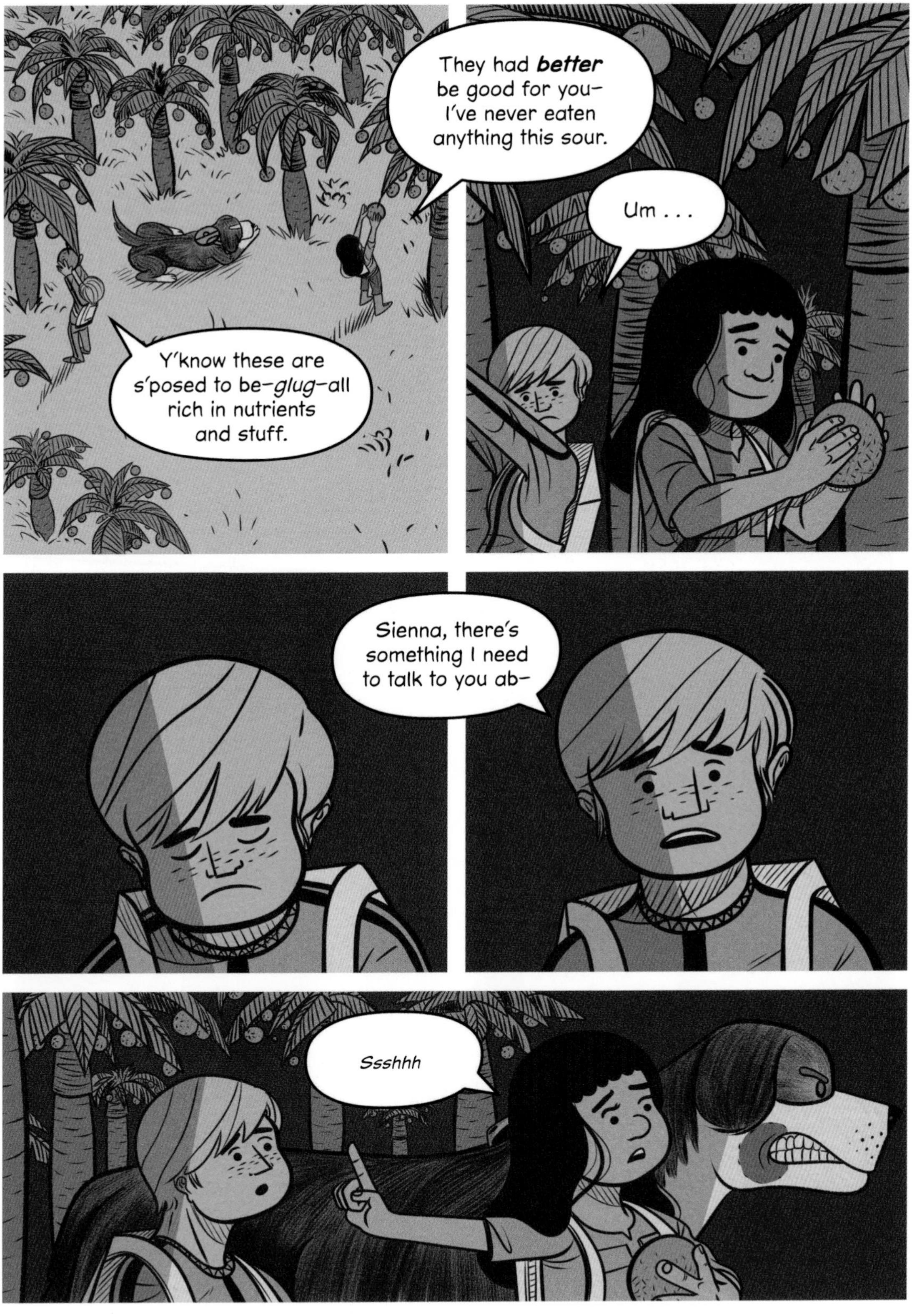
Y'know these are s'posed to be-*glug*-all rich in nutrients and stuff.
They had **better** be good for you- I've never eaten anything this sour.
Um . . .
Sienna, there's something I need to talk to you ab-
Ssshhh

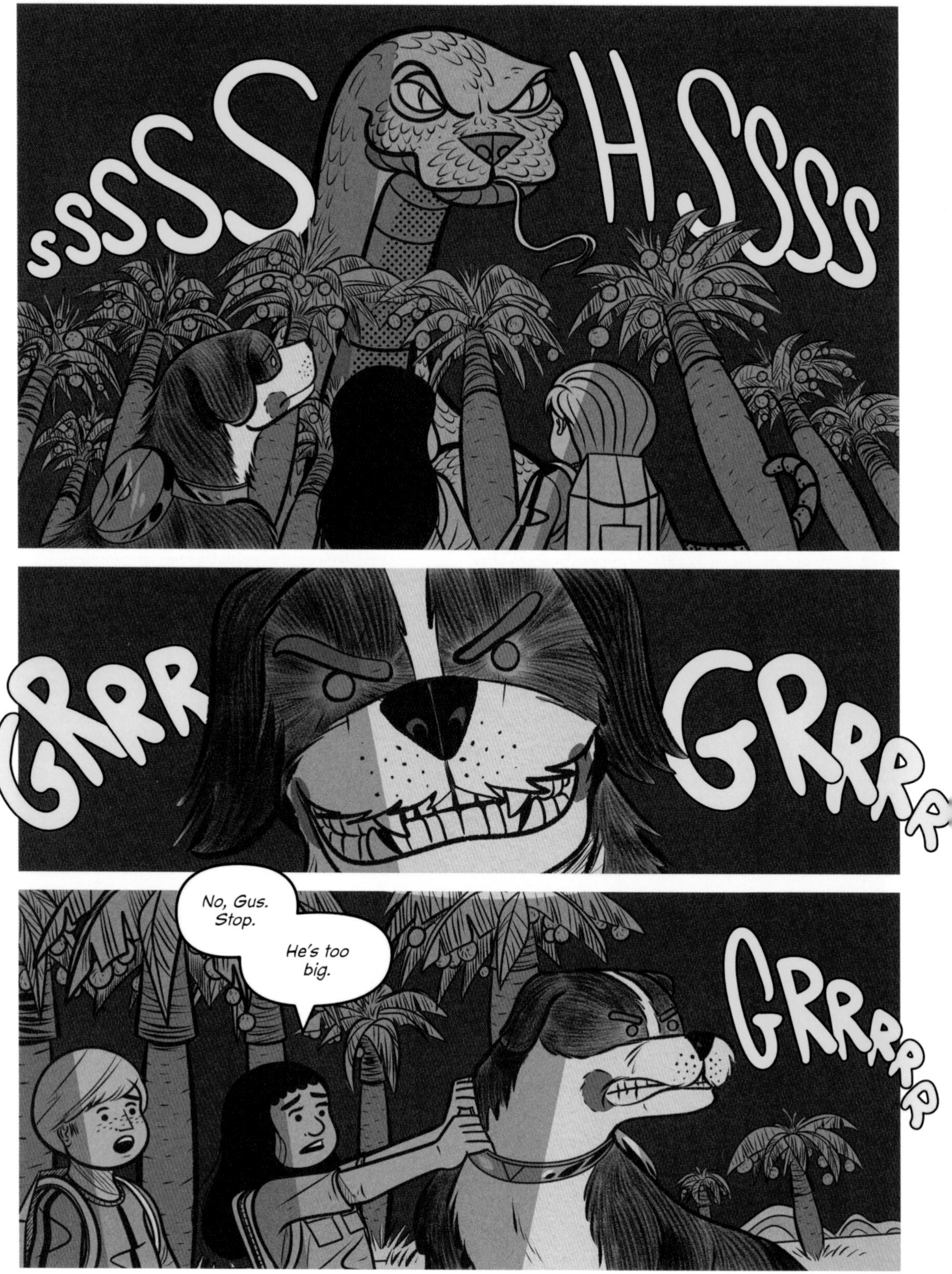
sSSSS
HSSSS
GRRR
GRRRR
No, Gus. Stop.
He's too big.
GRRRRR

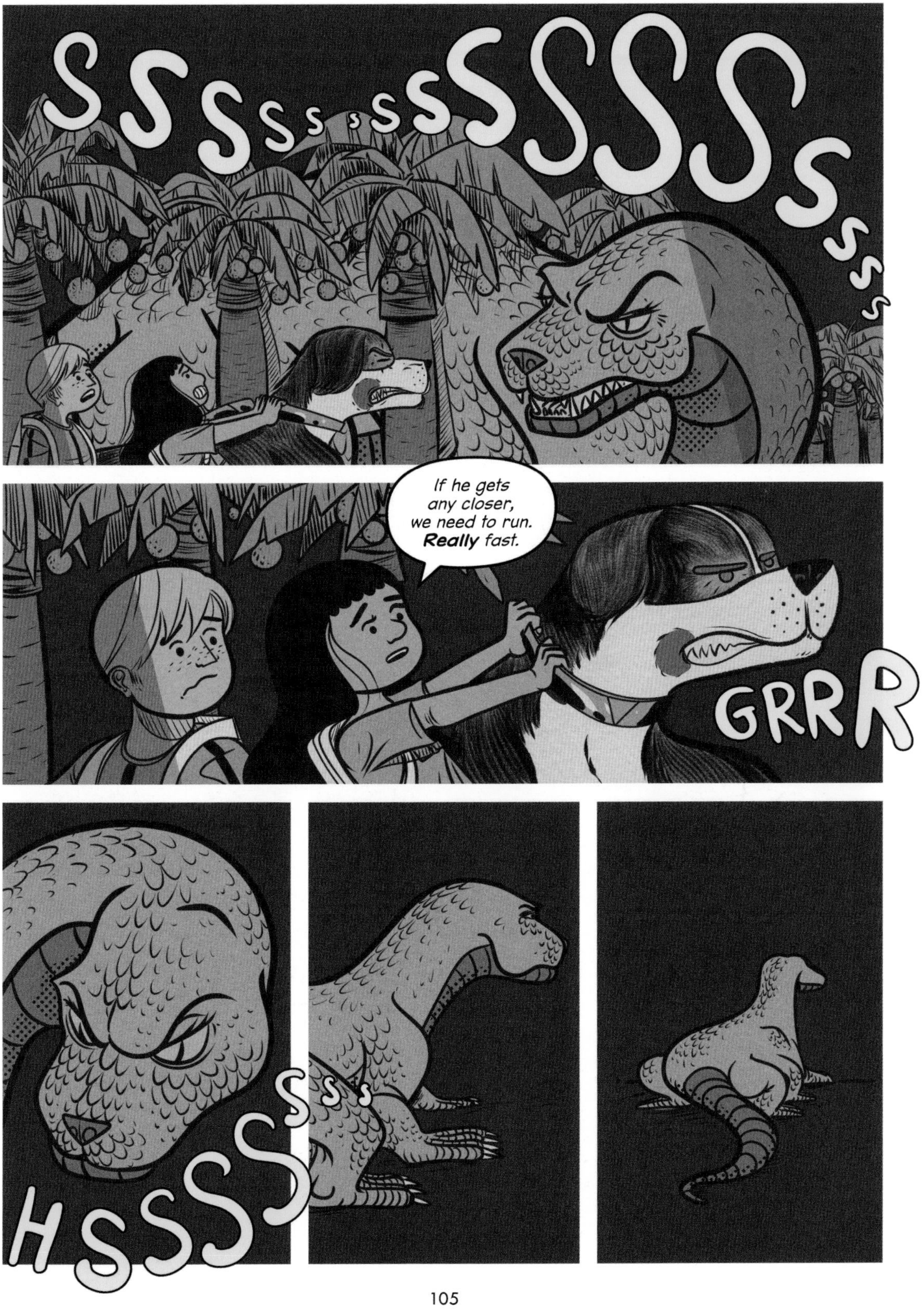
SSSsssssSSSSSsss
If he gets any closer, we need to run. **Really** fast.
GRRR
HSSSSsss

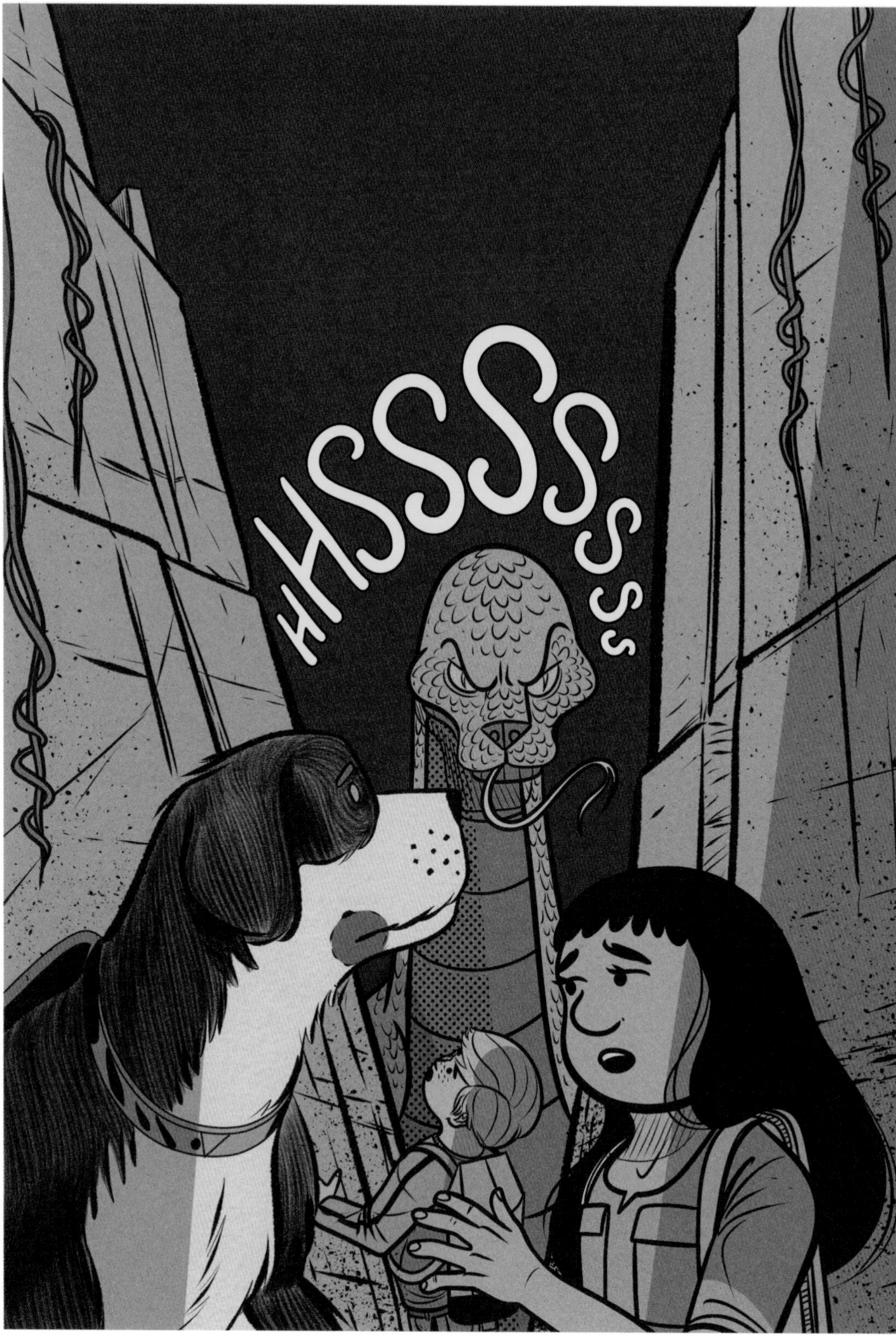
HSSSSssss

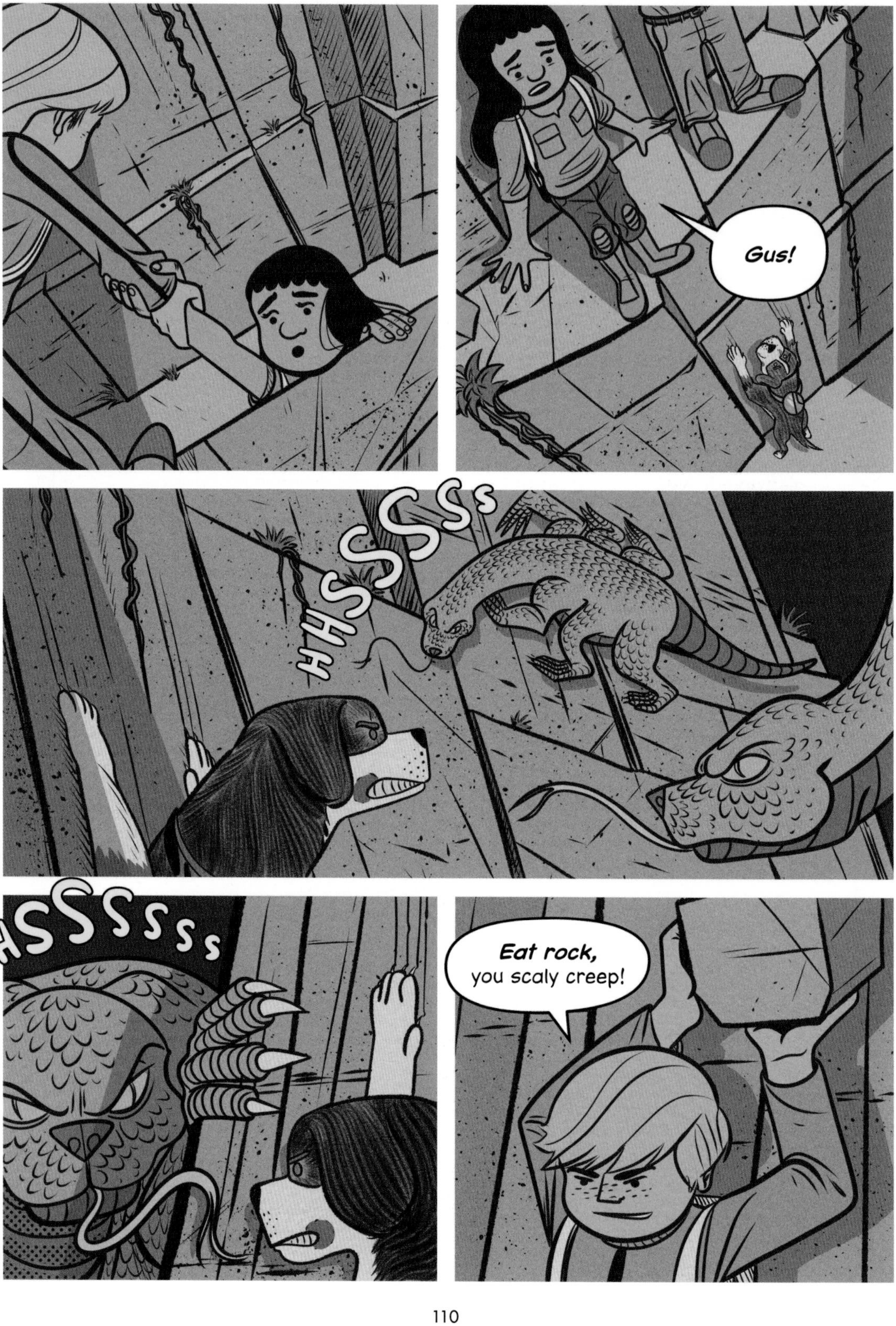
Gus!
HHSSSSs
HSSSSSs
Eat rock, you scaly creep!

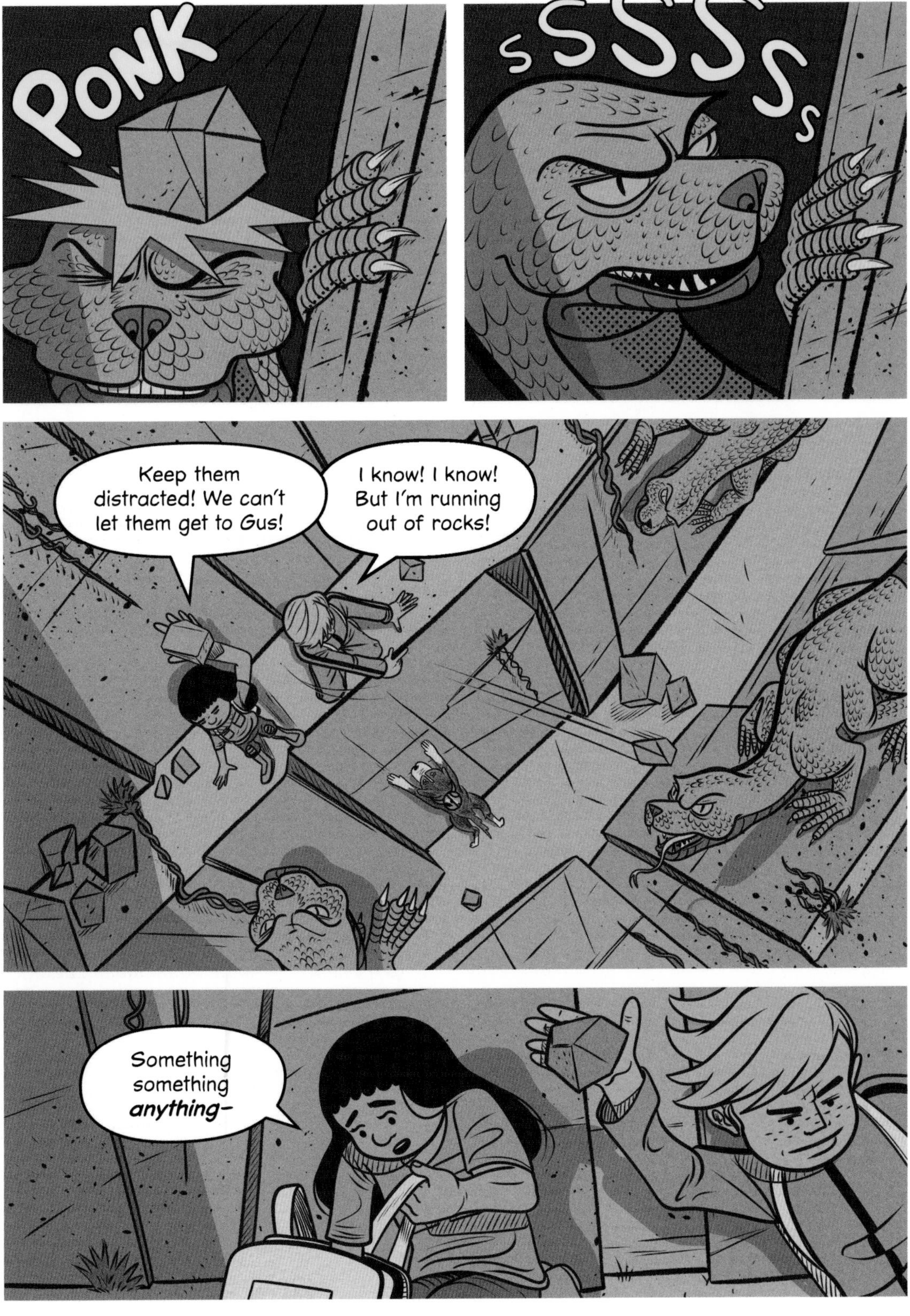
PONK
sSSSSs
Keep them distracted! We can't let them get to Gus!
I know! I know! But I'm running out of rocks!
Something something ***anything*–**

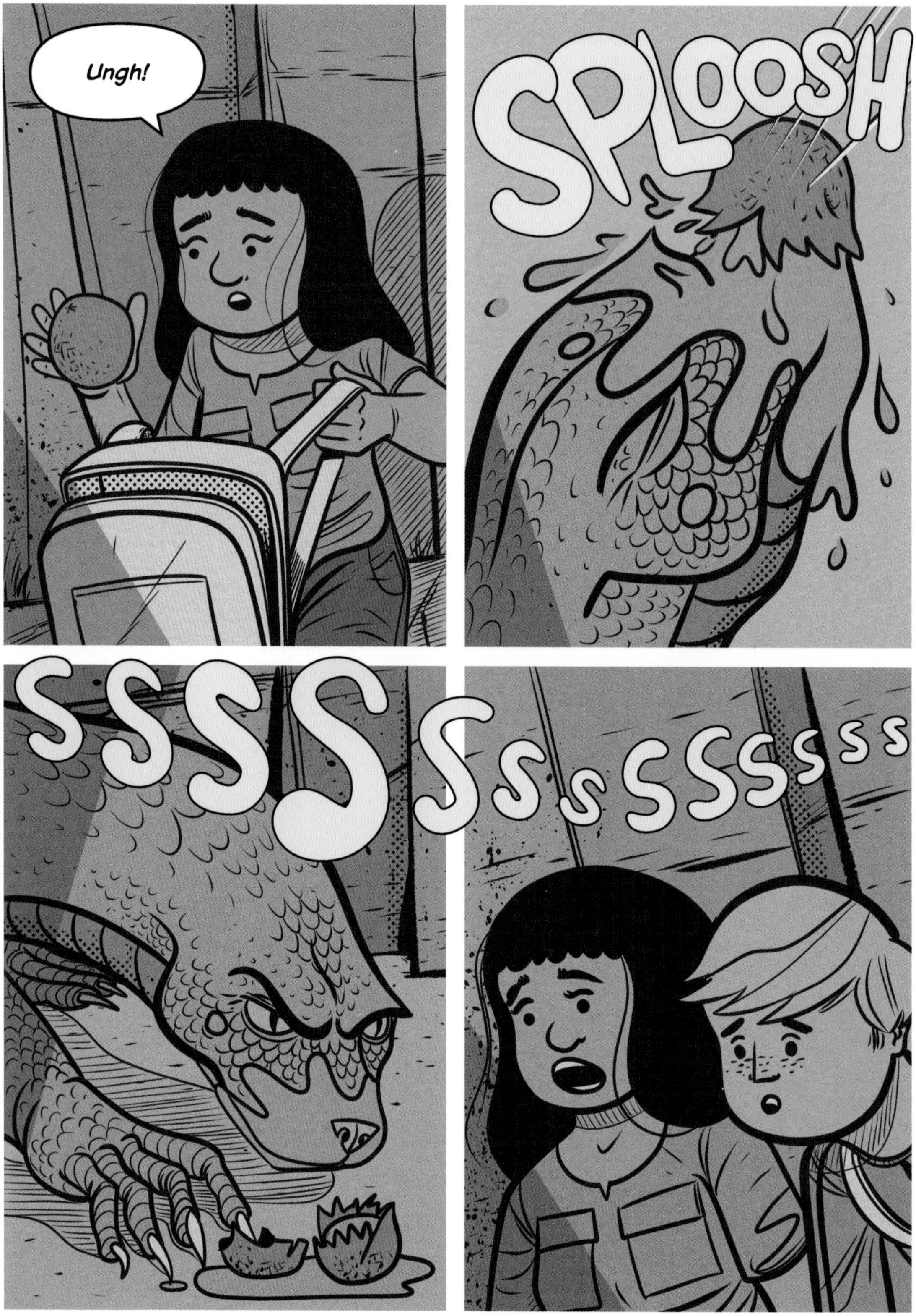
Ungh!
SPLOOSH
SSSSSsSSSSSS

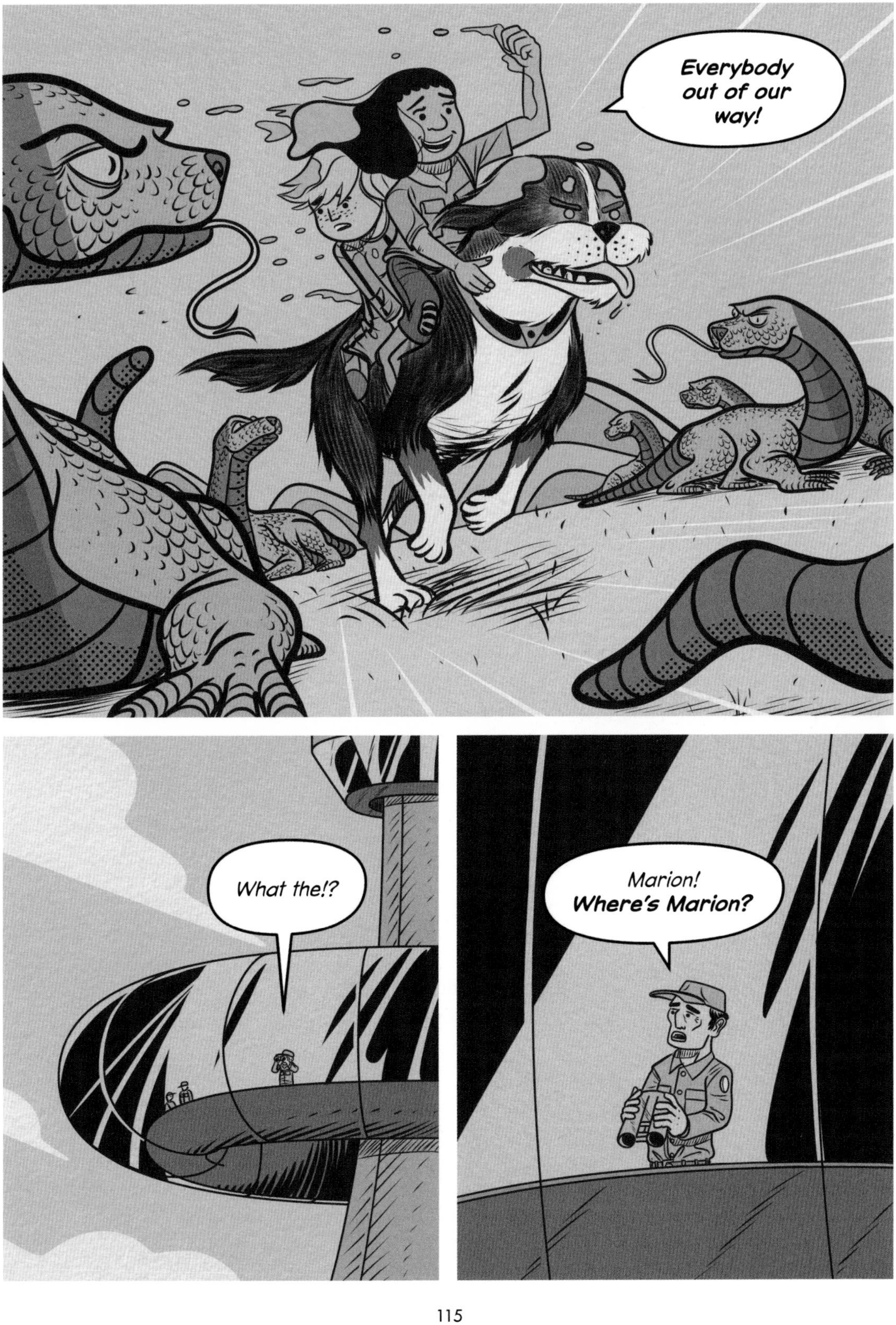
Everybody out of our way!
What the!?
Marion!
Where's Marion?

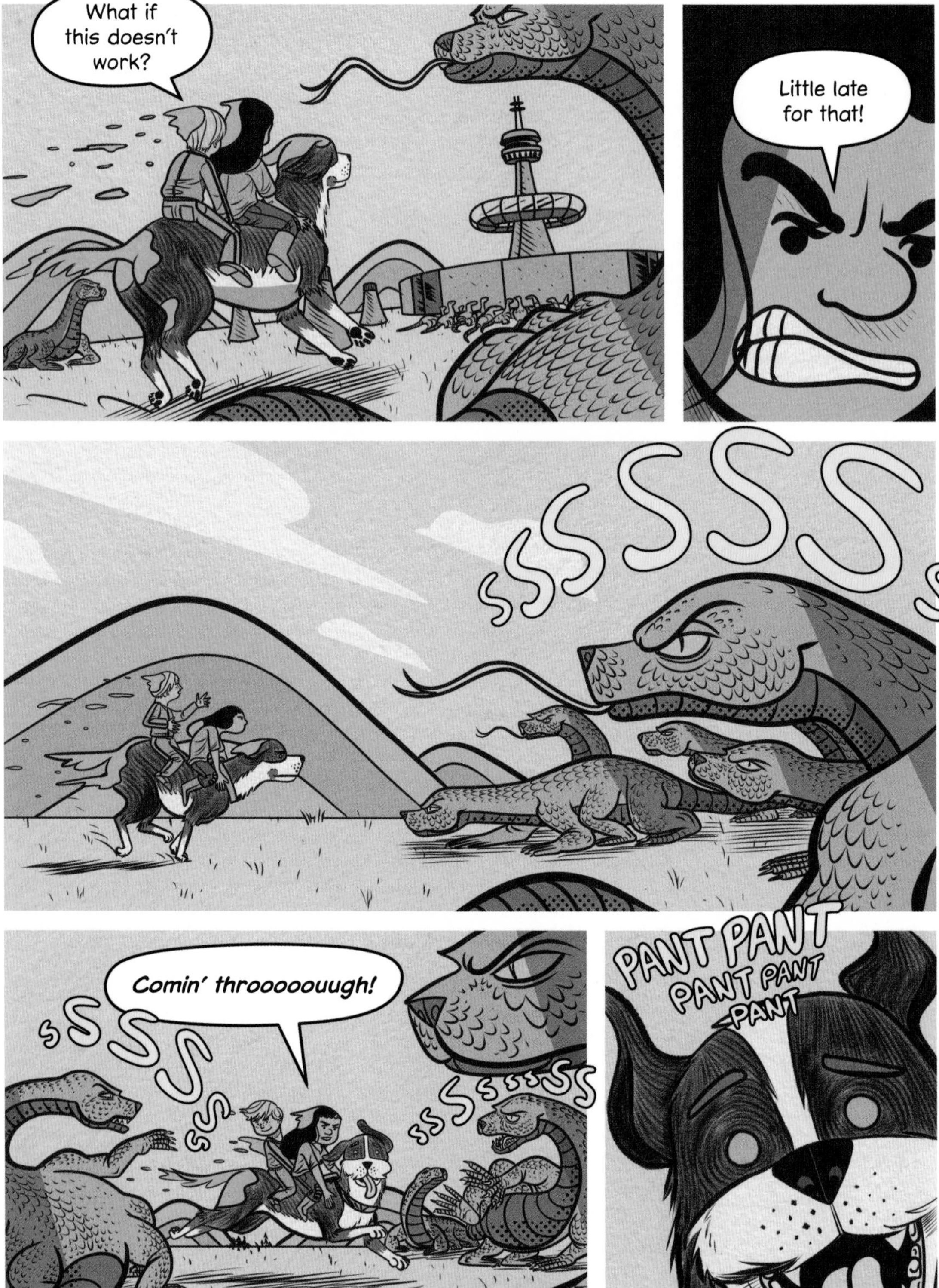
What if this doesn't work?
Little late for that!
sSSSSSs
Comin' throoooouugh!
sSSSsss
ssSssssSS
PANT PANT PANT PANT PANT PANT

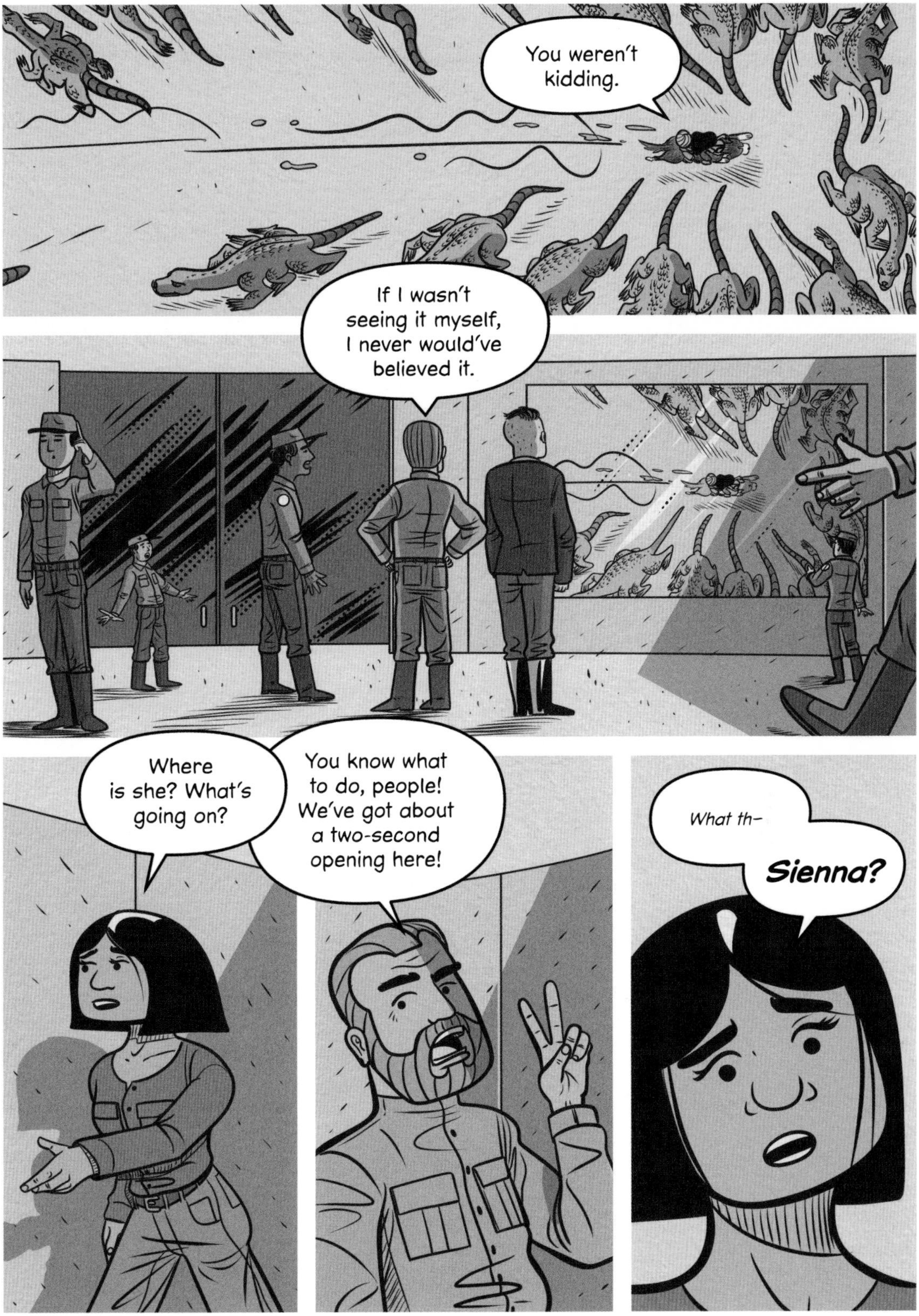
You weren't kidding.
If I wasn't seeing it myself, I never would've believed it.
Where is she? What's going on?
You know what to do, people! We've got about a two-second opening here!
What th–
Sienna?

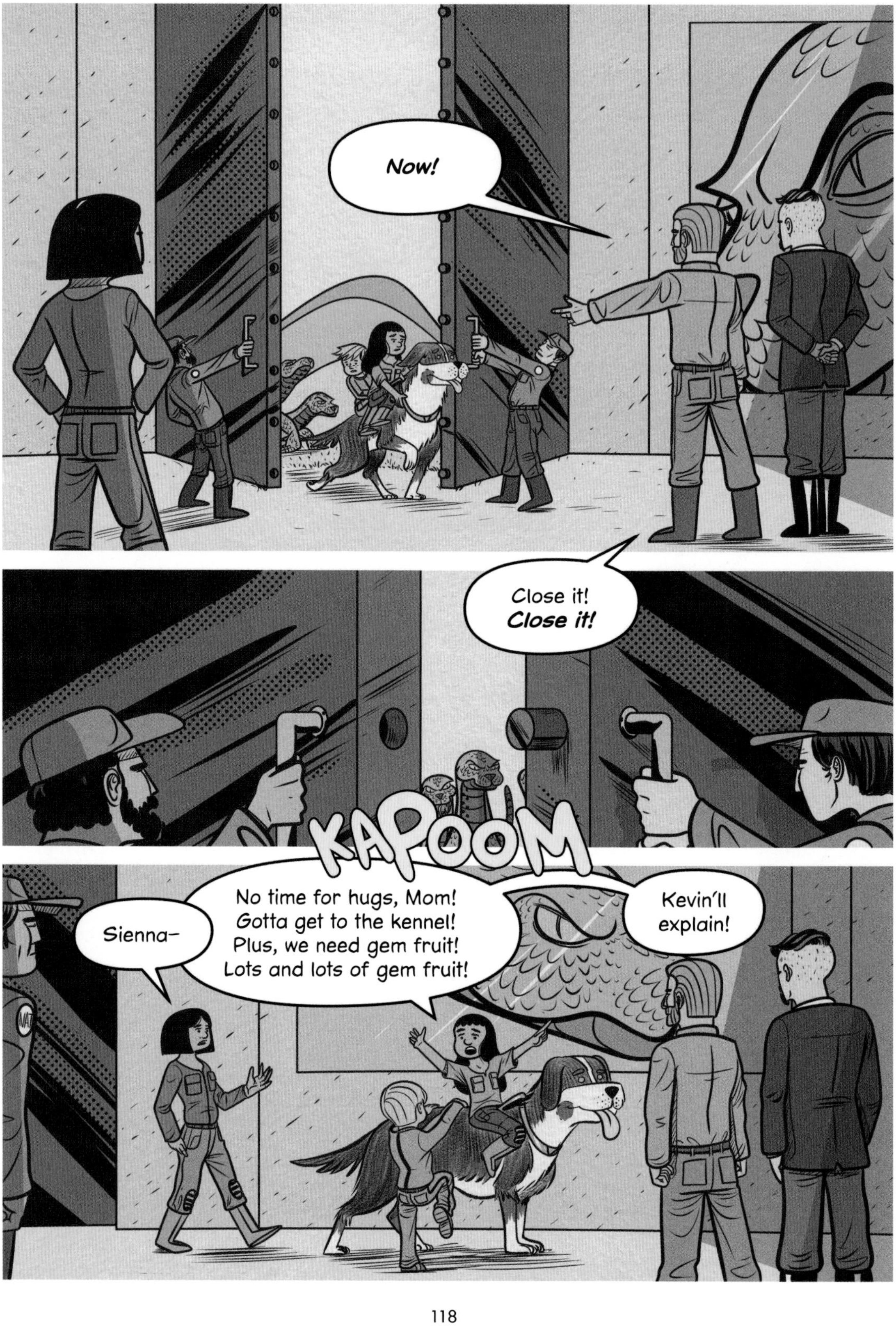
Now!
Close it!
Close it!
KAPOOM
Sienna–
No time for hugs, Mom! Gotta get to the kennel! Plus, we need gem fruit! Lots and lots of gem fruit!
Kevin'll explain!

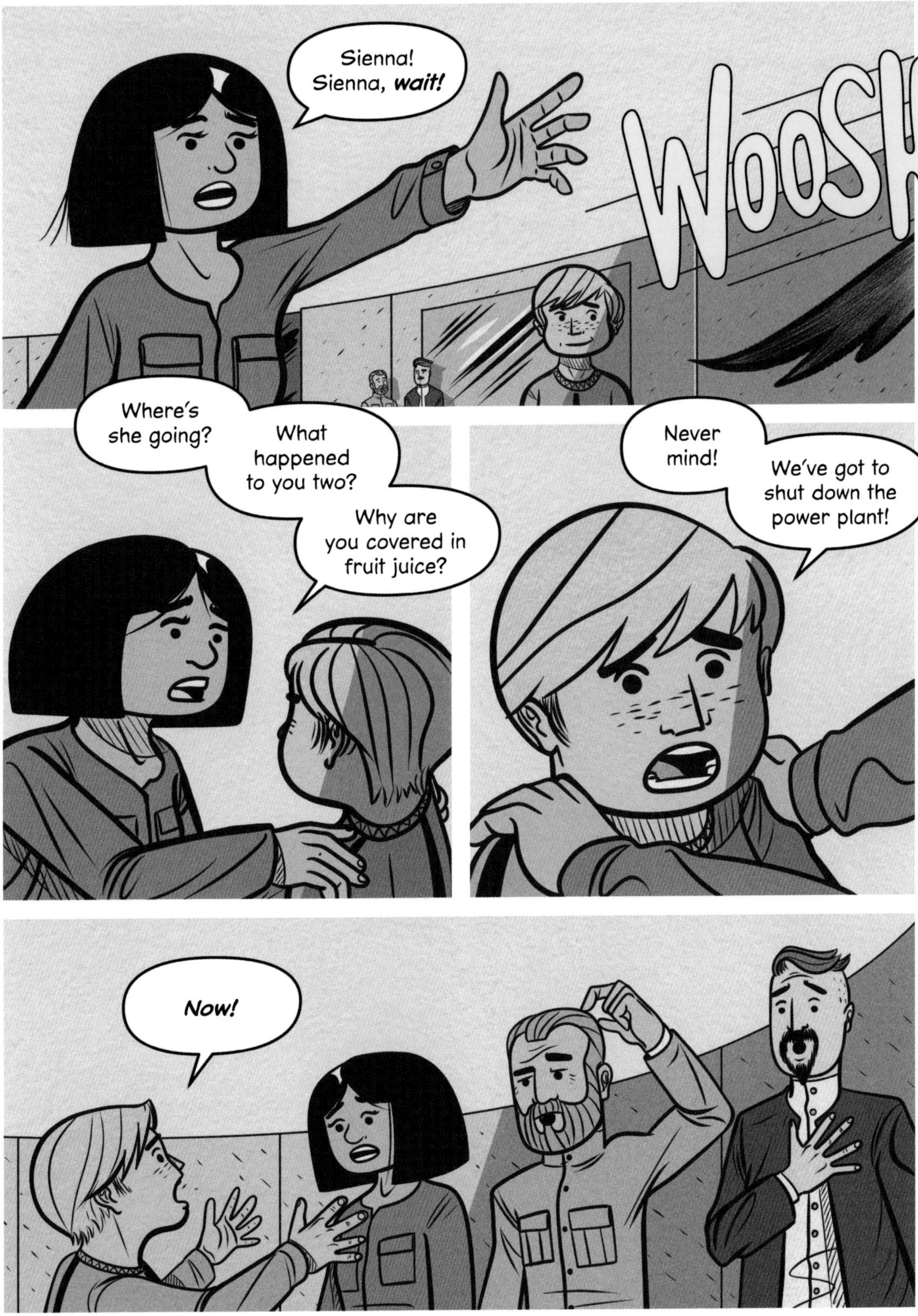

Sienna! Sienna, *wait!*
WOOSH
Where's she going?
What happened to you two?
Why are you covered in fruit juice?
Never mind!
We've got to shut down the power plant!
Now!

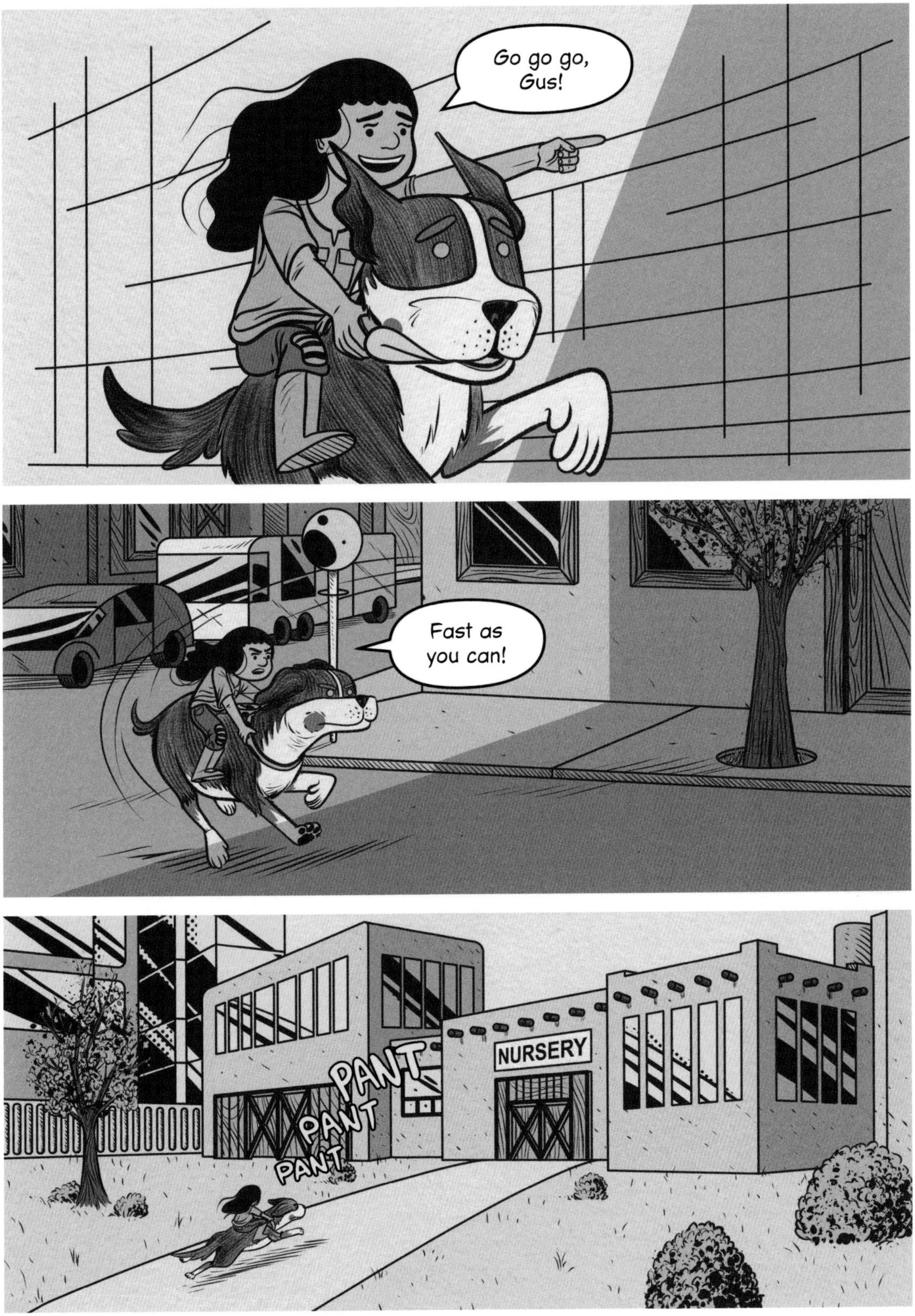

Go go go, Gus!
Fast as you can!
NURSERY
PANT
PANT
PANT

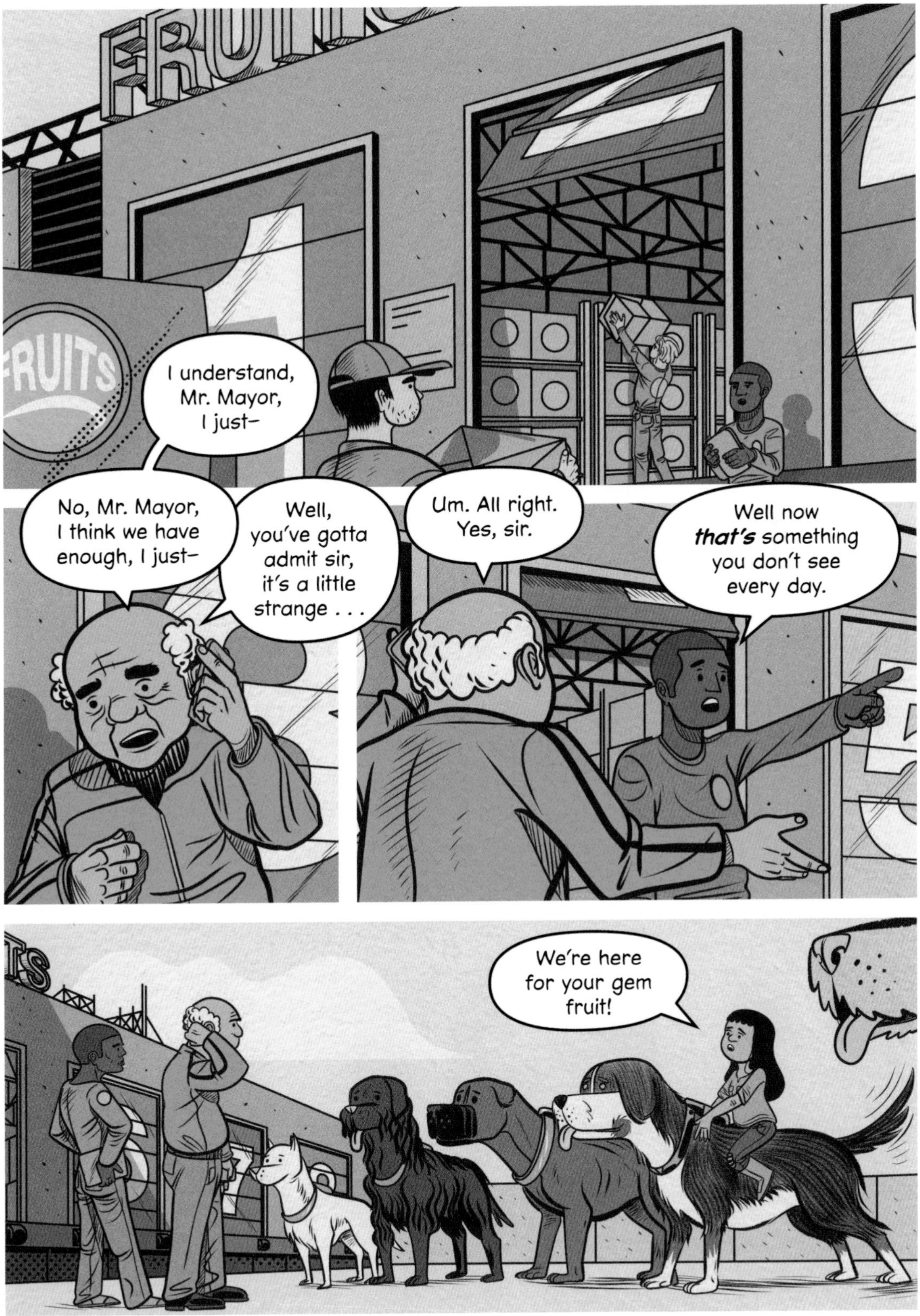
FRUITS
FRUITS
I understand, Mr. Mayor, I just-
No, Mr. Mayor, I think we have enough, I just-
Well, you've gotta admit sir, it's a little strange . . .
Um. All right. Yes, sir.
Well now ***that's*** something you don't see every day.
We're here for your gem fruit!

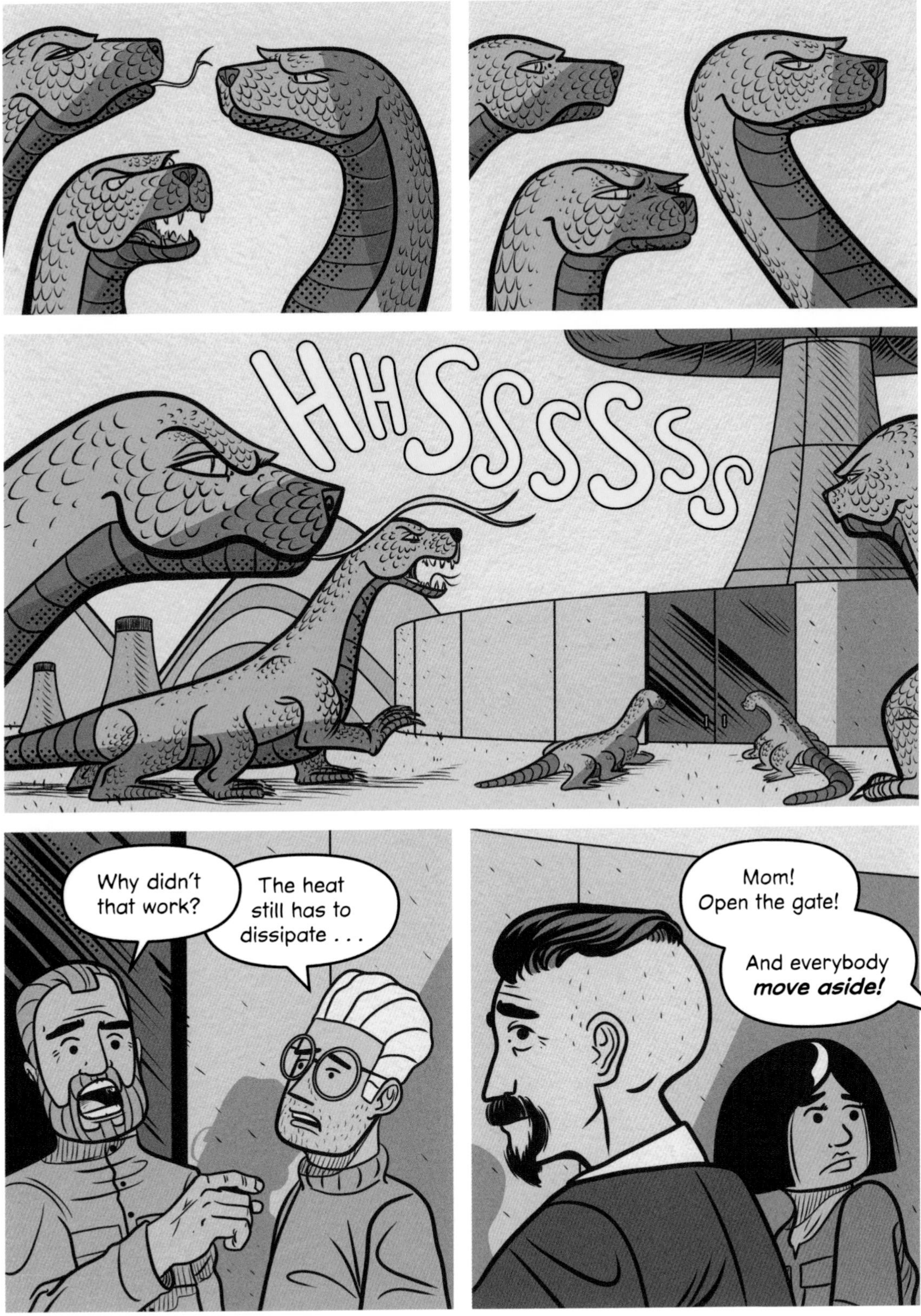
HHSSSSSS
Why didn't that work?
The heat still has to dissipate . . .
Mom! Open the gate!
And everybody *move aside!*

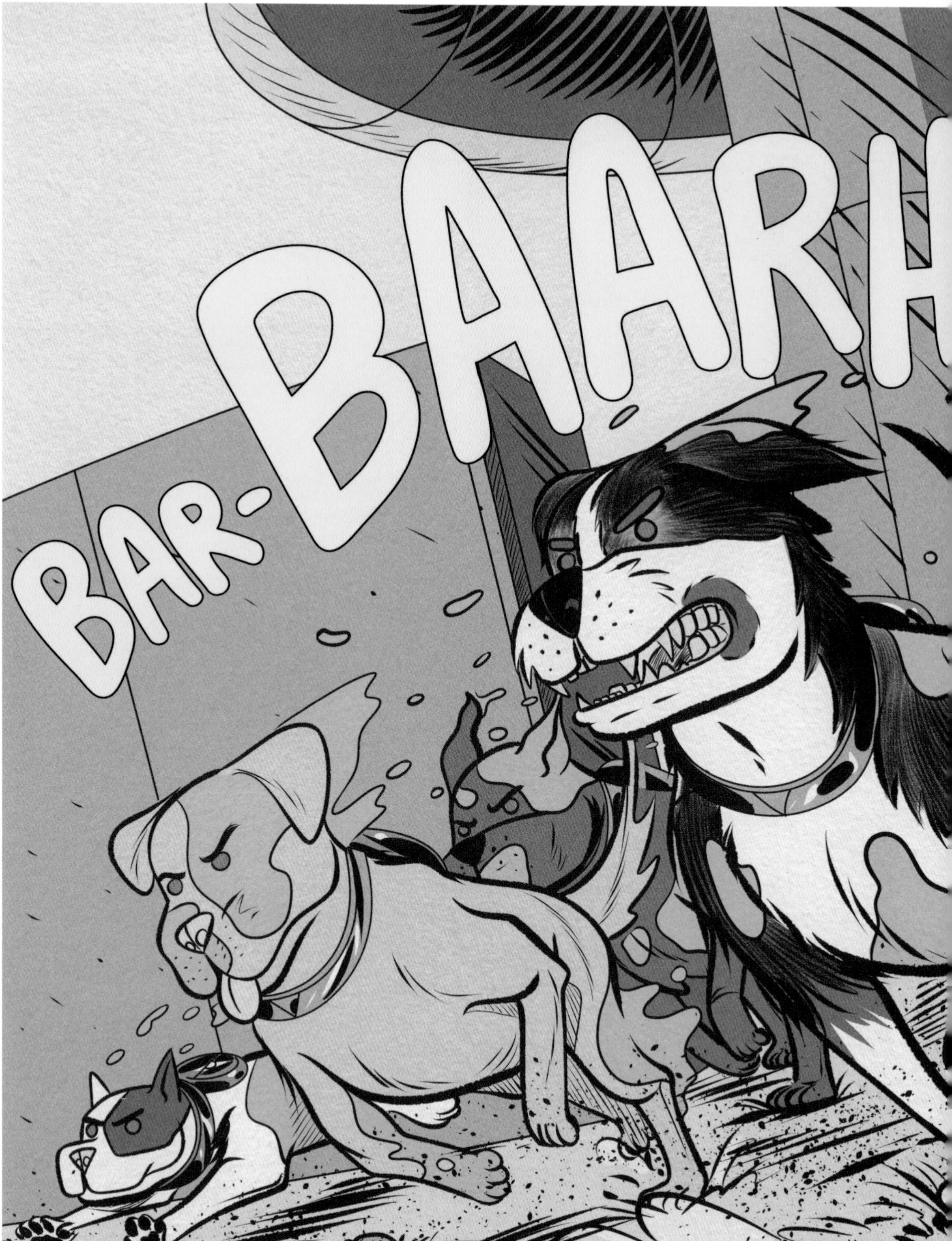
BAR-BAARR

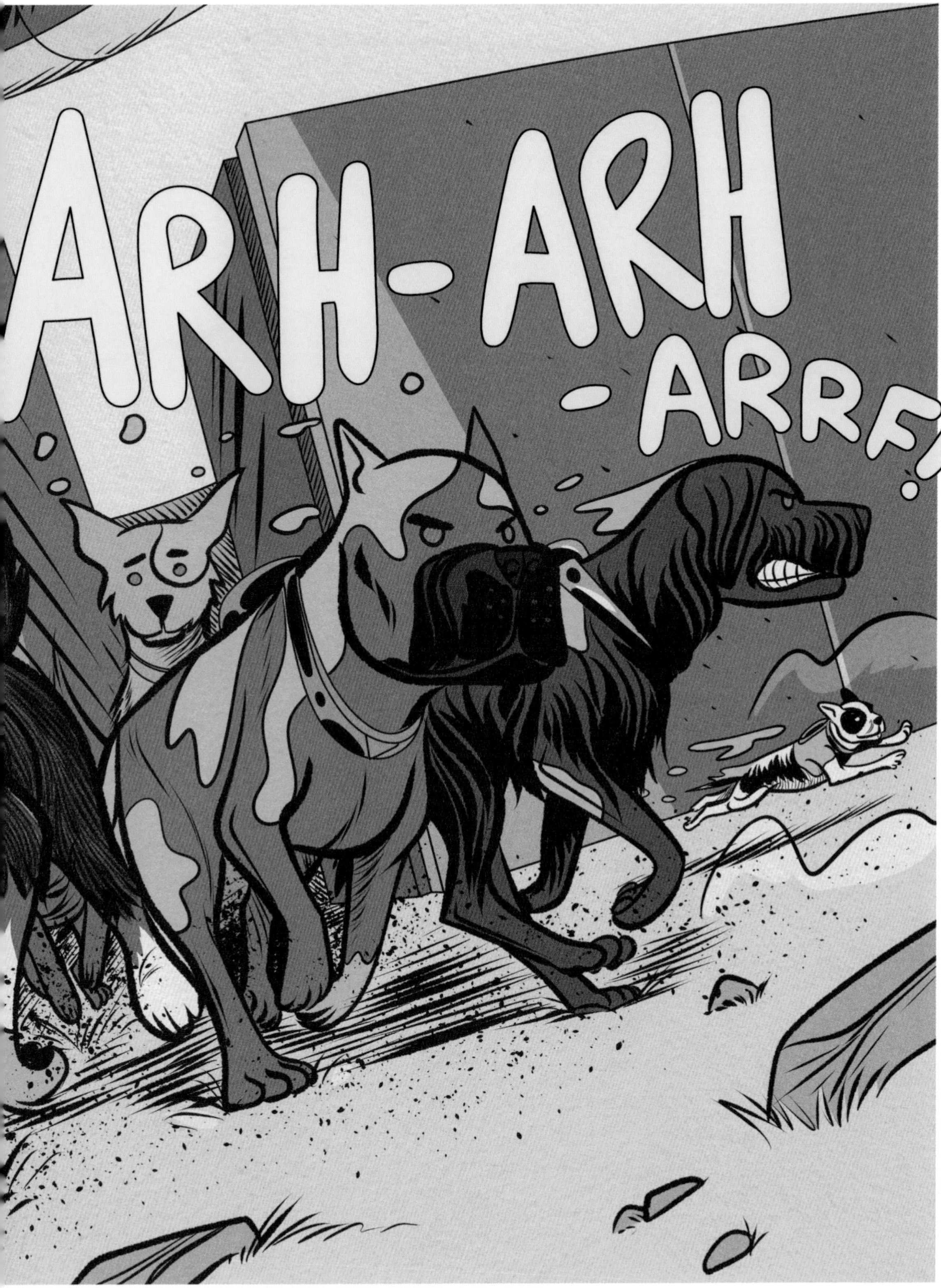
ARH-ARH
-ARRF!

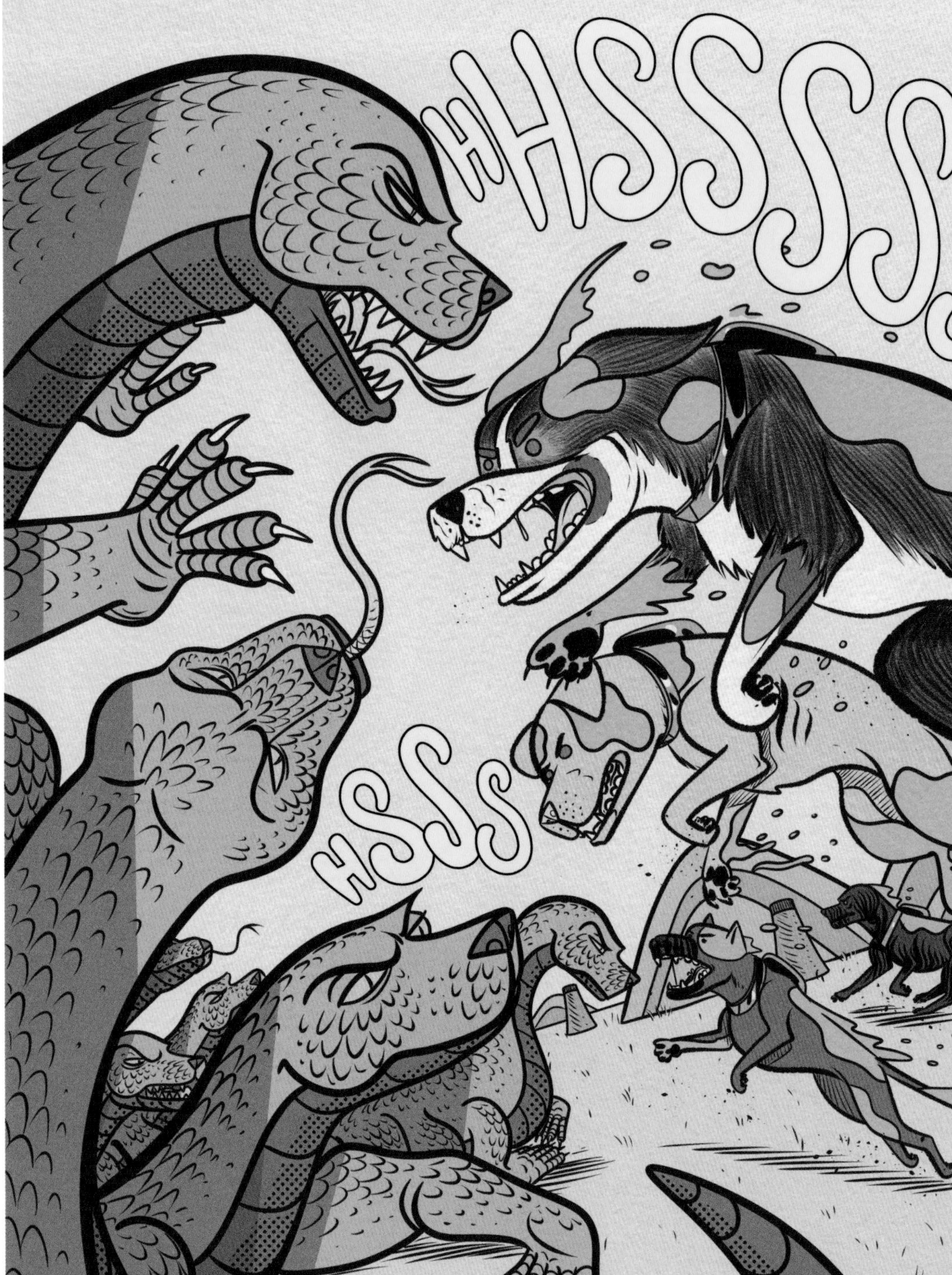
HHSSSSSS
HSSS

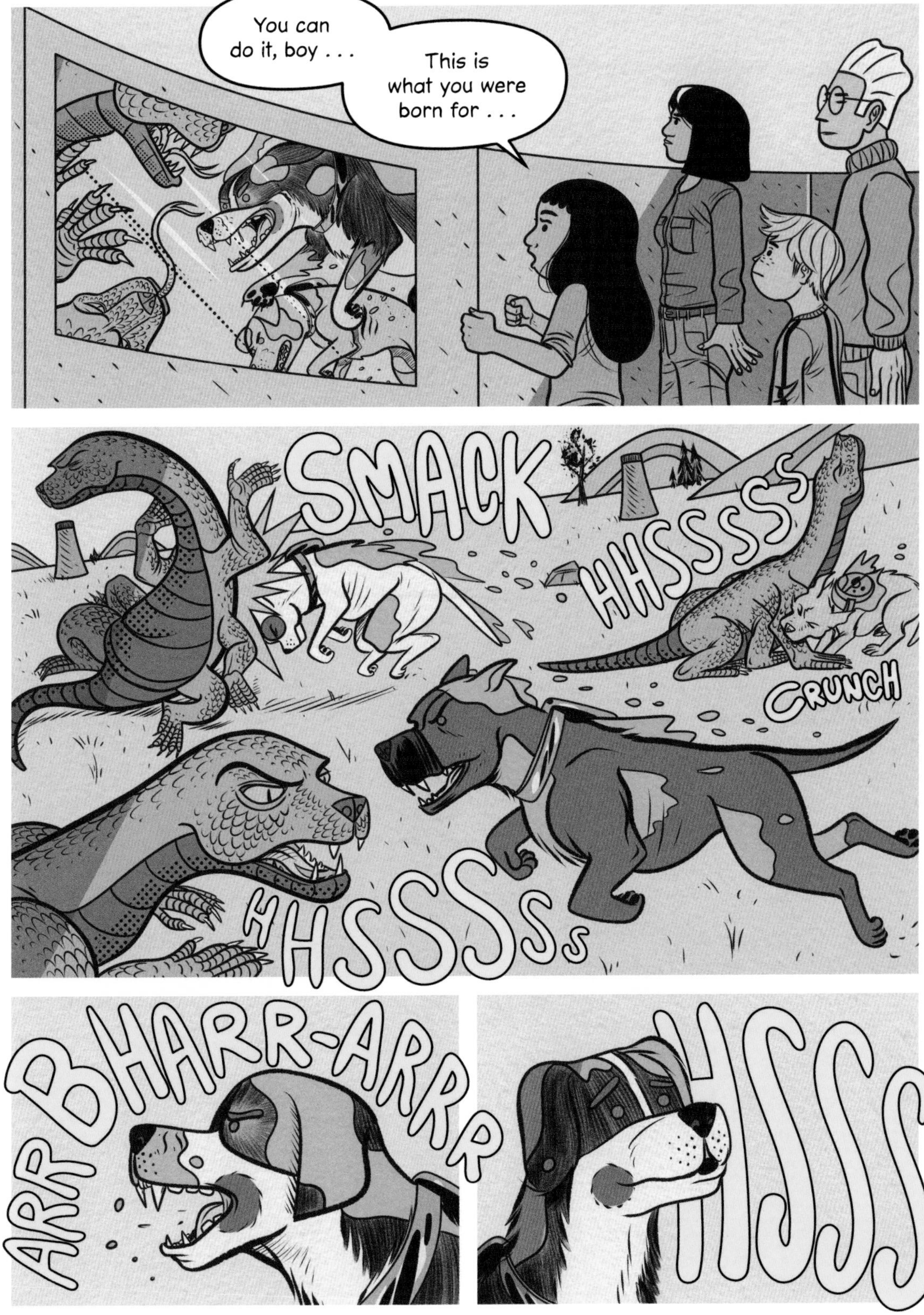
You can do it, boy . . .
This is what you were born for . . .
SMACK
HHSSSSS
CRUNCH
HHSSSSs
ARR BHARR-ARRRR
HSSSS

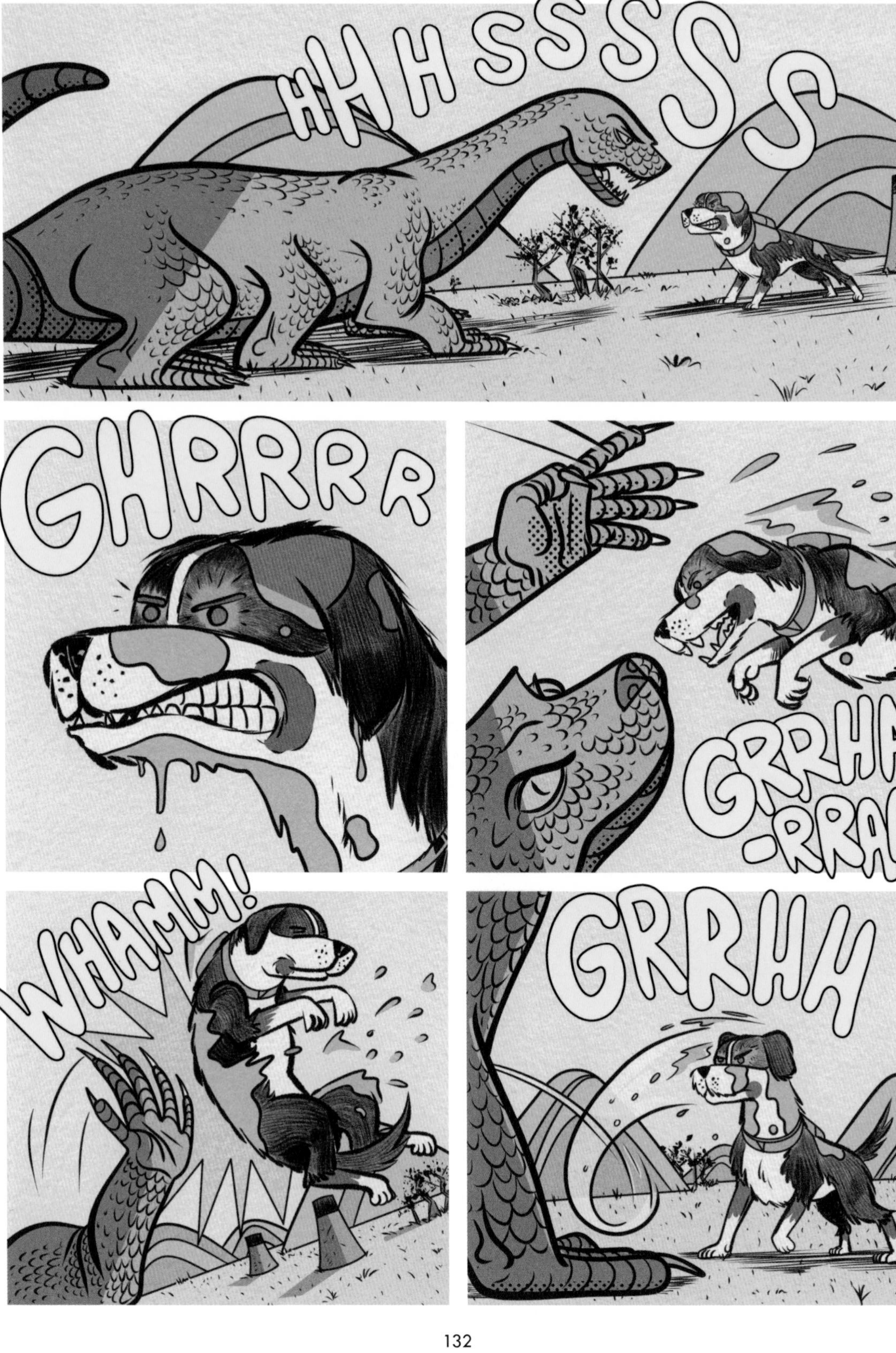
HHHSSSSS
GHRRRR
GRRHA-RRAA!
WHAMM!
GRRHH

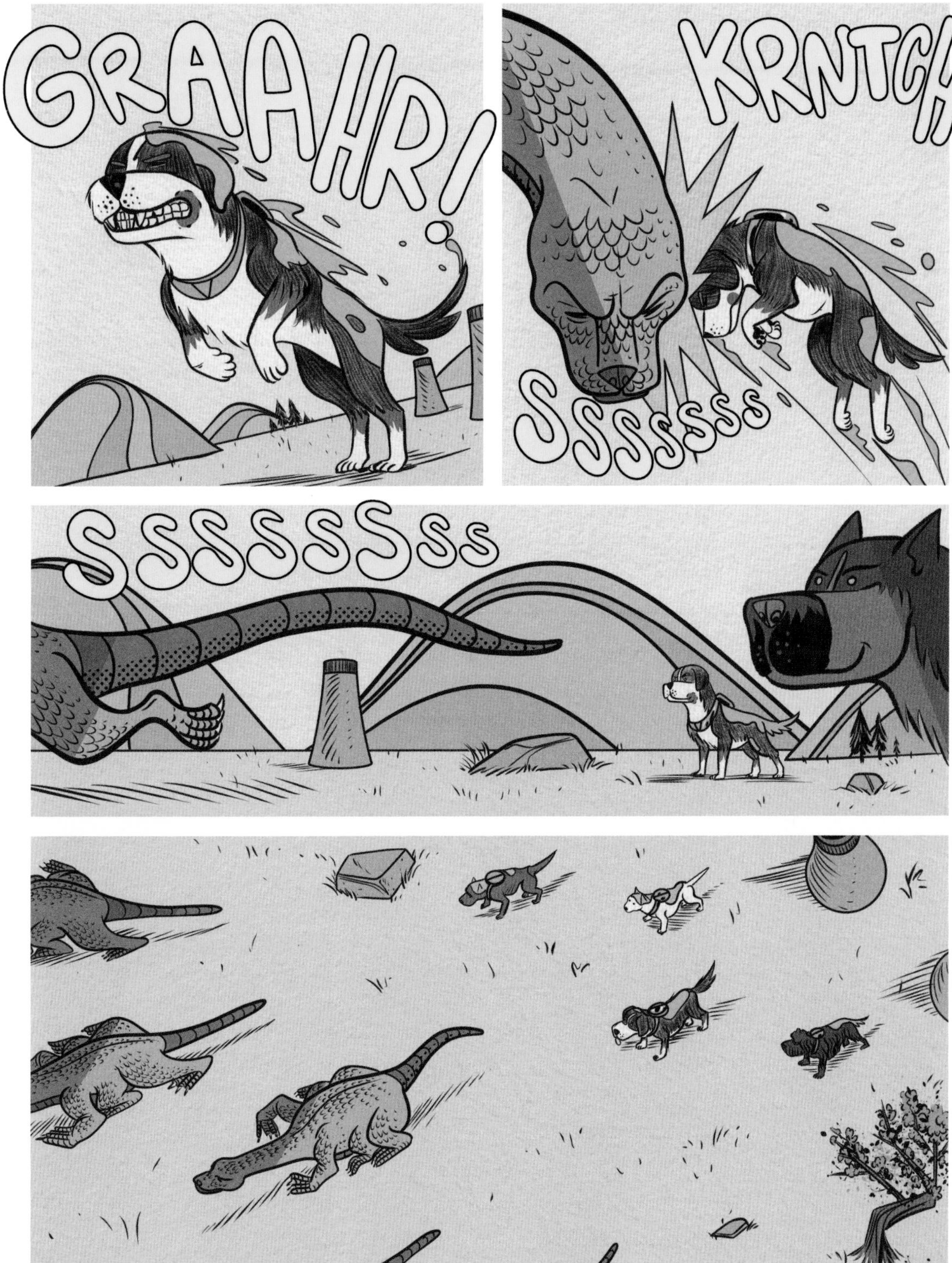
GRAAHR!
KRNTCH
SSSSSSS
SSSSSSSss

MAKING MEGA-DOGS

you are not a weirdo.

Everybody out of our way!

Whoa, hey! Wet dog, *wet* dog—

SHOOKA
SHOOKA
SHOOKA
SHOOKA

Dan Jolley: I'm a pretty huge animal lover, and after working for so long on stories involving the cats of Erin Hunter's *Warriors* universe, I thought it would be nice to write about dogs for a while. A few years ago, I was working on a video game at a development studio north of San Francisco, and one of my co-workers had an enormous Bernese Mountain Dog named Zod who'd come to work with him every day. I loved Zod. He was huge, and very friendly, and he'd go from desk to desk, collecting pets and ear scratches and belly rubs. Zod was my inspiration for Gus, and once I had the idea of this enormous canine, the rest of the story fell into place around him.

For the rippers, I was put in mind of a conversation I once had with a forest ranger. He said he really hated it when colonies of feral cats would show up in the woods, because feral cats are essentially the ultimate killing machines. One cat colony could wipe out an entire species of birds from a forest. I wanted the rippers to have that kind of terrifying, lethal quality, but I didn't want them to be actual cats, because I figured a cat-vs.-dog conflict would be super obvious. Then I remembered reading that some zoologists believe the reason cats hiss is that they're imitating snakes, a known deadly predator. I mixed up cats and snakes in my head, threw in a touch of the crocolisks from *World of Warcraft*, and the rippers were born.

Jacques Khouri: When I was first approached to work on this project, I was enthusiastic and anxious to start on it. I had never illustrated a book starring a dog as big as a pony. The proportions of *Gus* in relation to the kids were quite demanding, and I had to redraw them a lot of times. It's incredible how our mind wants proportions between familiar elements to look a certain way, like the size of a dog compared to a kid. I had to break away from that.

Another challenge was trying to get clear poses of Gus in action or expressing an emotion. How do you show sadness or curiosity on a dog's face and body? Thanks to the internet, I had the opportunity to learn a lot about canine behaviors and anatomy.

In inking, I find the biggest problem with longer books is keeping a consistent style. For example, if you choose one way to render the trees, then you better be able to do it for the whole book. At the start of the project, I did a lot of inking practice. In fact, one of the biggest challenges was once again Gus. How do you ink a shaggy dog? I tried a crosshatch effect, some patterns, some solid black colors . . . but nothing looked like the fur of a Bernese Mountain Dog. One day I attempted a dry-brush look, and voila! We had a shaggy dog.

All in all, I really enjoyed working on *Mega-Dogs*, and have to say I was a little sad when I drew the final panel with Gus in it. Love you, boy . . .

ABOUT THE AUTHOR

Dan Jolley began writing professionally at the age of 19. Since starting out in comic books, he has worked for DC (*Firestorm*), Marvel (*Dr. Strange*), Dark Horse (*Aliens*), and Image (*G.I. Joe*). He later branched out into licensed-property novels (*Star Trek*), film novelizations (*Iron Man*), and original novels, including the urban fantasy series Five Elements and the Audible Original *House of Teeth*. Working with Erin Hunter, he has scripted the manga stories set in the Warriors universe. Dan lives with his wife Tracy and a handful of largely inert felines in northwest Georgia. Readers can learn more about him at www.danjolley.com.

ABOUT THE ARTIST

Jacques Khouri makes animated films, works on commercials, teaches, and draws comics for a living. His influences range from animated cartoons to European and American comics. He currently lives in Montreal. You can find his work at ijotalot.com and jackkhouri.com. Please follow him on Tumblr or Instagram at @ijotalot.